TIME REP

PETER WARD

Time Rep

You can reach the author at:
Email: peterwardauthor@hotmail.co.uk
Blog: https://peterwardauthor.com/blog/
Website: Peterwardauthor.com

TIME REP

Imagine you've just been told you're the most insignificant person who's ever lived. A nobody. Somebody less important to the world than certain types of mushroom. Not very nice, is it?

That's exactly what happens to Geoffrey Stamp after a man from the year 3050 asks him to become a "Time Rep"—a tour guide for the 21st century, meeting people from the future who travel back through time for their vacations. You see, Time Reps need to be insignificant. Otherwise, when you go back in time and interfere with their destiny, the space-time continuum has a bit of a fit. And we wouldn't want that.

But when Geoffrey uncovers a conspiracy to change the course of history, he is sent on a mind-bending adventure through time and space involving an imaginary lake, a talking seagull, dinosaurs, aliens, the Great Fire of London, and the discovery that he might not be as insignificant as people thought…

DEDICATION

For my mother, Vivienne

ACKNOWLEDGEMENTS

First and foremost, I'd like to thank my beautiful wife Lucy for having the patience to read countless drafts of Time Rep over the years and for being there when I wanted to run various ideas, jokes, plot strands, character traits and dialogue past her. Her feedback made this book so much better than it would have been without her.

I'd also like to thank Erik Brown, Geoff Tachauer, Cammil Taank, Adam Malinowski and Mark Selby for reading early drafts of this book and giving me some very helpful suggestions to improve it—it was a long time ago now, but I still remember everything you did! Mark in particular is responsible for making sure readers were not subjected to some particularly awful jokes, whilst giving me the confidence to keep the good one(s) in.

Also thanks to Raelene Gorlinsky for putting up with all my questions around editing and production, and helping me make these new versions of the books as good as they can be.

Finally, special thanks to Ethan Ellenberg for all his efforts in representing me, and for taking a chance on the Time Rep series and reprinting these new editions.

Table of Contents

ONE

The front room of 23 Woodview Gardens was largely identical to every other front room along the street. It had some walls, a floor, and a pair of alcoves too small to accommodate anything useful. It had a bay window, a door leading out into the hallway, and a light hanging from the ceiling—in fact, as front rooms go, it had all the usual features you might expect. Unlike all the other front rooms along Woodview Gardens, however, this one was a complete mess. Crisps had been trodden into the carpet, newspapers were flung across the sofa, and the television was being used as some sort of makeshift clotheshorse—though by the size and smell of it you'd be forgiven for thinking it was an actual horse. Wallpaper was beginning to flake away around the skirting boards, the light switch had a one in ten chance of giving you an electric shock (even if you weren't touching it), and a strange smell lingered in the far corner like a ghostly vapor refusing to be exorcised. It was fortunate the curtains were permanently drawn—had any passersby caught a glimpse of this room, they might have thought they were walking past an animal enclosure.

In a sense they *were* walking past an animal enclosure, except the animal in question was the man who lived there—Geoffrey Stamp. Geoffrey was an average height, average looking man with pale skin, a round face, and olive green eyes. He had a skinny build, narrow shoulders, and arms that looked disproportionately thin for his body. At first glance, it was difficult to determine his age. With a week's worth of dark stubble blurring his jaw line and scraggy chestnut hair drooping over his forehead like an unkempt bush creeping over a garden wall, he could have been anywhere between twenty-five and forty.

In actual fact, Geoff had turned twenty-seven a few weeks ago. The occasion wasn't marked with him throwing a big birthday party or having a couple of friends over for a drink—the day just passed without incident, like the first two hours of *Star Trek: The Motion Picture*. He'd received a few cards. Some were from old friends he was on the verge of losing touch with, a couple were from some distant relatives he'd last seen when he'd just entered puberty, and one was from an insurance company who somehow knew his date of birth. "Happy Birthday Mr. Stamp," the impersonal, automated letter had wished him in two different fonts. "As you're now another year older, have you considered taking out one of our fantastic life insurance policies?" He hoped that whoever had decided send out that sort of letter to people had life insurance—they needed it.

His parents had also sent him a card all the way from America. They'd sold their house a few years ago, moving away from London because of his father's job, which was something to do with IT. Not very interesting. Apparently it was a big opportunity he couldn't afford to turn down, so they'd taken it, leaving Geoff behind to find a place to live and fend for himself. He was old enough now, they'd said. It would be good for him. Geoff visited them once a year and spoke to his mother on the phone every now and again, although the conversation was the same every time: Had he decided what he wanted to do with his life yet? Had he found a job? And did he have a girlfriend?

You could understand why she was concerned. Most people of Geoff's age had started to settle to down into a career. Perhaps been in a relationship for a few years. Started to think about marriage. Taken out a mortgage on a place. That sort of thing. But not Geoff. He was still single. And unemployed. The only job he'd ever held down for a significant period of time was as a paperboy (for ten years), and he'd been fired from that a couple of years ago because he was told he was too old. He wasn't sure why he'd stayed being a paperboy for so long. Maybe it was the same reason he'd made no real effort to find another job since. It wasn't a lack of ambition that was holding him back—he just lacked direction and any sort of skills or qualifications you would expect to find on most people's CVs. One thing was for sure though—he couldn't see himself working in an office environment. Sitting at a desk all day. Typing numbers into a computer. Passing someone the stapler every now and then. That wasn't for him. He knew he was capable of something more, but until he discovered what that was, he didn't want to burden himself with employment. He preferred to live a much more rewarding lifestyle, which basically consisted of him playing computer games.

Lots of computer games.

At this precise moment in time, however, Geoff was doing something else—he was asleep on the sofa, his feet hanging over the armrest at one end, his head nestled in a cushion of old magazines at the other. An empty cereal packet lay across his chest, rising and falling slowly with each breath, and his left arm had flopped over the side to the floor, his limp hand dangerously close to knocking over an old cup of tea. Every now and then he would mutter something incomprehensible or rub his face with the back of his hand. He was dreaming, although it wasn't about anything job related. In fact, if you really want to know, he was dreaming about fishing.

Fishing was somewhat of a recurring dream for Geoff, although he wasn't entirely sure why. He wasn't a fishing enthusiast, didn't know anyone who went fishing, and didn't even go fishing when he was younger. His childhood was spent sitting on the swings in concrete playgrounds, cycling up and down council estates with his friends in East London, or sitting in his bedroom playing *Sonic the Hedgehog*. He supposed there was an underwater stage in *Sonic the Hedgehog* that used to give him nightmares, but that was about the only connection he could think of. Otherwise, there was no reason for him to be dreaming about fishing whatsoever. He didn't even *like* fish, for goodness sake.

And yet here he was, sitting by his imaginary lake, fishing rod in one hand, pickle sandwich in the other, teeth chattering in the crisp morning air. He was slumped on his usual bench, feet squished into the gray mud beneath him, arms hunched close to his chest. The lake was quite large, probably the same size as a football pitch, with a small island of tall trees and thick vegetation in the middle. The water was calm, reflecting the overcast sky above, and a few reeds were sprouting up in odd clumps near the banks, as if the lake had undergone a failed hair transplant.

One thing that had been bothering Geoff recently was the fact that he could tell when he was dreaming. He didn't know whether it was because he was asleep so often that he was now accustomed to the sensation, or whether…A bite! Geoffrey dropped his sandwich, disbanded his psychological ramblings and grasped the rod with both hands. This was a slight overreaction since whatever he'd caught wasn't putting up much of fight. He reeled in his lifeless catch, wondering what kind of metaphor for underachievement would emerge from the water today. A boot maybe? A tire? An old rucksack? Every time he dreamt about fishing, he always ended up hooking some piece of worthless junk, so you can imagine his surprise when the thing on the end of his line turned out to be a fish.

Geoff looked at it. A fish. It began to writhe around desperately on the hook, trying to get back in the water. What did this mean? Was he actually going to achieve something today? Would something fish related influence his life in the near future? Or had he simply caught a fish? It spoke.

"Geoff?"

Geoff wasn't perturbed by this. All kinds of strange things happened in his dreams. Some things he talked about, others he didn't.

"Geoff?" The voice sounded familiar—it sounded like Tim.

Back when he was a paperboy, Geoff had faithfully delivered *The Times* to 23 Woodview Gardens for seven years, or rather to the person who lived there—Tim, who was much more interested in reading the paper than the house was. Tim was the reason Geoff had been able to remain out of work for such a long time, offering him a place to stay when he got fired. He was a little bit older than Geoff, a little bit taller than Geoff, and a little bit more employed than Geoff. At least, Geoff assumed Tim was employed—they never really spoke about what he did for a living. All Geoff knew was that Tim worked from home most of the time, analyzing reams of data on a computer. He had a small study next to his bedroom upstairs: walls plastered with line charts, desk overflowing with graphs and complex hand-written equations. Geoff didn't understand any of it. Quite often Tim would have to go traveling as part of his job. Wouldn't say where—he would just leave the house and return a few days later. For Geoff, this was perfect—he had no interest in whatever Tim did for a living, and Tim never really expressed a desire to tell him.

They'd struck up a friendship within the first year of Geoff delivering the newspaper to Tim's house when Geoff was caught staring at him through the front window. Tim had been playing a computer game in the lounge, and Geoff had stopped to watch. Their opening conversation was a little bit awkward, with Geoff having to explain why he'd been standing outside Tim's house for the last ten minutes, but they soon discovered that they both had a number of shared interests—namely the playing of computer games and the watching of someone else playing computer games.

As a landlord, Geoff couldn't really fault Tim. He tolerated Geoff's aversion to housework, never asked him if he was looking for a job, and rarely brought up the subject of rent, which he had consistently failed to pay for the past two years. In fact, if it wasn't for Tim, Geoff would have had no choice but to settle for the career he was dreading, sitting in a gray office in a gray suit, thinking gray thoughts. It was such an amazing coincidence that he should find himself living in a house on his old paper route with no pressure to do anything, sometimes he couldn't believe his luck.

But he wasn't happy about being woken up.

"What is it?" Geoffrey replied to the fish. He assumed Tim was talking to him in the real world—his voice manifesting itself in his dream as the voice of the fish.

Either that or he needed help.

"Come on Geoff. Get up."

Geoff rubbed his eyes. The fish now had hair.

"You're a fish."

"Yes, I'm a fish. Wakey wakey."

Suddenly, Geoffrey was blinded by an unbearable light—Tim must have opened the curtains. He felt a tugging on his foot.

"You need to wake up, Geoff," the fish said.

Geoffrey let out a small noise from his mouth and reluctantly opened his eyes, extending one hand in front of his face to shield his gaze from the sun. The picturesque lake slowly dissolved into the less pleasing aesthetic of the front room, and Tim now stood in front of him where there had previously been a talking fish. His friend wasn't quite in focus yet though—Geoff could make out the blurry outline of his tall figure, the blob of brown hair on top of his head, and the black-rimmed glasses, but that was about it. He closed his eyes and opened them again as if rebooting his brain. That was better—he could see much more clearly now: the unimpressed look on Tim's face, the slogan on his t-shirt that was far too witty for this time in the morning, and most importantly, the cup of tea in his hand.

"Is that tea for me?" Geoff said optimistically, brushing the cereal packet off his chest and sitting up.

"What's wrong with yours?" Tim said, nodding at the mug at the foot of the sofa.

"It's solidified."

"I see," he said, passing him the cup.

Tim looked around at the television screen and picked off the assortment of clothes Geoff had chosen to pile on top of it.

"You really have to stop using the television to dry your stuff out," he said. "It'll overheat again."

Five t-shirts and a pair of jeans later, he revealed a dusty screen displaying the words:

GAME OVER

Continue? Y/N

"Oh—I'd forgotten I was playing this," Geoff said, rummaging through the sofa cushions for a moment before pulling out a joypad. "Where did I get up to?"

"What game is this?" Tim said, tossing Geoff's clothes into a corner.

"*Space Commando,*" Geoff answered, positioning a cushion behind him and taking a sip of Tim's tea.

"I see. And what do you have to do?"

"You have to save the world," Geoff said, picking up a headset and putting the earpiece in his ear. "You play this commando guy who basically goes around shooting the crap out of aliens."

"And what is that thing you're wearing?" Tim said. "You got a job in a call center or something?"

"This?" Geoff said, positioning the headset's microphone in front of his mouth. "It lets you talk to other players over the Internet."

"Sounds fascinating," Tim said, picking up a large stack of plates and carrying them into the kitchen.

"Don't know whether you're interested," he shouted from the other room, "but there's a job being advertised in the local paper. I think you should apply."

"Get out of the way!" Geoffrey screamed into his microphone. "I can't hit it if you're in the way!!"

"What?" Tim said.

"Nothing," Geoff said. "Just talking to this idiot online."

"I don't know why you get so angry when you play that thing," Tim said. "It's not real, you know."

Regardless of it being real or not, Geoff was still getting very annoyed with *Space Commando*. His hand-eye coordination was never great after he'd just woken up, and he was having a bit of trouble aiming his character's ultimate weapon, the Death Bringer, at one of the alien's weak spots.

"So what do you think?" Tim said.

"About what?"

"The job."

"What job?"

"The job in the paper!"

Geoff wasn't really listening. He was taking too long trying to get a lock on a particularly large alien, and before he knew it, he was killed by enemy fire and greeted with another "Game Over" screen. He threw the joypad to the floor in frustration and thought about what Tim had just said.

"So there's a job in the paper?" he said. This was strange—Tim had never spoken to him about getting a job before. So why today?

"Yes," Tim said. "Not sure what it is, but you don't need any qualifications. You don't have any, do you?"

Having failed most of his exams at school due to a lack of interest in any of the subjects, the only qualifications Geoff had to his name were a knot tying badge from Scouts, a third place rosette from a talent show, and an "I beat PC Gamer at *Doom*" t-shirt.

"No," Geoff conceded.

Tim came back into the room. "I've circled it," he said, tossing a newspaper on Geoff's lap. "Not playing your game?"

"I think I need to wake up a bit first," Geoff said, taking off his headset. "I keep pressing the wrong buttons." He glanced down at the paper and read the job advert aloud.

"Long established tour operator seeks holiday representative to liaise with a variety of clients. No experience or qualifications required."

"Well?" Tim said.

"I don't know. A holiday rep?"

"It's not every day you see a job in the paper that says 'No experience or qualifications required.'" He stretched a hand out to Geoff, indicating that he wanted his tea back.

Geoff offered the tea to the pile of clothes Tim had chucked in the corner.

"You really need to see a doctor about your hand-eye coordination problem," Tim said, pulling Geoffrey's arm in his direction and taking the tea. "How long does it usually take to wear off?"

"I don't know," Geoffrey said. "I'm never able to look at my watch to tell."

Geoffrey didn't like this at all. He didn't want a job. He was happy sleeping all day and playing computer games all night. It was an unrewarding lifestyle that suited him just fine, at least until he'd discovered what he wanted to do with his life. But by midmorning, he had half-heartedly written a letter of application to this tour operator company, or whatever it was. If anything, just making the slightest bit of effort to get a job would prevent any rent-related conversations with Tim, which always made him twinge with guilt.

"It's finished," he called up the stairs.

"Good," Tim replied. He sounded like he was in his study. "Now go and post it, will you?"

"What, you don't want to hear it?"

"Not really. Envelopes are by the front door."

Geoff was still having some trouble controlling his hands, and it took him a couple of minutes to stick a stamp in the corner of an envelope and put the letter inside.

As he sat at the bottom of the stairs slipping his trainers on, he noticed a female silhouette approaching through the bubbly glass of the front door. It stopped on the doorstep, rifled through a large shoulder bag for a few seconds, and popped a letter through the mailbox.

Geoff was particularly fond of this silhouette. It belonged to Zoë, the postwoman, whom he had known for many years back from his paperboy days. In the past, they'd often keep each other company as they walked the streets in the morning, Geoff delivering newspapers, Zoë delivering everything else. She was a bit of a tomboy—always wearing baggy jeans that snagged under her grubby trainers and large jumpers that disguised her slim figure. She never wore dresses or skirts, rarely put on any makeup, and usually had her long dark hair tied in a pony tail. Her voice was slightly deeper than you might think to look at her, her left ear had four piercings in it, and she had a small tattoo of an owl on the back of her right shoulder. When she wasn't working, she played guitar in a band. With large eyes and a wide mouth, she didn't have classically beautiful features, but nonetheless Geoff thought she was incredibly attractive. She was just so easy to talk to. Conversations felt effortless and natural, he found it very easy to make her laugh, and she was always happy to offer words of encouragement or advice.

Somehow, he felt like a different person around her, as if she was able to flick a switch in his mind and fill him with a sense self-worth. He'd often thought about asking her out on a date but could never muster up the courage.

Geoff sprung to his feet and flung the front door open, smiling. Zoë stood right in front of him. They hadn't met up for a quite a few weeks, and seeing her again made him forget the world around him for a moment, so much so that he failed to notice that he'd just scared the living daylights out of her.

"Jesus Christ—you startled me Geoff," She laughed, pressing her hand to her chest.

"Oh, Sorry," Geoff said, "I'm, err…I was just leaving. Posting a letter, funnily enough." He held up the letter as if he somehow needed to prove it.

"So how you keeping, anyway?" she said. "Found another job yet?"

It was like asking a fridge if it had taken up tennis.

"No, nothing," Geoff replied, "But this letter is a job application, as it happens."

"Oh, cool—what's the job?"

"Holiday rep."

Zoe raised her eyebrows.

"What?" Geoff said.

"Nothing," she said. "It's just…not the sort of job I'd expect you to go for. Doesn't being a holiday rep involve meeting lots of people, being overly enthusiastic about everything, that sort of thing?"

"Are you saying I hate meeting people and being enthusiastic?"

"Yes, that's exactly what I'm saying. That's what I like about you."

"You're right," Geoff said. "But it was Tim's idea—I'm just applying to keep him happy."

"I see," Zoe said. "Oh—that letter is for you, by the way." She pointed down at the envelope she'd just delivered. "Don't see many addressed to you these days…"

"For me?" He picked it up. That was unusual. He hadn't received any mail for weeks.

"Have you applied for any other jobs recently? Maybe it's an acceptance letter."

"Nah. It's probably just another letter from the bank asking me if I'm still alive." He held the envelope in between his teeth, put his coat on, and stepped outside, closing the door behind him with a click.

Zoë laughed. "Seriously," she said, "aren't you going to open it and see who it's from?"

"I *was* being serious," Geoff said, stuffing the letter in his coat pocket. Since reaching his overdraft limit a while ago, Geoff hadn't been near a cash machine in months. The banks were nervous—after all, they were normally so careful about who they lent money to, so it was only natural that they wanted to make sure he was okay.

Zoë followed Geoff up the garden path and out onto the street, sifting through a few more letters.

"Which way you heading?" Geoff asked, hoping it was the same way he was going.

"Just to the end of the street, then back to the depot," Zoë replied, not looking at him.

"Oh, okay," he said, trying to hide his disappointment.

As he watched her walk away, a small voice in his head suggested perhaps now might be a good time to call after her and ask her out on a date. Nothing serious—just lunch or something.

"Hey, Zoë?" Geoff said.

"Yes?" Zoë said, turning around and smiling.

It was at this point that another, more forceful voice in Geoff's head pointed out that asking Zoë out on a date was a ridiculous, terrible idea, that she was way out of his league, and that he should quickly extract himself from this situation with some vague suggestion that they meet up again at an unspecified time before he seriously embarrassed himself and destroyed their friendship forever.

And on no account must he ever have any silly ideas about asking her out again.

Geoff found himself unconditionally agreeing with this new course of action. What was he thinking?

"Let's catch up again soon, okay?" he said.

"S-sure," Zoë replied, her smile fading.

Geoff watched as she walked off.

Within ten minutes, Geoff had posted his letter, bought a bar of chocolate from the corner shop and returned to the house. Tim was in the kitchen eating some cornflakes, examining a batch of papers he had sprawled across the kitchen table.

"How'd it go?" he said, not taking his eyes off his work.

"How'd it go?" Geoff replied. "I went out to post a letter, not run a marathon. Does posting a letter really warrant a 'how'd it go?'"

Tim rested his spoon on the table and looked up.

"What's gotten into you?"

"Nothing." Geoff sighed, sitting down next to Tim. "I saw Zoë just now…"

"Oh," Tim said, looking down at the floor. "And how did that go?"

"How it always goes. For a split second, I almost asked her out on a date, and then my brain went 'Noooooo! Don't do it! So I bottled it and just came across a bit weird."

"I'm sure you didn't look weird," Tim said. "At least, no more than usual."

"Thanks. Speaking of weird though—she had a letter for me."

"A letter?" Tim said, raising an eyebrow. "For you? Now that *is* weird. Who was it from?"

"Don't know," Geoff said, taking the envelope out of his coat pocket. "Let's find out, shall we?" He tore it open and pulled out a single, crisp sheet of paper. The paper felt thick and expensive with a soft grain to it that almost caressed the tips of his fingers.

Geoff looked at the letter in silence.

"Well?" Tim said, leaning over to read it as well.

"Dear Mr. Stamp," Geoff read aloud, his voice trembling slightly. "T-thank you for applying for the position of holiday representative.

I am pleased to inform you that you have been selected to attend an interview, which will take place at five o'clock this afternoon at our London office—please see the enclosed map. We look forward to seeing you. Y-yours sincerely, Ruth Ashmore."

The letter was written in very bad handwriting as if the person writing it had nothing to lean on. Geoff looked inside the envelope again. Tucked at the bottom was a small map. He took it out and laid it flat on the table. It showed a very small area of Westminster in central London with a red arrow pointing to a building off one of the main roads.

Geoff was more confused than the time he'd tried to work out why the words "flammable" and "inflammable" meant the same thing. How on earth had these people managed to reply to him before he'd even sent his application? He scratched his head in stereotypical puzzlement, thankful that at least his hand-eye coordination had improved.

"Err … That's *my* head," Tim said.

Two

"I'm here for a job interview," Geoff said to the receptionist. She was quite pretty, maybe in her early thirties, with a thin face, high cheekbones, and eyelashes that could double as window canopies.

"You must be Geoffrey Stamp," she said, looking him up and down. There was a slight look of uncertainty in her eyes as if she was inspecting a vegetable to see if it had gone off.

"Er … that's right," he replied, suddenly conscious of his appearance. The receptionist was dressed immaculately in a dark trouser suit and pale cream blouse, her shoulder-length hair so even it was probably cut using a spirit level. In contrast, Geoff looked like he'd turned up in the clothes he'd just slept in. Which he had.

The receptionist picked up a phone and began to dial a number.

"Please, have a seat," she smiled, resting the phone against her shoulder and pointing across the room to a row of black leather chairs. "We'll be ready for you in a moment."

The place was empty. Geoff eased himself into the nearest seat and stared up at a very high frosted glass ceiling. Looking around, he noticed that the whole lobby was made out of frosted glass: the floor was frosted glass, the walls were frosted glass, even the tables were made out of the stuff. In fact, so many things were made out of frosted glass that the words "frosted glass" began to lose all meaning in his inner monologue.

"Geoffrey Stamp's here for his interview," the receptionist whispered into the frosted glass phone. "Just give me a few moments to run a quick test and then I'll bring him up." She hung up.

Suddenly, the whole room flashed green for a moment. If Geoff had blinked at that second, he would have missed it. What was that about?

"Excellent," the receptionist said, pushing her chair out from behind her desk. She stood up. "Please follow me."

A panel clicked open at the far end of the room and slid across with a quiet hiss to reveal a brightly lit elevator.

Geoff got to his feet.

"I'm Ruth," the receptionist said, leading him toward the lift. "I'm the one who sent you the letter." Her high heels click-clacked on the frosted glass floor as she walked, the sound echoing all around the lobby as though a troupe of tap dancers had just arrived to practice a routine.

"Frosted glass." Geoff said.

There wasn't much to say about the elevator—it was quite large inside with brushed metal walls and a white tiled floor. The ceiling was made up of four grilled panels—the sort you could push to one side and climb through if you found yourself in an action movie, and the air smelled slightly stale. All very standard elevator stuff. But then Geoff noticed something strange—there were no buttons. No floor numbers. No alarm. In fact, this thing had less features than a Toyota Prius. What sort of elevator was this?

"Please state your destination," a synthesized female voice said.

"Top floor," Ruth replied.

The doors closed, and the elevator began to move.

"Can I ask you a question?" Geoff said, feeling the stubble around his chin. If he'd actually wanted this job, he might have bothered shaving.

Ruth turned to face him.

"If it's about how we knew you were going to apply for the job before you sent in your application, you'll find out if we hire you."

"That wasn't what I was going to ask actually," Geoff lied. He didn't like to be predictable. Now he just needed to think of something else to ask quickly.

"Sorry," Ruth said, shifting her weight back from one foot to the other. "That's what all the other applicants have asked me."

"Other applicants? How many people have you interviewed?"

"Nineteen—you're the last person we're seeing." She buttoned her suit jacket and tucked a few loose strands of hair behind her ears. "Here we are. Top floor."

The lift doors opened onto a huge empty room overlooking London, with tall windows stretching from floor to ceiling everywhere you looked. It was like walking into a large open plan office, except there was no furniture, no filing cabinets, and no overpriced vending machines that only sold flapjacks. A few cables were coiled around on the floor next to the elevator doors, a couple of ladders were leaning against a nearby wall, and few pots of paint were stacked next to a bare, concrete pillar. Either these people had just moved in, or they'd seriously misjudged the amount of floor space they needed.

In the far corner of the room, an old man was sitting at a large oak desk, back to the window, head buried in paperwork. Behind him, the scenery was spectacular, offering a panoramic view of both Big Ben and the London Eye—vastly superior to the view from Geoff's bedroom window, which offered a panoramic view of next door's shed and a nearby electricity pylon.

"Mr. Knight over there will be interviewing you," Ruth whispered, leading Geoff across the room. She seemed to be walking a little slower than she was downstairs as if she was somehow hesitant.

"Something the matter?" Geoff said.

"No, nothing," Ruth said, quickening her pace. "Just…"

Before Ruth could say anything more, the man in the corner looked up.

"Ah!" He bellowed. "This must be our final interviewee!" His voice echoed across the floor like an overly boisterous uncle cheering at the wrong point during a wedding speech.

"Yes," Ruth called out. "This is Geoffrey Stamp."

"Excellent!" Mr. Knight said, pouncing out of his seat and rushing over to meet them. He was tall and seemed quite agile for a man of his age, his long strides carrying him toward them at an impressive pace. His thick white hair was combed into a side parting, and he had deep wrinkles around his eyes that suggested he smiled a lot. Dressed in a brown three-piece tweed suit with shiny brown shoes and a yellow silk tie, Geoff guessed this man to be in his seventies.

"You'll have to excuse all this empty space," he said, giving Geoff a firm handshake. "We've only just moved in. Please—have a seat."

Ruth turned to leave.

"Good luck," she said over her shoulder, and left.

Geoff made his way over to the desk and sat down in a rather comfortable leather chair.

"Right, let's get on with this," Mr. Knight said, sitting down on the other side of the desk. He straightened his tie, pushed his work to one side, and placed a single piece of paper in front of him. Geoff recognized the coffee stain in the top corner—this was the letter he'd sent them only a few hours ago.

"'Dear Sir/Madam,'" Mr. Knight read aloud, "'I am writing to apply for the job you advertised in the paper. My name is Geoffrey Stamp. Yours sincerely, Geoffrey Stamp.'"

"How did you get that letter so quickly?" Geoff asked.

"This has to be the worst application I've ever read," Mr. Knight said, ignoring Geoff's question. "It doesn't tell me anything about you. Your hobbies, previous work, it's useless." He screwed up the letter and tossed it over his shoulder.

"But no matter," he said, pulling a clipboard and pen out from one of his desk drawers. "You're here now, so perhaps we can find out more about you. Your hobbies, for instance."

"I don't really have any hobbies."

"You must have a hobby. Football? Reading? What do you do in your spare time?"

Geoff thought hard.

"At the moment I'm trying to complete *Space Commando*."

"Space Commando?"

"It's a computer game."

"So you like to play games?"

"Computer games."

"And nothing else?"

"Not that I can think of."

"You mean to tell me you have no other hobbies besides playing on your computer?"

"No."

"Excellent," he said. "What about going out?"

"Did you just say 'excellent'?"

"Never mind that now. How often do you go out?"

"Not very often."

"How 'not very often'?"

"I don't know—I'd say today is first day I've been out this month."

"It's the first of September," Mr. Knight said, checking his watch. "This is the first day *I've* been out this month."

"It's September?"

Mr. Knight glanced down at his clipboard and made a note. "So you don't go walking?"

"No."

"Shopping?"

"No."

"Clubbing?"

"God, no."

"So if you don't go out, what do you do with your friends?"

"I've lost touch with most of my friends. The only person I see nowadays is the bloke I live with."

"No one else?"

"Well, there's Zoë, the girl who delivers the post."

"I see. So the only people you see are your flatmate and your postwoman."

"I suppose…"

"No friends… excellent," Mr. Knight muttered under his breath. He made another, much longer note.

"Is there something wrong?" Geoffrey said, trying to peek over the top of the clipboard. "I keep saying bad things, and you keep saying 'excellent'."

"Nothing's wrong," Mr. Knight said, placing the clipboard face down on the desk. "Now—tell me about any previous jobs you've had."

"I've only ever had one job, as a paperboy," he paused. "And I was fired from that two years ago for being too old."

"And what were your responsibilities as a paperboy?"

"I was a paperboy."

"Paperboy, yes," Mr. Knight echoed impatiently. "What were your responsibilities?"

"Well, when I say 'paperboy', I don't mean 'policeman'. I threw newspapers at houses. There wasn't really any life-or-death decision making that I can think of."

Mr. Knight leaned back in his creaky chair, placing both hands behind his head.

"So you've never had a proper job," he said, looking up at the ceiling, "You don't go out, you've got no hobbies to speak of, and with the exception of young Tim, you've got no friends."

Geoff nodded.

"You're not very observant, either." Mr. Knight stood up from his desk and turned to look across London. "Did you notice anything odd about what I just said?"

"Not really," Geoff said.

Mr. Knight turned around. "You haven't told me the man you live with is called Tim."

Geoff was so surprised, he got up from his seat. He stood there for a bit, looked around, then decided to sit back down again.

"Are you MI6?" he said.

"No."

"Oh," Geoff sighed, disappointed.

"We've had someone keeping an eye on you for a while," Mr. Knight said, returning to his seat. "Tell me—do you actually *want* this job?"

"Wait a second." Geoff stood up again, hoping this time that the gesture would express some sort of outrage. "What do you mean you've had someone 'keeping an eye on me'?"

"I mean exactly that. We've had someone keeping an eye on you."

"For how long?"

"It doesn't matter. Forget I said anything."

"Forget you said anything? You've been spying on me!"

"Does it really bother you?"

"Of course it does! What sort of holiday company is this, anyway?"

"There are a few things that make us a bit different from you're regular holiday company…" Mr. Knight said.

"Like the fact that you spy on people…"

"That's one of the things, yes. But I can't tell you anything more unless you accept the job."

"That's another thing you haven't explained."

"What?" Mr. Knight said, drumming his fingers impatiently on the desk.

"The job. What is it? Or can't you even tell me that?"

Mr. Knight said nothing.

"Right. So I have to accept the job before I know what it is." Geoff weighed this up in his mind. "Sounds a bit unreasonable."

"Nobody's forcing you to work here."

"Fine. I don't want the job," Geoff said, turning to leave. He felt defiant.

"Sit down," Mr. Knight said. "You're hired."

Geoff found himself doing as he was told, and slowly lowered himself back into the chair. It *was* pretty comfortable, after all. "What?"

"You've got the job," Mr. Knight said, loosening his tie.

"But I just turned the job *down*."

"I know." Mr. Knight looked at his watch. "That's why I'm hiring you."

"Ding!" Geoff said.

That was weird. He was planning to say something along the lines of "what the bloody hell is going on?" Instead, he'd opted for "ding!" He frowned, opening and shutting his mouth like a fish, before realizing the noise had come from the lift behind him. The door slid open and Ruth walked over to where he and Mr. Knight were sitting.

"Ruth—excellent timing," Mr. Knight called out. "Mr. Stamp here's got the job. The *real* job, that is."

"Brilliant," she said, leaning against the corner of Mr. Knight's desk. "Somehow, I had a feeling you'd pick him."

Geoff was confused. "This is some sort of joke TV show, right?" he said, flicking his eyes between Ruth and Mr. Knight. "'TV's Most Hilarious Interview Antics III' or something?"

"No, no no no. This isn't a joke, Geoff," he said.

Geoff flitted his eyes between the two of them again, waiting for someone to explain what the hell was going on.

"What would your reaction be if I told you that we were from the future?" Mr. Knight asked.

"Say that again?" Geoff said, leaning forward slightly. He tilted his left ear toward Mr. Knight in the hope that the question would somehow change if he heard it at a different angle.

"How would you react if I told you that we—myself and Ruth— were from the future?" he repeated.

"The future?" Geoff said.

"Yes."

"The *future* future?"

"The *future* future, yes."

"I'm not sure, really," Geoff said. "It's not the kind of thing I have to react to very often. I'm more used to reacting to things like 'There's a dress code, sir' or 'We've run out of milk.'"

"Fine. I'll just say it then—myself and Ruth—we're from the future. The distant future."

As it turned out, Geoff's reaction was to raise his eyebrows as high as they would go, take a lungful of air, hold it in his cheeks, and exhale slowly.

"I'm going to try to run through this quickly," Mr. Knight continued. "It always works best if I run through it quickly. We work for Time Tours Inc."

"Time Tours Inc?" Geoff said. "Never heard of them."

"You wouldn't have. It's a travel agent, based in the future, that sells holidays to different time periods. Anyway—we want *you* to be a holiday rep for the early twenty-first century—a 'Time Rep', if you like. Your job will be exactly the same as if you were a representative for tourists from another country, except the tourists you'll be dealing with will be from the future. You'll show them the sights. Take them on tours. That's the job in a nutshell."

The speech was concise. Sounded like he'd said it a hundred times.

Geoff was still slowly exhaling air from his cheeks. He'd understood roughly none of what Mr. Knight had just said.

"Any questions?" Ruth said.

"Yes," Geoff said. "Tell me—have you both recently been released from some sort of mental hospital?" Geoff asked.

"No," Ruth said. "We're just normal people."

"From the future," Mr. Knight added.

"Would it be terribly rude if I said that I didn't believe you?"

"You don't believe us?" Mr. Knight said.

"No."

"Why not?"

"Why not? Time travel is impossible!"

"That's what people once said about teleportation."

"That's what people *still* say about teleportation!"

"To be honest," Ruth interrupted, "this is something we've come to expect from all Time Reps when we first tell them. Disbelief. That's why we always orchestrate the little game with the application letters."

"Stops successful interviewees from walking out the door," Mr. Knight added.

"What are you talking about?" Geoff stammered.

"Think about it." Ruth said, leaning down to retrieve Geoff's crumpled letter that Mr. Knight had thrown to the floor. "How could we have known to send a response to your letter before you'd even posted it?"

"Well for a start, you could have … um … er …"

"It's impossible," Ruth said, "unless we were capable of time travel."

Geoff looked out of the window. It was beginning to get dark outside, the sun casting a soft red glow over the London skyline. A sea of streetlights began to flicker on in the distance like lighters in the air at a rock concert.

"Does this convince you that we're telling the truth?" Mr. Knight said.

"Not really," Geoff replied, standing up. "And it's getting late now, so I'm leaving."

"Wait!" Mr. Knight pleaded, leaping out of his chair. "Okay, Mr. Stamp—Okay. We don't normally do this, but if you really don't believe us, we'll prove it to you."

He reached into a drawer and pulled out a small set of earphones.

"Put these on," He said, handing them to Geoff.

"What are they?" Geoff asked, examining them in his hand. They looked like a regular set of shoddy earphones, but there were no wires, as if they were supposed to rest in his ears by themselves.

"Just … put them on," Mr. Knight said, taking a second pair out of his drawer and placing them in his ears. "See? It's fine."

Ruth pulled a similar set out of her trouser pocket and did the same.

"It's okay, Geoff," she smiled.

Geoff looked at Mr. Knight for a moment, rolling the earphones around in the palm of his hand. He didn't see what possible harm there could be in wearing a stupid pair of earphones (unless they were playing hardcore Belgian trance music of course), so he did what he was told.

Once they were in, he listened carefully, but they didn't appear to be making any sound.

"Good," Mr. Knight said. "Now, are you ready?"

"Ready for what?" Geoff said. He felt stupid.

"Ready to travel back in time," Ruth replied.

"Is that what these earpho …"

But before Geoff had a chance to finish his question, he felt his mind tingle as if it were being charged with electricity. His vision blurred, his palms began to sweat, and his heart started beating faster. He felt a bit sick, the same sort of feeling he got when Tim suggested it might be time to tackle the washing up. Suddenly there was a flash. Geoff shut his eyes and wrapped his arms around his face. What was happening to him?"

Then nothing. He felt normal.

"Geoff?" Ruth said.

"Uh-huh?"

"Geoff, lower your arms." He felt her touch his side and jumped.

"It's okay, Geoff—it's over. We're here. Lower your arms."

Geoff lowered his arms but kept his eyes shut.

"Now, open your eyes."

Geoff opened his eyes a crack, then a little wider, then wider still, until they were completely open. What he saw before him was nothing short of amazing. It was unbelievable. Impossible. Crazy.

Mr. Knight stood next to Geoff and placed an arm around his shoulder.

"Welcome," he said, pausing for a few seconds for effect, "To 65 million years BC."

THREE

Geoff couldn't comprehend how it was possible, but somehow, he was no longer standing in an empty, open-plan office, overlooking the streets of London. He was standing on the side of a tall, rocky mountain, overlooking a lush rainforest. His knees were shaking as if they were about to give way at any second. This couldn't have been some parlor trick or complex illusion—real dirt crunched beneath his feet as he stepped forward to take a closer look at his surroundings, the hot sun was beating down on his face from above, and the warm, humid air wrapped itself around him like a heavy, invisible blanket.

Geoff edged toward the side of the mountain and looked down—they were very high up, perhaps a few thousand feet above sea level. Beneath him, he could see all kinds of strange vegetation—species of trees he'd never seen before towering over the canopy of the rainforest, huge plants with giant curved leaves the size of bed sheets, and thick, green vines twisting in all sorts of different directions. This was nature unleashed—a dense, sprawling mass of jungle, totally untouched by mankind. In many ways, it reminded him of the back garden, which he really needed to deal with at some point if he didn't want it to take over the world.

Geoff turned around and looked at Mr. Knight, who was standing a little closer than he would have liked, given how close he was to the edge. Geoff moved away and sat down on a nearby rock.

"Well?" Mr. Knight said, removing his earphones. "What do you think?"

Geoff didn't know what to think. His brain felt as though it had turned to mush, as if he'd just watched something on *Fox News*.

"Have I...gone mad?" he managed.

"No Geoff, you haven't gone mad. You've gone to the Cretaceous Period. And you can remove your earphones now, by the way."

"The...Cretaceous Period?" Geoff said, taking the earphones out one at a time.

"Yes," Mr. Knight said, looking up at a strange bird hovering in the sky. It was small with blue wings and a long beak. Geoff had never seen one before. "The end of the Maastrichtian age of the Cretaceous Period to be precise. Are you familiar with the prehistoric timeline?"

Geoff shook his head. He'd seen *Jurassic Park* a couple of times, but that was about it. In the distance, he noticed the head of a something that looked distinctly dinosaur-like break through a layer of vegetation, its snake-like neck stretching toward the higher branches of a tall tree. The dinosaur snagged the branches in its mouth, stripped away a clump of leaves in its jaw, and began to chew.

"This...this is incredible!" he said, watching a herd of different dinosaurs drinking from a large lake at the foot of another mountain. "I mean...these are real dinosaurs! I'm looking at real dinosaurs!"

"Does this convince you that we're telling the truth?" Ruth asked, sitting down next to him.

"I'm...I'm speechless," Geoff stammered. "I never thought I'd ever see anything like this. It's...it's beautiful."

"Well, don't get too used to it," Mr. Knight said, looking at his watch. "In eight minutes and twenty-nine seconds, everything you see here will turn to dust."

"What do you mean?"

"You're about to see how the dinosaurs became extinct," Mr. Knight replied, looking up in the sky.

"Extinct?"

"You see that shiny dot?" Mr. Knight said, pointing at a faint speck of light in the sky.

Geoff nodded.

"That dot is an asteroid. A very large asteroid. And it's about to hit the Earth with such tremendous force that it will wipe out almost all living creatures on the planet. The moment it strikes, a cloud of super-heated dust will be thrown up in the air, blocking out the sun for years. Huge tsunamis will sweep the planet from one side to the other, and colossal shockwaves will set off volcanoes and earthquakes on a global scale."

Geoff gulped.

"Can I ask a question?" he said.

"Go on…"

"Where exactly is this asteroid going to hit the Earth?" he said, looking nervously up at the sky.

"Right in front of us," Mr. Knight said, pointing toward the middle of the rainforest. "By my calculations, we're about forty miles away from the impact point."

"I see," Geoff said, pausing for a moment. "In eight minutes, you say?"

"Seven minutes and fifty-three seconds," Mr. Knight said, checking his watch again.

"Can I ask another question?"

"Of course," Mr. Knight said. "What is it?"

"Well, don't get me wrong—this is all very interesting and everything, but isn't it a teeny tiny bit dangerous? I mean, shouldn't we be somewhere else? Like in a nuclear bunker?"

"Nonsense," Mr. Knight said. "We're perfectly safe. We'll just wait here long enough to see the moment the asteroid strikes, then we'll transport ourselves back to the future. It'll be fine."

Geoff starting rubbing his hands together. He always rubbed his hands together when he was nervous.

"I'd rather we just left now, if it's all the same to you…" he said, hastily inserting his earphones again. "I mean, I'm convinced—time travel is real. You guys are telling the truth. Good stuff." He pressed the earphones into his ears as far as they would go. "Shall we?"

"But this is the proof I promised you, Mr. Stamp. You are about to witness the most devastating event in the history of the planet. Difficult thing to fake, wouldn't you say?"

"Yes, but we really don't have to stay here on my account," he insisted, fiddling with his earphones. "How do you make these things work?"

Ruth turned to Geoff and placed a hand on his shoulder.

"Don't panic," she said. "Everything will be fine."

Geoff took a few deep breaths.

"So you guys… really are from the future?"

"That's right."

"And you really do send people on holidays to different time periods?"

"We do."

"And you need me to be a holiday rep… for the twenty-first century?"

"A *Time* Rep…" Mr. Knight corrected him.

"But… why me?" Geoff asked, looking up as a flock of strange birds glided overhead. The speck of light in the sky had grown ever so slightly bigger.

"Oh, you have no idea how special you are," Mr. Knight said, taking a handkerchief from his breast pocket and wiping a few beads of sweat from his forehead. "Our supercomputer has taken years to draw up a shortlist of candidates suitable for the job, and you were one of them."

No one had ever called Geoff "special" before. He was curious to find out more.

"Your… supercomputer?" he said, leaning forward. It really was quite hot out here, the sun shining directly down on them.

"Look, I may be getting ahead of myself, so stop me if this gets confusing. We've got this supercomputer in the future."

"Stop."

Mr. Knight ignored him. "This supercomputer has so much processing power, it can predict causality. In other words, it can tell us the precise effects of interfering with the space-time continuum in a particular way."

"And this computer picked me to be a … Time Rep?"

"Well, it short-listed you."

"But why?"

"Because it worked out that you're totally insignificant."

Geoff blinked. For a moment he forgot about the asteroid.

"Insignificant?"

"Yes," Mr. Knight said, walking toward a small piece of shade under a tree. "Every Time Rep must be a totally insignificant person. Imagine if we asked someone important or famous from the twenty-first century to do the job—we'd be in danger of changing the course of history. By only approaching people who don't matter to the course of the space-time continuum, we avoid that risk."

"And we avoid drawing attention to ourselves," Ruth added. "It goes without saying that time tourism is kept absolutely top secret to the destination time periods."

"I'm insignificant?" Geoff said, standing up from his rock. "I *don't matter?*"

"You don't matter to the space-time continuum, but you certainly matter to us," Mr. Knight said, leaning against the tree trunk. "You see, because most people have an influence on the course of history, we can't ask them to do this job because we'd be interfering with the past. You, however, are *so* insignificant, that even if I were to kill you on the spot, history would remain completely unchanged. That's why we need you to become a Time Rep. You're one of the only people we can ask because it doesn't change anything. Not even a little bit."

Geoff looked down at the ground and twisted his right foot into the dirt.

"Not even a smidge?" he said.

"The fewer people you know, the less you go out—the better. It's taken our computer seven years of temporal analysis to produce a list of people from this time period insignificant enough to be considered for the job."

"But your computer could be wrong," Geoff said, feeling a little hurt. "Surely I can't be *that* insignificant."

"Trust us Geoff," Ruth said. "You are. Apart from your suitability for being a Time Rep, you're worthless. You're less important to the world than certain types of mushroom. There's only you and nineteen other people living in the twenty-first century who are insignificant enough to be considered for the job. People who draw absolutely no attention to themselves. Lazy. Reclusive. Lonely. Unemployed. Uninteresting. Unattractive…"

"Stop, stop, stop!" Geoff said, glancing up again. The dot of light was now quite distinctive against the clear blue sky. "Uninteresting? Unattractive?"

"Maybe not unattractive…just normal. Bland. None of you would stand out."

"So what makes *me* so special?" Geoff said, looking down again. "Am I especially bland? Am I more uninteresting than anyone else? Am I the world's most boring, unsociable person?"

"No, no no. The only thing that marks you out from the others is the fact that you turned the job down. Everyone else accepted."

"That's it?" Geoff said. "Why is that so important?"

"When you turned down the job, you intentionally denied yourself an opportunity. You showed me that you had no aspirations— no desire to better yourself. All the other applicants saw this job as a chance prove themselves, a chance to change their ways. And that is exactly what we can't have—we need you to stay the way you are. We need you to stay insignificant."

"So…what did you tell the others?"

"The others?"

"Yeah. After they accepted the job offer."

"All the other applicants still got a job," Ruth said, "just not this job." She turned to look across the rainforest. Over in a small clearing a few miles away, something that looked as if it might be a tyrannosaurus rex emerged from the jungle. "We sent them all to Spain to work as regular holiday reps. They've got no idea that they actually failed the test."

"I don't understand," Geoff said, watching as the tyrannosaurus stomped toward a group of smaller dinosaurs. "If this whole time-tourism thing is such a big secret, why did you advertise the job in the paper?"

"We didn't," Mr. Knight smiled, emerging from under the tree. "We had your newspaper custom printed. The advert only appeared in the copy sent to your house."

"But how did you know I would see it?"

"Because we told Tim to show it to you."

Geoff stopped looking at the tyrannosaurus rex and snapped his gaze around.

"What?"

"Tim. Your housemate. He works for us. He's the one who's been spying on you."

Ruth wrinkled her brow and turned to Mr. Knight. "*Spying* might not be the best way of putting it," she said.

"Well, how else would you put it?" Mr. Knight scoffed.

"Wait a minute," Geoff said, only just starting to comprehend what he was being told. "Tim?"

"Yes, Tim."

"My housemate, Tim?" he said, taking a few steps toward Mr. Knight. "Not some other Tim?"

"Your housemate, Tim."

Geoff thought about this for a bit.

"Are you sure?" he said.

"Of course I'm sure!" Mr. Knight replied impatiently.

"And I suppose he's from the future too?"

"He is."

"Right. What year did you say you were from?"

"I didn't. I suppose the year would roughly be 3050, but we don't really measure time in Earth years anymore."

"No?"

"No. We use Outer Spiral Galactic Mean Time."

"Course you do," Geoff said. "Much easier system. I'm surprised we haven't started using it already."

"Look, Tim isn't a spy," Ruth said. "Think of him more as a headhunter. It's his job to make first contact with potential Time Reps, get them ready for the role, and keep an eye out for any disruptions in the space-time continuum as a result of our interference. And yes—he's had to conceal the truth from you for a number of years, but it's the only way we can be sure you're suitable for the job. Besides—now that you've been hired, he'll be a great mentor, as he is for all the other Time Reps he's identified throughout history."

"I don't believe it," Geoff said. He was so dumbfounded at what he was being told, he hadn't noticed the dot of light was even larger now, like a smaller, second sun in the sky.

"Think about it. He invited you to live with him when you lost your job, didn't he? Rent free?"

"So what?"

"Bit convenient, isn't it?"

"Convenient?"

"Don't you see?" Mr. Knight said, glancing down at his watch. "He invited you to live with him because he decided that you had potential."

"You're wrong," Geoff said. "He invited me to live with him because I'd lost my job. He felt sorry for me."

"He already knew you were going to lose your job," Mr. Knight said. "That's why the company bought a house on your paper route. We did it so that Tim would be able to establish a relationship with you. That way, he was able to convince you to move in with him when you got sacked instead of…doing what you would have done otherwise."

"You mean to tell me I was never supposed to live with this guy? That my life was supposed to follow a different path?"

"Trust us," Ruth said, "you're not missing out on anything."

"Once you'd moved in," Mr. Knight continued, "he bought the games consoles to keep you entertained, did all the shopping, everything. He's been keeping you as detached from the outside world as possible, minimizing your contact with other people. In essence, he been grooming you for the job from the moment he met you."

"I don't understand," Geoff said. "Wouldn't it have just been easier to ask me directly? Put all the 'Time Reps' to the test on day one?"

"Yes, but that's not allowed," Ruth said. "Contacting someone from another time period must be taken slowly. You can't just wander up and ask someone to be a Time Rep."

"Why not?"

"Regulations," she sighed, the lull in her voice suggesting that she didn't agree with half of them. "There are hundreds of regulations for traveling through time."

"Such as …?"

"Any alterations we make must be done as gradually as possible. Asking someone to be a Time Rep out of the blue is too immediate. As we said, people like Tim constantly monitor any changes in the space-time continuum when they interact with candidates, and as such we have to be *extremely* careful, take things very slowly. It's only when we're completely sure that a candidate is ready for the role that we bring them in for an interview."

"Anyway," Mr. Knight said, putting his earphones on again. "By my watch we have exactly fifteen seconds before the Earth is totally decimated, so we'd better get ready to leave."

Geoff's earphones were already firmly in place, hopefully ready to do their thing. *Don't panic*, he said to himself—don't panic. He looked up at the sky—the asteroid was now looming above them like a giant finger of death: black and jagged and devastatingly huge.

He panicked.

The next thing he knew, there was an almighty roar. All around, creatures stopped what they were doing and looked up as the asteroid broke through the upper atmosphere, the hulking mass of rock blazing through the sky in a trail of smoke and flames. Before Geoff even had a chance to take in what was happening, the asteroid pummeled into the forest before him, exactly where Mr. Knight had predicted. In an instant, every tree, plant and animal was vaporized.

Shockwaves thundered through the ground, plumes of scorched earth billowed into the air, and the sky turned black—the sun disappearing behind a thick cloud of ash.

"Time to leave!" Mr. Knight shouted as the mountain they were standing on began to collapse.

But Geoff didn't get a chance to hear what Mr. Knight had said because by now he was slumped on the ground, unconscious.

Four

Which was by no means unusual. Geoff often fell asleep while people were talking to him. Particularly relatives. But this was different though—the sight of a mass extinction event was obviously too much for him, and he must have fainted. Either that or the earphones were actually playing some kind of warped music designed to make you fall unconscious, like a Celine Dion album. In any case, one minute he was witnessing the end of the dinosaurs, the next he was back in his recurring dream, strolling down a hill toward his imaginary lake.

While there was no mistaking the fact that this lake only existed in his mind, Geoff was conscious that it was loosely based on a real-life lake he used to go to with Zoë, a lake they used to stroll around together when they'd finished their rounds in the morning. It had always been a place that had made him feel comfortable, and, in times of stress, it was somewhere he always went to in his dreams to help him relax.

This time was no exception. His imagination had done its best to make it a really nice day for fishing; it was crisp, early-morning kind of weather, the air thick with fog and sweet to taste. In most respects, he felt a bit like being at summer camp, except he wasn't eleven, and he wasn't being tricked by the older boys to go and ask the adults for a "Scrotum Scratcher" under the cruel misapprehension that it was a kitchen utensil.

No, this dream was refreshing. Even though he knew he was asleep, he felt awake, or at least more energetic than normal. Instead of spilling like a rag doll onto his usual imaginary bench, he stood upright, nearer the bank, and cast his line further out into the water than ever before. Almost immediately, Geoff's fishing rod was nearly tugged out of his hand—his imagination taking him completely by surprise. Digging his feet into the mud, he steadied himself and tried to maintain a better grip. Whatever he had snagged, it was huge, and he wasn't sure how much longer he'd be able to hang on. The rod was now squirming around uncontrollably, desperately trying to prize itself free from Geoff's hands, which were beginning to get a little sore. He didn't understand—he'd never dreamt anything like this before—rusty hubcaps and old boots didn't usually put up this much of a fight, unless of course they were still attached to cars or people.

Something began to emerge from the water. Was that ... a head? He tried to look a little closer—yes, it looked a head, hidden under some sort of black hood. But it wasn't just a head he had caught—as he pulled harder, the torso and arms began to emerge. This was a whole person! It was certainly heavy enough to be a whole person. His eyes began to water with the strain of trying to control the rod—it was starting to slip from his grasp. Then, just as suddenly as it had started, the battle was over. The rod broke free of Geoff's rather pathetic grip, sailed across the lake, and glugged into the water. The hooded figure disappeared back under the surface, leaving only a few bubbles to commemorate the struggle.

Geoff dragged his feet out of the muddy bank and slumped down on the bench. What was that all about? Was there some sort of significance to what just happened? Why was he dreaming about pulling a hooded figure out of the water? He rubbed his thumbs into his palms to try to bring some circulation back to his hands.

"There," a voice said. "He's waking up. Should be able to hear us now."

"Who said that?" Geoff said, snapping his head around. He couldn't see anybody.

"Speech has returned, too."

"How long before his sight returns?" Another voice. Sounded like Tim.

"He should be fully awake within a few minutes."

"Don't bet on it," Tim's voice said. "This guy slept through a burglary once."

"So what? Most burglars are quiet."

"So were these," Tim said. "Except they stole the bed he was sleeping in. Rolled him right off the mattress and into a pile of clothes and he didn't stir for a second."

The voices weren't really coming from any particular direction—they just seemed to be booming out of the sky.

"What's going on?" Geoff said.

"We're bringing you back into the space-time continuum," Tim's voice said. "Your senses are returning one at a time."

All of a sudden, his body froze. He couldn't move his arms or his legs.

"I can't move!" Geoff shouted.

"Don't struggle!" The other voice said, "That's just your sense of touch returning. We've got you strapped onto a table here, so your senses are just aligning with reality."

"You've got me strapped onto a table?"

"Just until your sight returns, Geoff," Tim said. "We don't want you walking into any doors, or anything."

It was at this stage that Geoff would normally pinch himself to make sure he wasn't dreaming. The difficulty here was that he already *was* dreaming, so he couldn't move to pinch himself even if he wanted to double-check. All he could do was close his eyes and hope that this would all be over when he opened them again.

FIVE

"Geoff?"

"What?"

"Open your eyes."

"No."

"We think your sight has returned."

"Oh good," Geoff said. "What about my sanity? How's that coming along?"

"Just open your eyes," Tim said.

"Can I open *one* eye?"

There was a pause.

"If it makes you feel better."

Geoff cautiously opened his left eye. He appeared to be lying flat on his back, his arms and legs firmly strapped to some sort of operating table. Unfortunately, that was all he could really see; above him, a large overcomplicated lighting rig shone in his eyes, blinding him from the rest of his surroundings.

"I've changed my mind," Geoff said. "I think I'll just close my eyes again."

"Wait," Tim said. "Let me turn those lights off so you can see properly."

The lighting rig folded in on itself and retracted into the ceiling in one graceful movement, as if it secretly wished it had chosen a career in ballet dancing.

"Is that better?"

With the lights no longer shining in his eyes, Geoff could now see that the room he was in was mostly empty. There were no sofas, no pictures hanging on the walls—nothing. With the exception of a door in the far corner, the room was featureless. Completely white. Average size. A room that would have serious trouble describing itself on a dating website.

Tim was standing in one corner, although at first Geoff didn't recognize him—he was wearing a long white laboratory coat, and his face was concealed behind a pair of large plastic goggles similar to the ones Geoff wore when he was doing his laundry. Next to him stood a much older man—probably the owner of the other voice Geoff had heard in his dream. The man's face was quite craggy with a thick white beard, his eyes nestled away behind a pair of bushy white eyebrows. He appeared to be leaning on an old wooden walking stick for support and, like Tim, wore a white coat and goggles.

"Right," Tim said, rubbing his hands enthusiastically, "Let's help him up."

The two men approached the table and began to unfasten the large leather straps securing Geoff's arms and legs.

"What's the last thing you remember?" Tim said, releasing Geoff's right arm.

"Dinosaurs!" Geoff said. "I saw…I mean, there was an asteroid, and fire, and earthquakes, and fire, and an asteroid! And earthquakes!"

"Good…anything else?"

"An asteroid!"

"Geoff, calm down."

Geoff tried to collect his thoughts.

"I remember someone telling me that you were a spy," he scowled, recalling his conversation just before the asteroid struck.

"I can't believe Knight still calls me that," Tim said, walking around to release Geoff's other arm. "Did he not explain to you what I do?"

"This other girl did. Ruth. She said you were a recruiter or something…"

"More like a headhunter," Tim replied, removing his goggles.

Geoff sat up and rubbed his wrists. It felt like someone had been practicing their Chinese burn technique on him.

"Well this is excellent," the bearded man said, removing his goggles. "He seems to remember everything. Sounds like he's suffered no residual memory loss whatsoever."

"Who's this guy?" Geoff asked.

"I am Dr. Skivinski," The man said, leaning on his walking stick. "But you can call me Eric."

"Turn and face me, would you?" Tim said, pulling out a small pen torch from his coat pocket.

"What are you doing?" Geoff said, swiveling his body around.

"Just removing your brain," Tim replied.

Geoff looked at him in silence. Despite having known Tim for several years, he never could tell when Tim was being sarcastic, and now would have been a pretty good time to start learning.

"That was a joke," Tim replied, shining the torch in Geoff's eyes. "You seem fine. Now—I just need to ask you a few simple questions to make sure you're okay to leave the room."

"Questions?" Geoff said, leaning back on his hands.

"Keep still. Do you feel disorientated?"

"Yes."

"Confused?"

"Very."

"Sick?"

"I want to throw up."

"Are these stupid answers, or is that actually how you feel?"

"I'd quite like somebody to explain what the bloody hell is going on," Geoff said.

"I think he's angry," Eric said. "Could be one of the side effects of bringing him back here while he was unconscious."

"Or it could be one of the side effects of being kidnapped and strapped to a table," Geoff said.

"You haven't been kidnapped," Tim said. "We've brought you to the future to understand a bit more about time tourism."

Geoff looked down at the floor.

"Tim—have you really been lying to me all this time?"

Tim thought about this for a moment, lolling his head from side to side.

"Not as such," he replied eventually, putting his torch away. "You never asked me what I did for a living, and I never told you. In that sense, it wasn't so much lying—I just…didn't volunteer certain information."

Geoff pulled his best unimpressed expression, like the one he used when Tim had tried to convince him to eat quiche a few years ago.

"Look, I'm sorry for deceiving you Geoff—I really am. But there was no other way of doing this. And hopefully you'll learn to appreciate what we've done when you see what this is all about—the things you'll see, the places you'll visit, the people you'll meet—your life is about to change in the most exciting way imaginable. And I know you're probably angry with me right now, but trust me—it will all have been worth it."

Geoff wasn't sure what to say. He felt conflicted. Part of him was furious with his friend. And a little scared. But at the same time, he had to admit that he was curious. He'd just been to 65 million years BC, for goodness sake.

"So where are we now?" he asked.

"You're in the future," Tim replied, helping Geoff down from the table. "And this is one of our arrivals chambers."

Geoff looked blankly at Tim. He had no idea what that meant.

"All time tourists leave for their destinations from a departure chamber and arrive back in an arrivals chamber," Tim clarified.

Geoff still looked blankly at Tim. He was sure all this would probably make sense at some point, but right now he felt as if someone was trying to explain to him the logic behind 90% of Nintendo's business decisions.

"You okay to walk?" Eric said.

"I think so," Geoff said, rolling his head around and stretching his arms in the air.

"Good. In that case, all we need to do is get you signed through at customs, and then we can start to show you around."

Geoff frowned.

"This place has customs?"

Tim walked over to the door and opened it.

"Just think of this place as you would an airport," he explained, motioning Geoff to follow him. "When time tourists come back from their holiday, they go through customs, collect their belongings from the arrivals lounge, hug some relatives, that sort of thing."

Tim led Geoff down a long, wide corridor, with Eric following a few steps behind. The corridor was a completely different architectural style to the cold, plain feel of the Arrivals Chamber, with dark stone walls, ornamental candelabras, and tall gothic archways towering overhead. Looking up, he noticed various posters hanging down from above, advertising what seemed to be different holiday destinations. One read: "Visit the 22nd century Varsarian invasion and see their final annihilation in the 28th century for one unbelievable price!" The picture underneath seemed to be an artist's impression of a huge flying saucer crashing into Big Ben. Or was that a photograph?

"Who are the Varsarians?" Geoff asked.

"That's a long story," Eric answered. "The Varsarians were a race of aliens who tried to wipe out humanity centuries ago. It's our most popular tourist destination."

After a few minutes of walking, the corridor began to curve to the right. Geoff began to hear a general murmur of chitter-chatter coming from ahead.

"We're nearly there now," Tim said, slowing down to walk alongside Geoff, "and it sounds like quite a few people have just come back from somewhere."

The corridor opened out into a massive hall with thin shafts of sunlight pinpricking their way through a spectacular stained glass ceiling. The visual effect was stunning, casting everything below in a variety of different pastel colors. The walls of the hall were a lighter colored stone, the ceiling was lined with an elaborate piece of decorative coving, and the floor was tiled with shiny marble slabs, polished to such a fine sheen that Geoff could see his reflection if he looked down. He noticed his flies were undone and tried to pull them up without anyone noticing.

What was Tim talking about? This place looked nothing like an airport—it was more like the hypothetical offspring of Grand Central Station and a cathedral. Where were the yellow signs sending you on a treasure hunt to find the nearest bin? Where were the sandpaper-like carpets you only found in airports and math classrooms? And where were the shops full of sales assistants trying to convince you to spent £20 on a giant Toblerone?

There must have been nearly a thousand people in front of Geoff, all snaking their way around in a long queuing system that split off through several manned gates at the opposite end of the hall.

"So what happens now?" Geoff said.

"We'll just have to wait our turn," Tim said, leading Geoff and Eric up to the end of the queue. "Then we can start showing you the departure lounge, the paradox-scanning facilities, everything that happens here before people are cleared to travel."

Geoff looked ahead at the people in the queue.

Something was a little strange.

The family in front of them were dressed in torn brown rags.

Further in front, a couple looked like something out of *Pride and Prejudice.*

The more he looked, the more he realized that everyone was wearing something unexpected. This included Geoff, since it was unusual to see him not wearing pajamas. But you didn't usually see people dressed in togas, politely waiting in line. Or men in pantaloons. He felt like he'd arrived at a birthday party without realizing it was fancy dress.

One of the children from the brown rag family in front began to stare at Geoff. He stared and stared through his freckle-framed eyes as if Geoff was the most interesting person he'd ever seen. He stared at Geoff's shoes. His clothes. His face. His legs. Just when this was starting to get mildly annoying, the child finally tugged on his mother's sleeve.

"Mum," he said out loud, not taking his eyes off Geoff, "look at that man's clothes!"

The mother flicked her eyes over to Geoff, then back to her son.

"What time period do you think he visited, Mum?"

"Oh, I don't know, Ollie," the mother said. The tiredness in her voice suggested that this was the hundredth question little Ollie had asked today.

"Hey, Mister," the kid said, cocking his head. "What time did you go to?"

"Er…what?" Geoff replied. He didn't speak child.

"What time did you go to?" The kid narrowed his eyes as if he was weighing up several candidate time periods in his mind.

"This is Geoffrey Stamp," Eric interrupted, sensing Geoff's struggle at answering the question. "New Time Rep."

"My goodness," the mother said, quickly tugging her son away. "Not *the* Geoffrey Stamp?" Her husband and a few other people up ahead began to look around.

"No, no," Geoff replied, turning his gaze to Tim and Eric. "I assume there is some other Geoffrey Stamp?"

Tim and Eric looked at each other, saying nothing.

Geoff looked back at the woman. "You've heard of me?"

"You're the new rep," she said. "For the twenty-first century?"

Geoff turned back to Tim and Eric. "How does she know that?"

"Your name's been all over the news for the past week," Eric said.

"It has?" Geoff said.

The woman in front of them turned to the rest of the queue.

"Can everyone please move aside?" She shouted, "Geoffrey Stamp is coming through!"

The chatter in the hall began to quiet down. A few more people began to look around.

"Oh, don't worry about me," Geoff said, stepping back in embarrassment. "I'll wait in line."

"You don't have to wait, Mr. Stamp," one of the cavemen said. "Please, go straight through!"

Geoff turned to Tim.

"What's going on?" he whispered.

"I thought this might happen," Tim replied. "Time Reps are starting to be treated like *ambassadors* these days."

"What?"

"You're now quite an important person to know," Eric said. "Did Mr. Knight take you through any of your responsibilities as a Time Rep?"

"He just said that I'd be showing people the sights," Geoff said. "You know, like a regular holiday rep. Why—is there a bit of international diplomacy involved as well?"

"Not quite," Tim said. "But the job is a little more complicated that just showing people around."

"Such as …?"

"Well, let's say one of your tourists gets in trouble with the police for breaking a law that no longer exists—most people are insured to have their bail paid and legal representation organised by their Time Rep."

"Or say one of your tourists is hit by a bus," Eric said. "You'll be expected to be at the scene within minutes to arrange safe passage back to the future where they will receive proper medical treatment."

"A good Time Rep can be the difference between life and death," Tim explained, "and these tourists know it. You'll be treated with a huge amount of respect while you're here."

Geoff looked back at the crowd of people, most of whom were now looking straight back at him. He took a few tentative steps forward, a little unnerved by the fact that people were moving aside as he approached them.

"That's Geoffrey Stamp," Geoff heard a Victorian-looking man point out to his daughter as he passed by. "He's a very important man from the twenty-first century…" The little girl looked up at Geoff, meeting his gaze briefly before burying her face in shyness into her teddy bear.

Geoff began to feel a little uncomfortable—he'd never known so many people to be looking at him at once, apart from that time when he'd accidentally fallen asleep on a train one night and woken up the next morning surrounded by a hundred commuters who had been trying to work out if he was dead.

He needed to get out of here as soon as possible.

"Mr. Stamp!" someone shouted. "Mr. Stamp!"

Geoff stopped walking and looked in the direction of the voice. It seemed to be coming from a medieval knight struggling to push his way through the crowd in a clunky suit of armor.

"Can I just say what a pleasure it is to meet you," the knight said, lifting his faceplate to reveal a fawning grin. "You can rest assured that my next trip will definitely be to the twenty-first century!" He extended a gauntlet-clad hand for Geoff to shake.

Geoff didn't really know how to respond to this, so he shook the man's hand, smiled uncomfortably, and continued toward the customs gates at the end of the hall. More and more people around him were beginning to mention his name to the point that he couldn't really hear what they were saying. All he could hear was "Geoffrey Stamp … Geoffrey Stamp … Geoffrey Stamp … Geoffrey Stamp," his name drowning out any other snippets of conversation. He could occasionally pick out the odd detail here and there—someone mentioning that he'd turned down the job, someone else saying he used to be a paperboy, but mainly he could just hear his name: "Geoffrey Stamp … Geoffrey Stamp … Geoffrey Stamp … Geoffrey Stamp." The words were now ringing in his ears, repeating over and over again, louder and louder, almost as if they were being chanted by the crowd. He waded past the last few people in the queue and hurried over to the nearest customs official, desperate to leave the overwhelming reverberation of "Geoffrey Stamp," which was echoing all around the hall.

"Name?" the man said, licking his pencil.

"Take a wild guess," Geoff said, staring blankly at the official.

"This is Geoffrey Stamp," Tim said. "New Time Rep for the twenty-first century."

"Another rep?" the official said, jotting something down on his clipboard. "This is the fourth one you boys have brought in today! Just signed through some pharaoh from 3000 BC. He was a new Time Rep, too."

"Well, we've got a lot of new destinations planned this year," Tim told the customs official. "How long is this going to take?"

"Well, you'll need to take a sample of his DNA. And you'll need to inoculate him."

"Inoculate me?" Geoff said, looking around at his minders.

"There's a few airborne viruses your twenty-first century immune system won't be able to deal with," Eric said. He turned to the customs official. "That's all been taken care of," he said. "I personally inoculated Mr. Stamp when he arrived, and we've already got his blood, hair, saliva, semen, and tissue samples on record."

"You've got what?" Geoff said, snapping his head around.

"Relax," Tim assured him. "It's just a precaution—we need to keep a record of everyone who goes in and out of here."

Geoff was appalled—this was such a blatant disregard for his human rights, it made the terms and conditions of using his games console's online service seem perfectly reasonable. He was just about to protest when his attention was distracted by a group of armed guards he noticed out of the corner of his eye.

He turned to get a closer look. There were ten of them, each dressed in bright blue uniforms. They all wore dark glasses and earpieces, held large rifles firmly in front of them with both hands, and had stony expressions on their faces. This was quite an appropriate description since each of them looked as though they were literally carved out of rock.

"Why all the security?" Geoff said.

"We've had a lot of attempted terrorist attacks this month," Eric answered. He put his walking stick under his arm and took the clipboard from the official. "So you can't be too careful these days."

"What the hell are you talking about?" Geoff said.

"Some people aren't just here to go on holiday," Eric explained, signing something off. "A few have other ideas. They try to use the time-travel facilities to go back and change the past for their own political agenda." He checked over a few more details on the clipboard, handed it to Tim, and rested back down on his walking stick.

"People try to change the past?"

"I'm afraid so," Tim replied, adding a few remarks underneath whatever Eric had written. "Ever since this place opened up, there have been various attempts to abuse the technology and change history: people trying to go back and help Guy Fawkes blow up the houses of Parliament, distant relatives of Holocaust victims trying to go back and assassinate Hitler, peace activists trying to prevent World War 4. There's even a rumor that some people are trying to…" He trailed off, as if he'd thought the better of finishing his sentence.

"Trying to… what?" Geoff said.

"Nothing. Let's just say that any attempt to change the course of history is considered an act of terrorism." He handed the clipboard back to the official.

"Did Mr. Knight tell you about my supercomputer?" Eric said. "The one that predicted your total insignificance as a human being?"

"He may have mentioned it," Geoff said, rubbing the back of his head—he'd been trying to put that to the back of his mind. "Listen—are you sure about this whole insignificance thing? Maybe this 'super' computer made some sort of mistake?"

"I spent seventeen years of my life writing the six-billion-character algorithm it uses to make those predictions," Eric said, stroking his beard. "Won my first Nobel Prize just for suggesting the initial theory in a bar. Trust me—in the fifteen years it has been operational, not once has it made a mistake. The very fact that nothing changed when we removed you from the twenty-first century should be a testament to that."

"Still could be a mistake," Geoff said.

Eric took a deep breath.

"The computer predicts *everything*. It is 100 percent reliable. It has never made a mistake, and it predicts that it never *will* make a mistake. It is infallible. That's why we use it to 'paradox scan' every person before they leave this time period. If the computer predicts any changes to the space-time continuum, deliberate or not, as a result of a particular journey, then that tourist is blocked from accessing the departure chamber and sent home immediately."

"We'll show you how it all works later," Tim said, suspecting that they were getting a little ahead of themselves.

"You gentleman are clear to proceed to the Arrivals Lounge," the customs official said. He motioned them to move along, handing Geoff a small badge. "Wear that if you enter any restricted areas," he said, and turned to the next person in the queue.

Geoffrey looked at the badge. On it was a hologram of his face, his fingerprint, and the words "GEOFFREY STAMP—TIME REP— 21st CENTURY." He didn't really want any more strangers knowing who he was and coming up to him to shake his hand, so he tucked the badge in his coat pocket and followed Tim and Eric through the customs gate.

The Arrivals Lounge was bustling with more strangely dressed tourists, the different outfits providing an insight into the kind of places you could visit. To Geoff's left, a few people dressed in Tudor clothes were collecting their luggage from one of the many conveyor belts. To his right, a group of children wearing nothing but fig leaves were chasing each other around. Tim and Eric pushed their way through the crowd, looking back every so often to make sure they hadn't lost Geoff. They seemed to be making their way over to a row of brightly lit elevators at the back of the hall. Geoff carefully negotiated his way through the crowd and followed Tim and Eric into the nearest one.

"Please state your destination," a synthesized female voice said. Unless he was mistaken, this was the same voice Geoff had heard in the lift with Ruth before his interview.

"Take us to the Departure Lounge," Tim said.

Six

The lift began to descend to its destination.

"These lifts," Geoff said, looking around at the shiny interior. No buttons again. "They recognize your voice?"

"That's right," Tim said.

"Is it easy to confuse them?"

"What do you mean, 'confuse them'?"

"Let's say we were talking about someone we knew in the basement. When one of us said the word 'basement,' would it think we wanted to go the basement, or would it know that we were just saying the word 'basement'?"

"Is that important?" Tim said. "Why do you want to know?"

"Just curious."

"The lift is programed to look at the context of the word to determine if it is a command," Eric explained. "It knows when it's being spoken to."

"So you can't fool it?"

"I don't know," Eric said. "I've got better things to do with my time than try to trick a lift into going to a floor I don't want to go to."

"I suppose it is a silly thing to do, now that you mention it," Geoff said.

The group stood in silence for a few moments.

"Basement!" Geoff blurted out suddenly.

The lift still didn't seem to change direction.

"Maybe this place doesn't have a basement," Geoff said.

"Or maybe the lift knew you were trying to trick it," Eric said.

"How would it know that?"

"You've just spent the last two minutes talking about whether you could confuse the lift by saying 'basement,' and then you said, 'Basement'. It doesn't take a genius to work out that it's a trick."

"But that would mean that the lift can understand everything we're saying!" Geoff said.

"Correct," Eric replied.

"But…don't you find that weird?" Geoff said, suddenly feeling a little intimidated. "I'd rather the lift wasn't listening to our conversation!"

"I'd rather *I* wasn't listening to our conversation," Tim said.

"Now arriving at the Departure Lounge," the elevator said, coming to an abrupt halt.

The doors opened to reveal another huge gothic hall similar in design to the arrivals lounge. There must have been tens of thousands of people here. Some were seated, looking up at huge glowing departure screens that appeared to be hovering in mid-air. Other people were in more of a hurry, barging their way through the crowds, luggage crashing around in tow.

"The Departure Lounge is the starting point for all time tourists," Tim said, raising his voice over the murmur of the crowd.

It really was *very* busy here, with all sorts of strangely dressed people rushing off in different directions. Geoff found it quite entertaining to look at the various costumes in the room and try to guess which time period people were going to visit. For the most part, this was quite easy: he assumed that the group dressed as cowboys were going back to the Wild West and that the group dressed as World War II Allied soldiers were going back to 1940s Europe. But other costumes posed more of a challenge. Silver jumpsuits? Bright yellow dungarees? Either these people were about to present some sort of nightmarish children's television program, or they were travelling somewhere later than the twenty-first century: a place where Geoff was not familiar with the fashion. This was not say that Geoff was particularly familiar with the fashion of his own time period—indeed, beyond knowing that it was inadvisable to step outside without any clothes on, his knowledge concerning what to wear was about as developed as a spoon's sense of smell.

"We should try to tag along with the next group that gets called up," Eric said to Tim.

"Agreed," Tim replied, forging his way into the crowd. "Stay close to me, Geoff," he said over his shoulder.

Geoff followed his hosts across the departure lounge, wading through groups of 1920s gangsters, astronauts and hippies.

"THIS IS A CUSTOMER ANNOUNCEMENT," a voice blared over the loudspeaker. "WILL CUSTOMERS TRAVELLING TO 1666 AD PLEASE MAKE THEIR WAY TO QUARANTINE CHAMBER SIXTEEN."

A group of people dressed as what Geoff could only describe as 'generic peasants attire' seemed to respond to this announcement. They got up from their seats, had a bit of a stretch, and ambled their way over to an exit marked "Quarantine Chambers 0–50."

"Here we go," Tim said. "Let's follow them."

Geoff tugged on Tim's sleeve. "Quarantine Chamber Sixteen?"

"All tourists are quarantined briefly before departure," Tim said over his shoulder, "just to make sure they're not carrying any diseases or viruses that cannot be cured in the past."

"Why?"

"Because we don't want someone going back in time and spreading today's cold virus," Tim replied. "It'd be the plague all over again."

The quarantine chambers looked a little familiar.

Frosted glass.

All the tourists were sitting patiently on frosted glass benches, looking aimlessly up at a frosted glass ceiling, leaning back against frosted glass walls. Everything was frosted glass.

"Frosted glass!" The words fell out of Geoff's mouth before he knew why he wanted to say them.

"What?" Tim said.

"This whole place is made of frosted glass!"

"It's not frosted glass," Eric said. "It's a special sensory material we use to detect any extraneous organisms. Viruses. Bacteria."

"Just takes a few seconds to scan everyone," Tim said, checking his watch impatiently.

"The door handles are frosted glass! The floor is frosted glass! There's not one piece of furniture in here that isn't made of frosted glass!"

"Yes, Geoff, everything is made of 'frosted glass'."

"Is your lobby a quarantine chamber, then?" Geoff asked. "The one I was sitting in this afternoon?"

"As a matter of fact, it is," Tim said. He sounded surprised that Geoff had made the connection. "We're all scanned before we go into the outside world."

Geoff thought about this.

"Wait a minute," he said. "Was I scanned before I went up for the interview with Mr. Knight?" He felt a little offended. "Did they think I was diseased or something?"

"I doubt it," Tim said. "Unless Ruth thought you looked really ill, she wouldn't have bothered with a scan."

The room flashed green for a split second.

"Looks like this group are safe to travel," Eric said.

A large set of double doors clicked open at the back of the quarantine chamber. The tourists got up from their seats and shuffled through in a semi-orderly fashion.

"Customs next," Tim said, following the last few people through the double doors, down a brightly lit corridor.

"Customs?" Geoff said.

"Yep."

"But didn't we just go through customs?"

"That was for arrivals. This is for outbound tourists."

The corridor opened out onto a large room. All the tourists were queuing up to go through a tall square arch, which to Geoff looked a bit like an airport metal detector. One by one the tourists passed under the arch and made their way over to a group of customs officials who were adding a few finishing touches to various costumes as they saw fit—a little more mud rubbed into the cleaner outfits, hair being messed up if it looked too styled. The attention to detail was amazing.

"This should be quite familiar to you," Tim said.

"People having their hair messed up and mud rubbed into their clothes?" Geoff was sick of Tim making fun of his personal hygiene.

"That's not what he meant," Eric said. "This is quite similar to the kind of checks you have before you board a plane in the twenty-first century. If I recall, they used to check for potentially dangerous items like sharp objects and cigarette lighters along with the usual bombs, guns and other things it's probably best to stop someone taking on a plane. Here, we make sure everyone is dressed appropriately to blend in, and we screen everyone to make sure they are not carrying any technology that doesn't exist in their destination time period."

"Think of it this way," Tim said, sensing Geoff's confusion. "Ever been to Australia?"

"No." Geoff said. He hadn't even been to the bottom of the garden.

"Course you haven't," Tim muttered, remembering that he probably knew more about Geoff than Geoff did. "Well, when you visit Australia, you're not allowed to take any foreign biological materials into the country that might upset the balance of the ecosystem. Travelling through time follows the same principle: anything that does not exist in the time period you are visiting must be left at your departure time. We certainly don't want a stray piece of technology changing the course of history or exposing the time-tourism industry to the past."

"Does it really make that much of a difference?" Geoff said.

"Like you wouldn't believe." Eric said. "Last week we caught someone trying to take a bottle of Viagra back to the Battle of Waterloo. If they'd left it there by mistake and someone had worked out what it was, we think the world population would have doubled by the year 3000."

"Wow—that would have been an almighty cock-up," Geoff smirked.

Eric ignored him.

"Hang on a minute," Geoff said. "If you're so strict about making sure everyone blends in when they go back in time, how come I was able to go back to 65 million years BC without going through all these checks?"

"That's different," Tim said. "A tyrannosaurus rex isn't exactly going to come up to you and say, 'Excuse me sir, but why are you wearing those strange clothes?' And everything was about to be vaporized anyway, so if you'd left anything behind like a watch or a phone, it would have been destroyed."

"Besides, that was a one-off trip," Eric said. "It's not a destination we offer to our regular tourists. However, if you want to go back to any point in *human* history, the only piece of technology you're allowed to take with you are the earphones you need to get back again. Apart from that, you're not allowed to take anyth…"

BEEP! BEEP! BEEP! BEEP!

Eric was interrupted by a loud beeping sound. As beeping sounds go, it was fairly polite but piercing enough to suggest that someone should probably go and find out what all the beeping was about rather than just ignoring it in the hope that it would eventually turn itself off. It was the square arch. The beeping got louder, and a few lights began to flash for good measure. The tourist who had just walked through the arch had obviously triggered something. He stopped and looked sheepishly toward the customs officials, who had all snapped their gaze in his direction.

"Jesus," Eric spat under his breath, gripping the top of his walking stick a little more tightly. "Another idiot."

"I was hoping you'd get to see something like this," Tim whispered to Geoff. "Looks like this guy might be trying to smuggle something back in time."

The other tourists stared at the man, some nervously backing away. Parents squeezed their children's hands a little tighter. One of the more senior-looking customs officials approached cautiously.

"Excuse me sir," he said, "but are you carrying anything on your person that may not be indigenous to the time period you are about to visit?"

"Me?" the man said, pointing to himself as though there was some confusion around who was being addressed.

"Step over here, please sir," the official said, grabbing the tourist by the arm and pulling him over to one side. Another official made a few adjustments to the arch to stop it beeping and motioned the remaining tourists to continue through.

"It infuriates me that some people still try to get away with this," Eric said to Tim. "How many more adverts do we need to run warning people of the implications?"

"I'll ask you again," the official said to the tourist. "Are you attempting to take something back in time that won't have been invented in 1666?"

"This is ridiculous," the man said. "It's the tiniest, most insignificant thing. What possible harm could it do?"

"I don't know sir," the official said. "Hand it over and I'll tell you."

The tourist dug into his pocket and removed a small metal disc. "See?" he said, handing it to the official. "It's just a hologram."

The official turned the disc over in his hand and pressed a small button on the side. Sure enough, the disc projected a small flickering image in mid-air of the man with a woman and two kids.

"My family," the tourist explained.

"Lovely," the official said. "Dangerous thing to try to take back with you though," he said, switching the disc off again.

The tourist looked blankly at the official for a moment. "I don't see how."

"All it would take is for you to lose this in the past, someone else to pick it up and find out how to switch it on ..."

"So what?" the man interrupted. "So I lose it. How would someone else finding it change anything?" He sounded frustrated.

"Are you some sort of moron?" Eric spat at the tourist from across the room, waving his walking stick in the air. "They still have the death penalty for practicing witchcraft in the seventeenth century!"

"Witchcraft?" the tourist said. "What has this stupid hologram got to do with witchcraft?"

"Oh, we don't think anything of a simple hologram these days," Eric said. "But can you imagine what would happen to someone in the seventeenth century if they were able to produce a flickering image in the palm of their hands? People would think it was magic. If that person was then accused of consorting with evil spirits, they could be killed. What if that person should have been your ancestor? Or my ancestor? Or anybody's ancestor? Suddenly, a whole family tree could be wiped out!"

"Couldn't have put it better myself," the customs official said, turning back to the tourist.

"I won't drop it," the tourist said impatiently, reaching out to try to grab the hologram back. "I'll keep it on me at all times. Promise."

"I guarantee the computer will never let you through with this," the official said, tossing the device over to one of his assistants. "Now please—follow the rest of your group through to the paradox-scanning facility. You can have this back when you return."

"Stupid computer," the tourist said, reluctantly doing as he was told.

Stupid computer indeed, Geoff thought. This was the computer that thought he was less significant than certain types of mushroom. Said he was unpopular. Uninteresting. Unattractive. So what if it used a six-billion-character algorithm to reach this conclusion? *Sunset Beach* had loads of characters in it, and that was rubbish.

The paradox-scanning facility was a short walk from customs, leading the tourists down a dimly lit corridor past several advertisements for lectures and guidebooks designed to increase their chances of passing the scan. "Thirty percent of tourists were turned away last year because they lacked the knowledge of local customs needed to blend in," said one billboard. "Those people should have read *Tipping in Restaurants: 1950 to 2150.*" Apparently it was a bestseller.

Geoff felt himself walking a little faster. He wasn't sure why—it was as if some sort of invisible force was beginning to pull him down the corridor, like having an overexcited dog on a leash. And it wasn't just him—everyone seemed to be breaking into a bit of a jog.

"What's going on?" Geoff said. "I feel like I'm in that Olympic event where everyone walks like a cockney."

"It's the computer," Eric said. "It's actually a massive neutronium-encased lattice of artificial micro-black holes. Only one of its kind in the world. Unfortunately the side effect of its design is that it emits a mild gravitational pull." He ran his hand along the wall to try to slow himself down.

"Sounds powerful," Geoff said, humoring Eric.

"You can't begin to imagine."

"But can it run *Nascar Racing* in full detail? Even on my old 486 DX4, that game chugged along like a bastard."

"Nascar Racing?"

"Old computer game. You've never heard of it?"

"This computer is *not* used to play games," Eric said sternly, clearly insulted at the suggestion. "Its sole function is to store huge amounts of information."

"You haven't tried *any* games on it?"

"It's not that sort of computer!" Eric fumed. "Do you have any idea about the kind of temporal calculations this computer is capable of? Can you even begin to understand how difficult it is to read back information through Hawking radiation? We're not going to waste that kind of processing power by plugging a joystick into it and playing *Pac-Man*!"

"I've been meaning to ask you—what exactly are these 'temporal calculations'?" Geoff made no effort to hide the skepticism in his voice—he was determined to prove that this computer had made some sort of mistake about him.

"Simple," Eric replied calmly, relieved that Geoff was beginning to ask some sensible questions. "The computer is effectively a simulator. It recreates a precise model of the space-time continuum in its memory banks."

"And how precise is this 'model'?"

"Precise enough to map out the vibration of every molecule on this planet for the next one hundred thousand years."

Geoff blinked. "Reasonably precise, then."

"You could say that," Eric said. "The computer takes a snapshot of the final nanosecond of this model, one hundred thousand years in the future. Once it has that as a point of reference, it runs the model again, changing the appropriate variables to reflect who is traveling through time and where they are visiting. If the final nanosecond is different in any way from the original snapshot, the tourist is blocked from traveling."

"Is that what happened with me?" Geoff said. "You ran a simulation of me being plucked from my own time, and there was no difference?"

"That's right."

"Well, there was one small difference," Tim interjected. "But the computer decided it was well within acceptable tolerance levels."

"What was the difference?"

"A seagull in Brighton was facing right instead of left."

Geoff frowned. "That was it?"

"Yes."

"No other differences?"

"No."

"A seagull?"

"A seagull."

"What was it looking at?"

"Nothing, as far as we could tell," Tim said. "Everything else on the entire planet was exactly the same. It just chose to look in the opposite direction."

"But…why did it do that?"

"We've got absolutely no idea. It just did."

"You mean everyone else was standing in exactly the same place? Doing exactly the same thing?"

"Not exactly," Eric said.

Geoff waited for Eric to elaborate, but no further explanation seemed to be forthcoming. "Come on," he said, "you can't just leave it at that!"

"It's complicated. One hundred thousand years from now, Earth will be a very different place. According to our simulations, mankind will have left the planet to explore other galaxies, and Earth would have been given back to Mother Nature. Towns and cities will have decayed into dust, air pollution will be non-existent, and the ice caps will have re-formed. Eventually, the entire planet becomes like a massive nature reserve. Quite beautiful, really."

Before Geoff could really think about what possible influence he could have over a seagull, he noticed the corridor around him beginning to change. The unremarkable gray walls were giving way to a much more glamorous, shiny metallic black material. The gravitational pull on his body started to weaken.

"This is all neutronium around you now," Eric said. "We're passing into the computer's core."

"The gravitational pull will normalize as we reach the paradox-scanning facility in the center," Tim said.

Geoff could see an opening up ahead. Sure enough, everyone appeared to be slowing back down to a normal walking speed.

"How big did you say this computer was?" Geoff said, reaching out to touch one of the walls. It was warm. Come to think of it, the farther they walked down the corridor, the hotter it was becoming.

"It's basically a huge sphere," Eric said, shrugging off his white coat and folding it over his arm. "I guess if you were to look down on the computer from above, it would be about the size of a hover-ball pitch. Except we're underground."

"Right. And how big are hoverball pitches?"

"About double the size of a lazer-tennis arena."

Geoff blinked.

"Well thanks for the useful comparison," he said. "Really helpful."

The corridor finally opened out to reveal a large, dome-shaped chamber. The walls and ceiling looked like they were made from the same shiny metallic material he had seen in the corridor—neutronium, was it? As for the rest of the room, it was empty. If it wasn't for a large, vertical shaft of light beaming down on a pedestal in the middle of the room, it would have been pitch black in here. Geoff tugged at the neck of his t-shirt—he was boiling.

An overweight official met the tourists at the mouth of the corridor and motioned them to gather around. He had a receding hairline, red cheeks, and a nose slightly too big for his face. His clothes were tight around his frame, his trousers struggling to contain the large belly that bulged over the top of them. Two patches of sweat were beginning to form under his arms.

"Ladies and gentlemen," the man bellowed, his voice echoing around the chamber. "For those of you who have not been here before, this is the paradox-scanning facility. In a moment, I will call out each of your names, one by one, in alphabetical order. When you hear your name, please walk over to the beam of light behind me, step into the beam and wait for the computer to scan you." The man paused for a second to wipe his brow on his sleeve.

"The scan should take no longer than 10 to 15 seconds," he continued. "If the beam turns green, congratulations—you have been cleared for travel. Step out of the beam and proceed to the departure chamber." He pointed toward a brightly lit corridor on the opposite side of the room. "However, if you fail the scan, the beam of light will turn red. If this happens, please step out of the beam and come back to this part of the chamber. As a precaution against time terrorists, the corridor to the departure chamber will instantly seal itself. Any questions?"

"What happens if we fail the scan?" one person called out. "Will we find out why?"

"And will we get our money back?" another person shouted.

"One at a time," the man said, holding his hands up. His voice sounded a little strained in the heat. "The computer will transmit a report of every failed scan to my handheld terminal should you wish to know why you were not cleared for travel. And yes, you will receive a full refund from your tour operator." He looked from one end of the crowd to the other. "Any other questions?"

Everyone seemed reasonably comfortable with the process.

Geoff was still thinking about his seagull.

"Right," the man said, looking down at his handheld terminal. "David Atkin—you're up first. Step into the beam when you're ready."

A tall, thin man squeezed his way out of the crowd and walked over to the center of the chamber. He paused for a second, as if this was a big moment for him, and stepped up onto the pedestal, his body enveloped in the thick beam of light. Everyone else in the room stared at the man in silence, waiting in anticipation for the first result.

10 seconds passed.

David Atkin was shivering. Was he nervous?

15 seconds.

20 seconds.

This was taking a long time. The man looked back at everyone and shrugged his shoulders. He began to blush, obviously a little embarrassed at the delay. All of a sudden, the beam turned green.

"Yes!" he said, punching the air. A few people in the crowd cheered. He stepped off the pedestal and disappeared down the opposite corridor with a distinct spring in his step.

"Andrew Baker," the official called out.

It was the man who'd had the argument earlier about his hologram. He strolled aggressively up to the pedestal and stepped into the light, his arms folded tight across his chest. He didn't look happy. It was almost as if he expected to fail.

The beam quickly turned green. Again, a few cheers and claps came from the crowd, who seemed happy to rally behind whoever's turn it was to go up. A look of surprise swept across the man's face. He stepped out of the light and swiftly made his way to the departure chamber as if he was afraid the computer was going to change its mind.

"Christine Bennett," the official said.

A girl near the front of the crowd whooped in excitement and walked toward the beam of light. Geoff's eyes widened—this girl was gorgeous. Despite the unflattering peasant's costume, the mud on her face, and the twigs in her hair, there was undoubtedly something mesmerizing about this woman—confident eyes, a glistening smile, a sexy swing to her hips; Geoff could almost feel himself drooling as he watched her step up onto the pedestal. Or was that sweat? He sniffed under his arms.

"Am I beginning to smell?" he whispered to Tim.

"Beginning?" Tim replied.

The girl shut her eyes and arched her neck back in the light, waiting for her result. Her fingers were crossed.

All of a sudden, the light turned red. The crowd responded with a collective sigh of disappointment. As the official had mentioned, a large metal door immediately slammed down to seal off the corridor to the departure chamber.

"What?" the girl said in confusion, her voice trembling slightly. "W-what did I do wrong?" She stepped off the pedestal in shock and staggered over to the official in disbelief.

"I'm sorry, miss," the official said, looking down at his handheld terminal. "Says here we'd have lost five family trees if you'd gone back in time today."

"But…that can't be possible," the girl said. "I've spent weeks studying all the customs—I know exactly how to blend in, I…"

The official interrupted, reading aloud from his terminal. "Five separate gentleman would have fallen in love with you from afar and not pursued their destined partners as a result," he said, offering the girl his handheld terminal to read it for herself. "In layman's terms, the computer reckons that you're too attractive to 'blend in' in the seventeenth century."

The girl took the terminal in her hand and read a few of the details out loud. "An earl, three market traders and a blacksmith all die single as opposed to married with kids because they become infatuated with me and don't pursue other relationships? I don't believe it."

"Computer!" the official said into thin air. "Could you please bring up a video simulation of this prediction for the benefit of Miss Bennett?"

"A video simulation?" the girl said.

Within moments, a large hologramatic screen materialized in thin air in front of them, and everyone watched as it showed a life-like simulation of everything the official had just described. Sure enough, while the girl was minding her own business, walking around various seventeenth century London landmarks, a few gentlemen in the background were staring lustfully in her direction. Geoff couldn't believe this was really just a simulation—the graphics were good enough to be a film. He also felt weirdly in tune with what he was watching, as if he could hear the inner monologues of the people on screen—indeed, some of the blacksmith's thoughts toward Miss Bennett were really quite disgusting. Was this simulation somehow managing to transmit something to them on a more subliminal level?

"I've seen enough," the girl said. "Make it stop."

The screen flickered off and disappeared in a brief flash of vapor.

"Sorry," the official said, taking his terminal back. "I'm afraid you'll have to leave the way you came in. Why don't you pick up one of our leaflets on temporary plastic surgery on your way out?"

The girl walked off in silence, removing the twigs from her hair and snapping them in half as she left.

"Cheer up, everyone!" the official said, sensing a slump in the crowd's mood. "Matt Davies—you're up next." The corridor to the arrivals chamber opened up again.

Geoff watched as the rest of the tourists were scanned by the computer. Many were cleared for travel; many were not. In one case, a family of five were sent home because their eldest son failed the scan. Turned out he had secretly skipped a few of the lectures on seventeenth century swearwords and would have unwittingly drawn attention to himself when he accidentally shut his fingers in a barn door. His mother was furious, demonstrating her own knowledge of thirty-first century swearwords as they left. Geoff smiled to himself—at least *some* things hadn't changed much.

"Well, this little tour of our facility is nearly over," Eric said, watching the last person being cleared for travel. "Ever fancied going back to 1666?"

"To be honest, it's never been on my list of places to visit," Geoff said. "The only place I thought about going to this year was that new fish and chip shop that opened around the corner."

"How about it then?" Eric said. "It'll be useful for you to experience one of these trips for yourself."

"But I've already been back to 65 million years BC," Geoff said. After the trauma of his last trip, he was a little nervous about going back in time again. "Is it really necessary to go somewhere else as well?"

"I think it is," Tim replied. "I'm sure seeing the Cretaceous Period was all very interesting, but you wouldn't have seen one of our Time Reps in action back then."

Geoff mulled it over. "Will I need toothpaste?" he said. "I didn't bring any toothpaste."

"No, you won't need toothpaste," Eric replied. "You're not allowed to take anything like that, remember? Besides, we'll only be there a little while—just long enough for you meet another Time Rep and see the sort of thing you'll be doing."

"Well, what do you say?" Tim said. "You didn't have any other plans, did you?"

Geoff thought about this for a moment. As a matter of fact, he did have other plans—plans that generally involved a lot of sitting down, drinking some tea, and not doing anything too stressful. But he had to admit he was curious.

"Sure, why not?" Geoff said.

"Great," Tim said. "Step into the beam of light and we'll be on our way."

Geoff hesitated. "Is it safe?" he said.

"Of course it's safe!" Eric snapped. "You just watched everyone else step into it, and they didn't blow up, did they? And besides—we wouldn't be in business very long if it was *unsafe*, would we?"

"I suppose not," Geoff replied, cautiously approaching the pedestal and stepping up into the beam. He was surprised to discover that it was actually refreshingly cool compared to the rest of the room; so much so that goose bumps were beginning to appear on his arms. That explained why so many people were shivering when they stepped into the light. He closed his eyes and decided to enjoy it while it lasted.

"So how come I wasn't scanned before I went back to see the dinosaurs?" Geoff asked, waiting for the light to turn green.

"Because we didn't need to scan you," Eric replied. "That trip to 65 million years BC was already taken into account by the computer when it scanned Ruth and Mr. Knight—it already knew they were going to take you there when they left here to interview you."

"The computer can go back that far?" Geoff said, suddenly feeling very hot. He opened his eyes. The light had turned green.

"It's not called a *super*computer for nothing," Tim said. "Now, are you ready to go back to 1666?"

"I guess," Geoff said. "Just as long as I'm not going to see the world end again. You know—death, destruction, flames, things collapsing around me, that sort of thing."

"Hmm … Well, you might be out of luck there," Tim said.

"What do you mean?" Geoff asked, rubbing his hands.

"Don't you know your history?"

"Erm, I know there have been a few wars here and there, but that's about it. What happened in 1666?"

"1666 was the year of the Great Fire of London."

"The Great Fire of London? People want to go back and see that?"

"Major disasters are always very popular," Eric said, stepping up to be scanned. "Nothing better than a bit of death and destruction to spice up a holiday."

Great, Geoff thought. At least he wouldn't have trouble thinking of something to write on the postcard.

Seven

Now, given all the fuss that had been made to ensure every tourist fit in with London's seventeenth-century population—the removal of watches and earrings, adding dirt to people's costumes and making sure no one's hair was conspicuously styled, you would have thought the time-tourism officials would have made at least a couple of alterations to Geoff's wardrobe, or rather to the clothes he was wearing at that moment, since large wooden pieces of furniture tended to be a bit cumbersome to carry around. As it happened, the general consensus amongst the officials was that Geoff was very suitably dressed for the seventeenth century; his hair was scruffy, his shoes were dirty enough to disguise their design, and his clothes were plain and crumpled. While Eric and Tim had to get completely changed, Geoff was allowed to travel back in time with no modifications to his appearance whatsoever. One official even told him to keep up the good work.

Just as when he had travelled back to 65 million years BC, the journey through time had felt almost instantaneous—upon putting on the earphones, his brain had tingled slightly, his heart raced a little, and his body suddenly materialized down a dark, cobbled back alley. Now that he understood what was happening to him, the experience was almost pleasurable. He removed his earphones and looked around. The alley was quite narrow, sandwiched between two tall wooden buildings. It smelled faintly of rotting vegetables. He glanced up—it was nighttime, the black, starry sky dotted with a few clouds here and there. Beneath his feet the ground was a little bit wet, as if it had rained recently. A few meters in front of him, the tourists who had passed the paradox scan were all gathering together by a stack of wooden crates, chatting excitedly amongst themselves.

It wasn't long before Eric and Tim arrived, the outline of their silhouettes quietly materializing out of thin air and fleshing out into solid humanoid forms. Geoff had to admit to being a little bit disappointed with the aesthetics of their entrance—the re-materialization process must have lasted only a couple of seconds and had none of the exciting bells and whistles he was expecting to accompany what was clearly an amazing technological feat. Not that he was expecting *actual* bells and whistles, because that would have been a bit stupid, but he would have at least liked to have seen a few sparks or a bright flash of lightning or something. The intention was obviously to draw as little attention to a time traveler's entrance as possible.

"All right?" Tim asked nonchalantly, as if they'd just stepped off a bus. It took Geoff a moment to recognize his friend—without his glasses and dressed in what could only be described as a potato sack with sleeves sown onto the sides, he looked slightly ridiculous.

"Nice costume," Geoff sniggered. "You look like you're about to audition for the role of the scarecrow in *The Wizard of Oz*."

"At least I actually had to get changed before coming here," Tim retorted, placing his earphones in his pocket.

"Shall we join the others?" Eric said, leading them over to the rest of the tourists. He appeared to be having a bit of trouble negotiating the cobbled street with his walking stick, but eventually made it over to the rest of the group, leaning on one of the crates for support.

"So what happens now?" Geoff said.

"We wait," Tim replied. "William should be here any minute to collect us."

"William?"

"William Boyle. He's one of the Time Reps we've got working for us in this time period."

"*One* of the Time Reps?" Geoff said. "How many have you got?"

"Oh, a few hundred," Tim said.

"A few hundred?"

"You've got to remember that the Great Fire of London only happened once Geoff, and we've got thousands of people paying to see it. You don't think we've got just one Time Rep to accommodate that kind of demand, do you? They can't be in several places at once."

"Well, they can," Eric interjected, "if we keep sending the same Time Reps back in time to conduct tours of the fire over the same few days. But we'd risk them being spotted in two places at once. Not the best scenario if you're trying to keep the whole thing a secret."

"It isn't fair on them either," Tim added. "It would be like *Groundhog Day*. Can you imagine living through the same day for years of your life?"

Geoff *could* imagine this actually. Sounded a bit like the last seven years, watching the same daytime chat shows every afternoon.

"So I have a question," Geoff said. "How does time travel actually work?"

Eric looked up.

"What do you mean, 'How does it work?'" he said.

"I mean, is it complicated?"

Eric shut his eyes and sighed.

"You could say that," he said. "Do you know much about the quantum physics? How the whole universe is actually a complex type of hologram?"

"Not really. Can you explain it to me?"

"Not a chance," Eric said. "It would take me two years of continuous talking just to explain how to manipulate quantum entanglement to send a photon back in time by one nanosecond, let alone organic matter. Forget it."

"Oh go on," Geoff said. "Can't you just sum it up?"

"Sum it up?" Eric said, his jaw hanging open. "Sum it up? The founding theories behind what makes time travel possible aren't something I can just 'sum up!'"

"Keep your voice down," Tim said, putting a hand on Eric's shoulder.

"But I've travelled through time now," Geoff said. "Surely I'm entitled to know *something*?"

"No!"

"Just a little bit?"

Eric shut his eyes again and let out a deep breath.

"Can you drive?" he said.

"Erm … I've got a license."

"And do you know how to build an internal combustion engine?"

"Erm … not quite."

"Well there you go, then. This is the same thing, only a hundred billion times more complicated. Trust me—explaining the rules of time travel to a time traveler would be like explaining the rules of golf to a golf ball."

"Golf has rules?"

Eric took a deep breath and shut his eyes.

Call it a hunch, but Geoff got the feeling that if he continued to pursue this line of questioning much longer, Eric would most likely take the analogy one step further and hit him with the nearest golf club-like object. He looked aimlessly up and down the street and tried to think of some way of changing the subject.

"Ah," Tim said, pointing toward a young man heading toward them. "Here's William."

Geoff watched intently as William approached, curious to see what another Time Rep looked like. As it happened, William looked like a perfectly average guy—he had no real distinguishing features, wasn't particularly handsome, and had all the mod cons you would normally expect to come with your standard human being: hair, eyes, arms, legs—everything about him was just … normal. He was short, and maybe two or three years younger than Geoff. The only thing remotely unusual about him was the fact that he was dressed as a peasant, but Geoff guessed this was probably due to the fact that he *was* a peasant. His face was little bit grubby, his lips were chapped, and his thick hair had a few bits of straw stuck in it, as though he'd been rolling around in a barn earlier in the day.

"Good evening everyone," he whispered, looking cautiously over his shoulder and motioning the group to huddle around. "Greetings, and welcome to the seventeenth century. My name is William Boyle and I will be your Time Rep for the duration of your stay in London."

"Watch and learn," Tim whispered to Geoff. "William is *very* good."

"The year is 1666," William continued, his voice crackling with anticipation as if he was telling a story around a campfire, "and the time has just gone ten o'clock at night. In just over two hours, a fire will start down Pudding Lane in the bakery of Thomas Farynor. At first, the threat of this fire will be ignored by senior authorities, but over the next four days, it will spread across the whole of London: tearing through the Royal Exchange, devastating St. Paul's Cathedral, and stopping just short of the court of Charles II, who is the King of England at this present time."

"My goodness," one of the tourists said. "Will we be in any danger?"

"None whatsoever," William replied. "There were actually very few recorded deaths from the Great Fire—the main casualties came in the aftermath, with tens of thousands of people left starving and homeless. As long we all stay together, you'll all be able to experience the fire in a safe, educational, and exciting way."

"While everyone around you has their lives ruined," Geoff added under his breath.

Tim frowned at Geoff.

"Well, that's what I would have added if I was the Time Rep for this place," Geoff said. "It's all very well these people showing up for a jolly holiday, but it's a bit weird to want to come and see something like this, don't you think? What are the plans for next year? A nice little jaunt to Pompeii to watch Mount Vesuvius erupt?"

"William's speech has come along very well," Eric said to Tim, ignoring Geoff.

"Yeah," Geoff said. "Come to think of it, how come he doesn't sound someone out of Shakespeare play?"

"Some of the earlier Time Reps required a little coaching," Tim said. "William responded very successfully."

William looked over the group and noticed Tim and Geoff talking.

"Will you all please excuse me for one moment?" he said, walking over to speak to them. "Why Tim, my good friend," he said, shaking Tim's hand. "Good to see you again!"

"William, I'd like you to meet Geoffrey Stamp," Tim said, slapping Geoff on the back. "He's the guy I told you about a few weeks ago, remember?"

"Ah yes—this is the one you were hoping they'd pick to be the rep for the twenty-first century?"

"That's right."

"Then I take it he was successful?"

"Yes, he was. In fact, it's his first day today, so I thought I'd bring him here today to see a good Time Rep in action. Kind of like an induction. You don't mind, do you?"

"Not at all," William smiled. "After everything you've done for me, how can I say no?"

"Hey—I didn't do anything," Tim said, looking like he was about to blush.

"Nonsense—Tim was the man who helped get me this job," William explained to Geoff. "Without him, I don't know what I'd be doing now."

"I do," Tim said. "That's exactly why I chose you."

"So you recruited this guy too?" Geoff said.

"Not recruited," Tim corrected him. "I told you—I don't hire people. I only hunt out potential Time Rep candidates, make them ready for the role, and then put them forward for consideration. Whether or not they actually get the job is entirely up to them."

"So how many Time Reps have you found in the past?"

"Twelve, including you," Tim said.

"Twelve?" Geoff said. "But…isn't that quite a lot considering how many years it takes before we're ready? I mean, you were looking after me for how long? Seven years?"

"That's true, but I'm usually taking care of at least two or three at any one time, at various points in history. That's why I always had to be leave home for a few days now and again—if I wasn't with you, I was usually with one of my other candidates in another time period."

"I see…" Geoff said. "So all those times when you came home dressed as a Victorian, you told me you had a friend who kept holding these weird fancy dress parties. Had you actually been back in time to visit one of your other candidates?"

"You got it," Tim replied.

"And all those boring charts," Geoff said. "Were they…"

"Space-time continuum analytics," Tim said. "I use them to keep track of any paradoxes or loopholes that might emerge in the timeline as a result of making contact."

"Huh." Geoff smiled. "Sounds like quite an interesting job when you think about it."

"Oh I love it," Tim said. "I can't tell you how rewarding it is to see a Time Rep candidate grow over time. To see someone considered to be useless by society proving that they are capable of so much more. It's extremely satisfying."

"Well, I suppose we'd better get a move on," William said, turning his attention back to the group. "Ladies and Gentlemen, the fire is due to start just after midnight, and I suppose you're all eager to see a bit of the old London before it goes up in flames. Just a final word of caution—please be mindful of your conversations when we're out in public. I don't want to hear anyone talking about last night's hoverball game for instance, okay?"

The group let off a quiet laugh and followed William as he led them out of the alleyway.

"Great costume by the way, Mr. Stamp," William whispered as they stepped onto the main street. "Nice to see someone did their research."

Most of seventeenth-century London looked as though it had been inspired by a badly played game of *Jenga*. Indeed, Geoff found himself nervously looking up at the tall wooden tenements to either side of him as he followed the tourists down a series of narrow streets, unsure as to how safe these structures really were. Most of the buildings were made entirely of wood and were so top-heavy and haphazard in their design that he was amazed they weren't already collapsing around him. One thing was for sure: the impending fire would certainly succeed in bringing these buildings down to the ground, where gravity had obviously failed.

"Now, this is a typical London street," William said, turning to face the group. "Notice how all the buildings have a very narrow footprint at ground level but gradually increase in size toward the upper stories. In the seventeenth century, overcrowding was a real problem, and as you can see, some people would go to any means necessary to give themselves more space to live in." He pointed up in the air. The two timbered houses to either side of the street were so wide at the top that they were practically touching, as if the owners were having a competition with each other to see who's structure could be the most dangerous.

"Shall we move on?" William said, turning on his heels and leading the way through a bustle of pedestrians toward Pudding Lane.

In the absence of cars, buses, cyclists and overzealous people working for charities, Geoff was somehow expecting seventeenth-century London to be a much quieter place than the city he was used to. But this was not the case. Even though it was nearly midnight, the streets were still filled with merchants, prostitutes, peasants, noblemen, and many more people. Some were dressed in such a strange way that Geoff found himself unable to guess what they really did for a living, a bit like people who worked in PR.

He was curious to find out from William what it was like to be a Time Rep, so he walked ahead of the tourists and caught up with him.

"Erm … hello," Geoff said.

"Ah! Mr. Stamp," William said. "What do you think of London? Magnificent place, don't you think? Pity it won't be here much longer."

"Yeah, it's pretty good," Geoff replied, not knowing whether he found William's overenthusiasm for everything a little irritating. "I'm from London as well, actually."

"Really? What's it like? Has it changed much?"

Given the entire place was about to burn down, Geoff didn't think this was a particularly intelligent question. Did William expect it to still be on fire or something?

"I think they've made a few improvements here and there," he said, stepping over a large pile of horse manure. "Electric lighting, proper drainage, wider streets, an underground railway system—little things, really."

"Sounds delightful," William said. "I might go and visit it one day."

"You're allowed to visit other places?"

"Oh yes. I've been on plenty of holidays to different time periods. The Wild West is my favorite—late nineteenth-century America."

"So I take it you enjoy being a Time Rep?" Geoff said.

"Oh, it's marvelous," William replied, looking over his shoulder to make sure the group were still following him. "Simply marvellous. Before I became a Time Rep, I had no food, no money, and no home. But now…"

"Now you're rich with a beautiful wife and a massive house in the country?" Geoff said optimistically.

"No, no," William said, leading the group around a corner. "I can't ever get married because I was never supposed to get married in the first place. If I did, I'd be interfering with someone else's destiny. And I'm not allowed to have a home either because I'd be living somewhere that would have belonged to someone else. The same goes for money—if I had any, I'd be buying things someone else should have been buying."

"Whoa," Geoff said. "You're telling me we don't get paid?"

William shook his head. "Did they not explain that to you?"

"No." Geoff narrowed his eyes. "For some reason they decided to leave that part out…"

"Don't worry," William said. "It's really not so bad."

"Are you sure?" Geoff asked. "Isn't the fact we don't get paid…actually a bit of a problem. In fact I'm pretty sure there are some laws against that sort of thing."

"That may well be, but you've got to understand—before I became a Time Rep, I had absolutely nothing."

"But you've still got absolutely nothing!"

William shook his head as if Geoff was somehow missing the point.

"You should have seen me back then, Mr. Stamp. I was riddled with disease, barely able to walk—the only way I managed to stay alive was by eating any dead rats I could find in the street. Then Tim found me. Now, I'm given food whenever I need it, and I can travel to different time periods whenever I wish. They even inoculated me against last year's outbreak of bubonic plague. This job might not pay me anything, but it's a damn sight better than the way I used to live. It saved my life."

"Yeah—that's great and everything," Geoff said. "But I still don't like the idea of doing all this for free. I've got video games to buy…"

"Think of it this way," William said. "Your payment may not be in the form gold or silver, but you do get the satisfaction of being part of something special: of meeting all these fantastic people, teaching them about their past. Given what you might have been doing with your life otherwise, isn't that payment enough?"

"Not really," Geoff said. "I can't exactly go into a shop and say, 'Listen, I don't actually have any real money, but I do have a very satisfying and worthwhile job. Please can I have a new television?'"

"What's a television?" William asked.

"A television is something you can use to dry your clothes on," Geoff replied. "They're really handy."

It wasn't long before they arrived at the bakery of Thomas Farynor—a building which looked so rickety and unstable in its construction that you'd be forgiven for thinking the architect designed it on an Etch-A-Sketch. It reminded Geoff of one of those crooked houses you sometimes got at funfairs: the ones where you go in, stagger along some sloping corridors, fall down some disproportionately sized stairs, look at yourself in a bendy mirror, and walk out again feeling as though you could have got more value for money just by walking around your own house drunk.

William had huddled all the tourists together in a dark corner of the street. From here, they were out of sight but had a perfect view of the building. Geoff looked around. Unless he was mistaken, there was another group of tourists with their own Time Rep hiding across the road and another group gathered on a balcony overlooking the street. He remembered what Tim had said about the number of Time Reps they had covering the Great Fire of London and wondered how many other tourists from the future were hiding nearby.

"Here we are," William whispered. "The bakery of Thomas Farynor. At this moment, the Farynor family is fast asleep upstairs. But in a few seconds, a single burning ember will fall out of the fireplace downstairs and set fire to a stack of papers on the floor. The burning paper will drift around the whole room, spreading the fire to the rug, the curtains, the furniture, and eventually the whole house. I'm sure you know the rest—within days, this fire will destroy the whole of central London, even leaping over the River Fleet to threaten the adjacent town of Westminster."

The tourists all looked very excited.

"What a shame no one was allowed to bring their phones back in time," Geoff said. "I'm sure a selfie with London burning to the ground behind you would have looked great on Instagram."

Geoff was surprised at just how quickly the fire was able to spread—within a couple of hours, the whole street was ablaze. Thomas Farynor and his family had been trapped upstairs in their house but had managed to escape from their bedroom window to the building next door. Unfortunately, their maid had been too scared to follow them, and the tourists watched uncomfortably as she became the first victim of the flames.

By now, a large crowd had gathered to witness the blaze, which had also caught the attention of London's fire authorities. They arrived at the scene on several wooden carts with water tanks in the middle and two long pumping handles to either side.

"What are those things?" Geoff whispered to William.

"That's the very latest firefighting contraption," William replied. "They use it to pump water out through a hose to put fires out."

Geoff thought about this. Essentially, what he was looking at was a seventeenth-century fire engine. There was, however, one fundamental design flaw to these machines: a flaw you would have expected to be ironed out in the conceptual stage—these 'fire engines' were made of wood, and if Geoff remembered correctly, wood was particularly good at catching fire. If the inventor of these machines was up for an award for using the most inappropriate building material, the only way he could have lost was if he was up against someone who had chosen to make a space shuttle out of asparagus.

Some of the firemen were arguing with a group of homeowners on the adjacent streets about something. Geoff tried to listen through the load roar of the flames.

"Don't you understand?" one of the firemen shouted at a blacksmith, "The fire will continue to spread unless we pull your house down! Grab everything of value from inside and get out of our way!"

"I know my rights!" the blacksmith said, standing in front of his property, his bulging arms crossed across his chest. "You ain't got the authority to pull me house down! Only Bloodworth has the authority to pull me house down! I want to speak to Bloodworth!"

Geoff tugged on William's sleeve.

"Why do they want to pull his house down?" he said.

"Stops the fire spreading," William said. "If there's nowhere for it to go, it burns itself out."

"And who is 'Bloodworth'?"

"Thomas Bloodworth. Or *Sir* Thomas Bloodworth. Lord Mayor of London. He'll be here any minute."

Sure enough, it wasn't long before a horse-drawn carriage arrived, pulling up a safe distance away from all the commotion. The carriage door opened, and a tall, middle-aged man stepped out. Geoff watched as he approached the nearest fireman. He had an extremely large moustache and was dressed smartly in a slashed doublet with wide lace cuffs, a dark gray pair of britches, a full-length fur-lined gown, and a broad-brimmed hat. His appearance was so extravagant that he looked as though he'd just been called away from one of Elton John's birthday parties.

"That's Thomas Bloodworth," William said to the group. "The fire authorities want to pull down the adjacent buildings to stop the fire from spreading any further, but this is classified as destruction of property, which is a very serious matter. So they've had to summon the Lord Mayor to assess the threat of the fire and see if he will permit them to take whatever action they deem necessary."

Geoff strained to hear the conversation between Bloodworth and the firemen, who didn't appear to be having much luck in convincing the Lord Mayor that this fire might become a bit of a bother if they weren't allowed to contain it quickly.

"You woke me up for this?" Bloodworth said, looking up at the blaze.

"My Lord," the fireman said, wiping a film of wet soot from his face. "We've got to pull down all the surrounding buildings immediately! The fire is out of control! My men ..."

"Now, now," Bloodworth said, straightening his white lace collar. "I'm sure your men are more than capable of dealing with this."

"You ain't gonna let him pull me house down are you, me Lord?" the blacksmith shouted from across the street. "That house is all I've got!"

"No one's going to be pulling anyone's house down," Bloodworth replied. "I forbid it."

The fireman looked visibly distressed at this decision, which was understandable, as it was quite clearly the wrong one.

"God bless you, sir!" the blacksmith shouted. "Hooray for Lord Bloodworth!"

Bloodworth smiled at the blacksmith and turned to leave.

"My Lord, I beg you to reconsider," the fireman said, pulling on Bloodworth's gown. "With the greatest respect, I think you're making a terrible mistake! This is one of the worst fires I've ever seen!"

"Pish!" Bloodworth said, snatching his gown from the fireman's grip. "A woman could piss it out!"

It was clear to everyone that this was slightly underestimating the danger the fire presented.

The tourists all watched in silence as Bloodworth stormed back to his carriage, slammed the door behind him, and ordered his driver to take him home. The fireman stood shaking on the spot as Bloodworth left, the flames behind him beginning to spread further and further. It took a few moments before he managed to regain his composure, turning his attention back to his men to coordinate their futile efforts.

"So there you have it," William said to the group. "That is how the Great Fire of London started and how one man's inaction led to the destruction of most of the city."

As William spoke, a large building on one side of the street began to topple over, its charred wooden structure splintering out in all directions as it crashed to the ground in a suffocating cloud of ash. Local people began to scream as they watched two more buildings catch alight, with everyone staring in horror as the fire grew more and more out of control, and even the tourists now seemed to be appreciating the tragedy that was unfolding.

Amidst all the chaos, however, there was one person who seemed quite calm: a person who wasn't screaming, wasn't running around in a blind panic, and wasn't even looking at the fire.

In fact they seemed to be looking quite intently at Geoff.

Geoff couldn't quite see who it was—the person's face was obscured by a dark hooded cape, and they stood a good few meters away on the other side of the street. At this distance, he couldn't even tell if the person were a man or a woman. The figure reminded him of something, but he couldn't think what.

If this wasn't disconcerting enough, the figure looked as though it was slowly drawing something out from under its cape and pointing it at Geoff. With all the smoke billowing through the streets it was hard to make out exactly what it was, but if he had to guess, he'd say it was some kind of crossbow.

This guess turned out to be quite accurate, as all of a sudden a bolt shot straight toward him.

"Jesus!" Geoff cried, just reacting fast enough to jerk his body out of the path of the bolt, which narrowly missed piercing his right hand.

Geoff looked over at the figure, who looked as though they were hurriedly loading another bolt into the crossbow.

"Tim!" Geoff shouted out, ducking behind a cart to get out of his assailant's line-of-sight. "Tim, where are you?"

"I'm here," Tim said, wading through a few tourists and looking down at Geoff. "What are you doing down there?"

"Um … I think someone just tried to shoot me."

Tim shifted his weight from one leg to the other.

"You what?"

"Someone across the street just fired a crossbow at me!"

"Geoff, stop messing around."

"I'm not messing around!" Geoff said. He picked the stray bolt up from the floor and thrust it toward Tim. "You see? Damn thing nearly took my hand off!"

Tim took the bolt from Geoff and looked at it.

"What the hell?" he muttered under his breath. "Did … did you see what they looked like?"

"They were wearing a cape," Geoff said, half getting to his feet to scan the other side of the street. For a moment he thought the figure had vanished, but then he noticed them running away to the right, through the growing crowd that had gathered to watch the fire.

"There they are!" Geoff said, pointing after them. "You see?"

"I see them," Tim replied, running across the street. "Hey!" he shouted. "You there!"

The caped figure looked over their shoulder at Tim and ran faster.

"Wait!" Tim called out, breaking into a sprint.

Geoff got to his feet and followed a few paces behind, quickly sidestepping his way past various groups of people and shielding his face from the cloud of burning embers drifting through the air. Up ahead, the caped figure darted down a side street and ducked into the nearest burning building. It looked as though the place was going to collapse at any moment, with a cross section of red-hot timbers smashing to the floor as he entered.

Tim stopped short of going inside himself—the flames around the doorway were just too fierce, the heat almost unbearable.

Geoff caught up a few seconds later.

"Where…are they?" Geoff wheezed. He was out of breath—this was the first time he'd done any exercise since he ran for a bus twelve years ago.

"They're in there," Tim replied, pointing through the burning doorway. "Right in the middle of the fire. Can you see them?"

Geoff leaned forward to get a closer look. The heat was painfully intense on his face, but he could just about see the hooded figure crouched down in the middle of the room. As Tim had said, they was surrounded by flames, the ends of their cape beginning to catch alight. There didn't seem to be any means of escape.

"My God," Geoff said, looking away for a moment to rub the sting of ash out of his eyes. "They'll burn alive in there!"

But when Geoff looked around again, the hooded figure began to turn transparent like a ghost. A few seconds later, they'd completely disappeared into the ether.

"Son of a bitch!" Tim said, kicking a loose stone on the floor.

"Did I see that right?" Geoff said. "Where did they go?"

"I don't know," Tim said, backing away from the doorway. "But it looks as though they just escaped to another time period. Clever bastard must have already been wearing his earphones under that hood."

"Earphones? You mean they were from the future?"

"Most likely," Tim replied. He looked down at the bolt, which he was still holding in his hand. "But the big question is—why did they try to attack you?"

Geoff and Tim made their way back to the tourists, who had been moved to a safer spot by William, near the edge of the River Thames. The fire was now so widespread it lit up the night sky like a horrific firework display. Grand wooden tenements had been reduced to charred piles of ash, the ground was covered in a thick film of soot, and the air was heavy with a black, billowing smoke.

Eric was leaning against a tree stump near the riverbank, watching as another structure collapsed to the ground in the distance. He seemed to be preoccupied with something, barely reacting to the devastation around him.

"Eric!" Tim called out.

Eric looked up.

"Where did you two disappear off to?" he asked.

"We may have a problem," Tim said, wiping a streak of soot from his forehead.

"Problem?"

Tim handed Eric the bolt.

"What's this?" Eric said.

"It's sharp, it's pointy, and someone just shot it at me!" Geoff said.

"What?" Eric said. "Who would do something like that? *Why* would someone do something like that?"

"We don't know," Tim replied. "But it seems they were from the future, like us—when we tried to apprehend them, they dashed into a burning building and put their time-travel earphones on to escape."

"Hmm. Strange that computer cleared them for travel if they intended to do something like that. Did you see what they looked like?"

Tim shook his head. "They were wearing a cape with a hood. Didn't get to see their face."

Eric sat in silence for moment, looking through Tim and Geoff as though they were a mirage in the heat.

"What are you thinking?" Tim asked, brushing a few sparks from his clothes.

"I'm thinking we need to report this," Eric said, rummaging through his pockets and pulling out his earphones.

"No kidding," Geoff said.

"And besides—we all have to get back to the future anyway."

"We do?"

"Yes—tonight is the tenth Time Rep inauguration party," Tim explained, placing his first earphone in place. "Mr. Knight holds one every year to welcome new reps to the business. You'll be meeting all the other Time Reps, key investors, politicians and scientists."

"It'll be quite a bash," Eric added.

"Hang on a minute," Geoff said. "Is now really the best time to be going to a party? I mean—shouldn't we be trying to find out why someone was just using me as target practice? What if I'm in some sort of danger?"

"Don't worry," Eric said. "All the people who need to know about this will be at the inauguration party anyway, so that's the best place for us to be if we want to get to the bottom of what happened here."

"Who do you think they were?" Geoff said. "I mean, do you have any idea?"

"Eric, I hate to say it, but it could be one of *them*," Tim suggested.

"One of who?" Geoff said.

"One of the people who've worked out the loophole in my algorithm," Eric conceded. "Time terrorists who know how to cheat the paradox scan."

EIGHT

Geoff was surprised to find a luxurious stretch limousine waiting to take them to the inauguration party when they arrived back from the Fire of London. With blacked out windows, gleaming bodywork, and blinding halogen headlights, he felt like a film star being driven to a movie premiere or a politician going to a big summit. Basically, he felt like someone more important than him, although as he now knew, that was pretty much everyone.

He reclined into the soft leather comfort of the limousine's back seat, stretched out his legs as far as they would go, and let out a long sigh—he hadn't sat down for the last three hours, which must have been a new personal record. Eric sat next to Geoff, typing something into a small phone-like device. Tim sat opposite, his back to the driver.

"Okay," Eric said, slotting the device back in his jacket pocket. "I've just sent a report to Mr. Knight and a few other key personnel about what just happened, so let's see what they come back with ..."

Tim was looking at Geoff.

"How are you feeling?" he asked.

Geoff wasn't sure how to answer. Part of him was still a little bit rattled at being shot at, but at the same time he felt a strange sense of relief—if this hooded figure had just tried to injure him, surely that meant he couldn't be as insignificant as Eric's computer had predicted?

Geoff sat up in his seat and looked at Eric.

"Could your computer be wrong about me?" he said. "I mean, if there's a loophole in your algorithm, could it mean I might not be an 'insignificant nobody' after all?"

Eric sighed. "I don't want to get into this again," he said, closing his eyes. He looked exhausted, his face sagging like a tire with a slow puncture. "Like I said before, the loophole potentially allows the computer to be manipulated into using its own powers of prediction against itself. That's all I can say. It has nothing to do with the assessment it made of you, which is still accurate."

"Prove it," Geoff said. "If you're so sure your computer hasn't made a mistake about me, explain more about this loophole."

Eric shifted his weight in his seat. He looked uncomfortable.

"I'm sorry, but I can't discuss the details with anyone until I've rewritten the algorithm. It's simply too dangerous."

"It's not just you, Geoff," Tim added. "Even I'm not allowed to know about the loophole."

"I don't understand," Geoff said. "How do you even know these 'time terrorists' have worked out a flaw in your code?"

"Because a few months ago, I made a frightening discovery— I found out that someone had been hacking into the computer, running different simulations to see the outcome of making certain changes. This wouldn't normally be a problem—the computer would still detect a change was being made and block anyone from going back in time if they were to attempt it in real life. But in this case, the scenario they ran was different. Someone had worked out how to change the course of history without the computer even realizing it. The scenario was perfect in every way. Brilliantly devised. And totally devastating."

"What was it?"

Eric glanced out of the window of the limousine.

"Like I said, I can't talk about it. But it involved visiting a time period we don't currently offer as a holiday destination—yet."

"And you have no idea who the hacker was?"

"No. But whoever it was, they must have had someone on the inside helping them. There's no way they would have been able to access the computer and analyze the algorithm otherwise. And the code is protected by a rolling encryption, so someone would need to have top, top, top level security clearance to get to it—a senior physicist maybe, or a board member."

"What's a 'rolling encryption'?"

"It's like an encryption, but it rolls."

Geoff gave a slow nod to pretend he understood Eric's explanation.

"So anyway, until the new algorithm is ready, my work on rewriting it is absolutely top secret."

Geoff was just about to ask another question when something unexpected caught his eye outside. He leaned forward and looked out of the window. It was a Ford Focus. He had travelled over a thousand years into the future and he was looking at a Ford Focus driving just ahead of them. Either Ford Focuses were extremely resilient cars, or something wasn't quite right. He looked out of the other window. A couple of Audis and a BMW were overtaking them. On the other side of the road, a Volkswagen Golf was tailgating a Chrysler. What was going on? Come to think of it, why were *they* travelling in a car? Weren't people supposed to be flying around in jet-powered shoes by now? Or teleporting—hadn't Mr. Knight mentioned teleportation?

It wasn't just the cars—the more Geoff looked around, the more things looked a little too familiar: buildings, streetlights, road signs, shop names, postboxes. Hadn't anything changed in over one thousand years?

"Am I missing something here?" Geoff said, still staring out of the window. "Isn't this to be the year 3050? Why does everything look exactly the same as I remember it?"

"I was wondering how long it would take you to notice," Tim said. "Things may look exactly the same, but this is not the original London you remember. It's actually a huge re-creation of the old city, right down to the last brick."

"A re-creation?"

"Remember earlier you asked me about the Varsarians?" Eric said.

"You mean when I saw that poster advertising a holiday to the twenty-second century? The one with Big Ben being blown up?"

"That's right. Well, the original city of London was mostly destroyed in that invasion."

"Crickey," Geoff said. "I guess they didn't like Earth very much then?"

"Oh, they liked Earth," Eric replied. "Only they preferred it to not be inhabited by the human race if at all possible—they wanted it for themselves. You see, the Varsarians were a particularly aggressive alien species hell-bent on some mission to colonize every planet in the universe capable of sustaining organic life."

"And you say people go back to the invasion on holiday? That it's one of your most popular destinations?"

"It is *the* most popular destination we offer," Tim said. "As you know, death and destruction are big selling points, and believe me—that invasion had it in spades. It's a dangerous time to visit, but the battle was one of the most spectacular in human history."

"It really is worth seeing if you ever get the chance," Eric said.

Geoff mulled this over.

"Can't you just tell me what happened briefly," he said, "in the comfort of this very nice, very safe limousine?"

"As you wish," Eric said, taking a deep breath. "In 2181 a huge fleet of Varsarian ships took Earth completely by surprise and annihilated several major cities in the space of a few hours. New York, Beijing, London, Basingstoke, Berlin—all were practically wiped off the map in one hit."

"Basingstoke?"

"Historians are still arguing over why they picked Basingstoke," Eric said. "The latest theory is that the name meant 'potatoes galore' in their language, and that they decided to blow it up because they didn't know what a potato was and thought it might be dangerous."

"That's just silly."

"It's a cultural thing. Apparently, certain words and phrases carried extreme importance to the Varsarians, causing them to behave in an over-the-top way. Basingstoke was just one of those words."

"Earth's counterattack was laughable," Tim continued. "Nuclear missiles, fusion bombs, proton clusters: the aliens took such little damage from the onslaught, they actually thought Earth was firing gifts into the sky as a peace offering."

"So what happened?" Geoff said. "How did Earth survive?"

"Unknown to the Varsarians, and indeed most of the world, a small university in Malta had just made a major scientific break-through," Eric said. "They had discovered how to create a temporal vortex."

"A what?"

"They had discovered time travel."

"Time travel was discovered that long ago?" Geoff said. "In Malta?"

"Discovered, yes," Eric said, "but not applied to anything. We had to develop a supercomputer powerful enough to control the technology before we could really exploit it—the time-tourism industry, for example, is only ten years old. Back in the twenty-second century, the university decided to veto the technology and kept it a secret from the public on the grounds that it was too dangerous. However, fearing the probable extinction of the human race, the university powered up its particle accelerator, tracked the Varsarians' orbit in space, and projected a vortex directly into the flight path of the invading fleet. The fleet was instantly transported six hundred years into the future. From humanity's point of view, this was actually quite funny—not only had they eliminated the Varsarian threat for the time being, but they also knew the precise moment when the fleet was going to reappear—they knew the exact year, the exact day, the exact minute. When the fleet therefore reappeared in the year 2781, Mankind was expecting them. By this time, the human race was fairly experienced at intergalactic travel and had built a huge battle fleet of its own to counter the attacking force. They wanted revenge for those who had lost their lives so long ago, and in six hundred years they had developed some pretty nasty weapons that were more than capable of delivering it. For the Varsarians, however, the six-hundred-year jump was instantaneous—they were completely unaware of what had just happened, so they carried on attacking. Unfortunately, they soon discovered that their opponents had suddenly become quite an even match. Energy beams that were moments ago wreaking destruction on the planet's surface were now being reflected back at them, mother ships were starting to take damage, and space fighters were being shot down. The battle lasted many days, but in the end, mankind was victorious—all of the invading ships were destroyed, and the Varsarians were finally defeated."

"Bit unlucky for them, really," Geoff said.

"Could have been unluckier," Eric replied. "If that university in Malta had sent them *two thousand* years in the future, they would have been wiped out in seconds. Most vacuum cleaners will be more powerful than the alien's weaponry by then."

"So what happened to London?" Geoff said.

"Well, this is the interesting part," Eric said as if the previous part about the near-extinction of humanity had been a bit dull. "Toward the end of the battle, one of the damaged Varsarian spaceships actually broke through the Earth's atmosphere and crash-landed in North America. When it was recovered by the military, they discovered an amazing piece of alien technology: a molecular rearrangement beam."

"A what?"

"A particle beam capable of rearranging mass into any formation."

Geoff thought about this.

"A what?" he said.

"On a small scale," Eric sighed, "if you fired this beam at an apple, it could turn it into an orange. On a large scale, if you fired it at the desolate, radioactive remains of a city once destroyed by an alien invasion, it could transform it back into that city."

"And that's what happened with London?"

Eric nodded. "Once the scientists had figured out how to program it, they flew the ship back into space and fired the beam at London. Within minutes, the city was completely reformed."

"But why does it look exactly like the London of the twenty-first century? Why are there still cars driving around?"

"Because when the scientists were making their calculations, they could only refer back to what London looked like before it was destroyed. The government of the day took advantage of this and decided to recreate London exactly as it had existed in the early twenty-first century. They then passed a bill that made it illegal to build or change anything, and the city became preserved as a memorial: a symbol of the city's strength in times of adversity. Since then, London has stayed exactly the same: Big Ben is still Big Ben, buses are still red, and the Tube still suffers from signal failures. We weren't even allowed to build the time-tourism facility in London unless we agreed to convert an old railway station, and the rest had to be built underground—even the supercomputer," Eric said.

"Blimey," Geoff said. "That's quite a story."

"Unfortunately, it doesn't end there," Eric said. "There's still one loose end that exists even to this day."

"You mean you still get those annoying people on the street handing out free newspapers?"

"Not quite. When the scientists first tested the molecular rearrangement beam, they fired it at a monkey. The results were terrifying."

"Why? Geoff said. Was it horribly mutilated?"

"No," Eric said. "The monkey turned into a human being."

"A human being?" Geoff said. "What's so terrifying about a human being?"

"Think about it. Why would the monkey have turned into a human being?"

Geoff shrugged. He had no idea.

"Because that was the way the Varsarians had last configured the molecular rearrangement beam. The theory is that some of them actually survived the crash, turned themselves into humans before the ship was recovered, and disappeared into society. What's worse, we have reason to believe that descendants of the Varsarian race still live among us today, plotting to use time tourism to change the outcome of their failed invasion. They may even be the ones who were able to gain access to the computer."

"In other words, they want to use the technology that was responsible for their downfall against us," Tim said, looking out of the window. It was beginning to get dark outside.

"We're about five minutes away," Eric said to Geoff. "You'd better take your pants off."

"I beg your pardon?"

"Take your pants off. Your clothes still reek of smoke from the Great Fire of London, and there's probably a load of holotographers waiting outside for you. We can't let you get out of the car dressed like that."

"I'd rather be wearing these pants than no pants," Geoff said, protectively tugging them up as far as they would go.

"Relax," Tim said. "I'm not suggesting you get out of the car in your underwear. There's a dinner suit under your seat in your size. Give me your clothes and put it on."

"Can't I just wear these clothes?" Geoff said. "I don't really like the thought of getting undressed in front of you two."

"We'll look away if it makes you feel better," Tim said, "but you're talking to two guys who took a semen sample from you four hours ago. We've already seen everything, believe me."

Geoff couldn't really argue with this and reached under his seat, pulling out a rather expensive-looking tuxedo.

It wasn't long before the limousine pulled up outside the building Geoff had been to for his interview over one thousand years ago. It looked exactly the same as he remembered it—tall, oblong, and cladded in glass. The only difference was that this time, a bright blue sign stretched over the main entrance that said "Time Tours Inc.", If he recalled correctly, there was nothing to suggest this place was the headquarters of the time-tourism industry in the twenty-first century. A luscious red carpet concertinaed its way up the short flight of stairs to the entrance, lined with thick rope cordon. And on either side of the carpet, huge crowds of people were jostling each other for a better view. What was all the fuss about?

"Don't forget this," Tim said, handing Geoff his badge. "All the other Time Reps will be wearing theirs."

"Why are there so many people here?" Geoff said, clipping the badge onto his jacket. "Is someone important coming?"

Eric straightened his tie.

"Like we said, there'll be the odd politician here and perhaps a few celebrities, but these people aren't here to see them. They're here to see the new Time Reps.

It took a moment for what Eric had just said to sink in.

"Wait a minute—you mean they're here to see me?"

"Don't worry," Tim said. "All you need to do is wave to the crowds and walk inside. Ruth should be waiting in the lobby to take us upstairs."

Geoff pressed his face against the car window and looked at the crowd. He couldn't believe it—these people had actually gathered to see him. Some were already trying to take his picture.

"I'm not worrying," Geoff said, rubbing his hands in excitement. "I think this is great! The limousine, the crowds—I'm being treated like a bloody film star! Just wait till I tell Zoë!"

"This could have been a mistake," Eric said, raising his eyebrows at Tim. "The file said he didn't like being the center of attention. It said…"

"I know what the file said," Tim interrupted, turning to Geoff. "Listen very carefully," he said, lowering his voice. "I know it's hard, but you've got to try to ignore all this attention. You mustn't let it affect who you are."

"What are you talking about?"

"Remember what Mr. Knight told you earlier—the only reason you got this job is because he thought it wouldn't change you. It's imperative that you remain the same uninspired, unambitious Geoffrey Stamp that he interviewed this afternoon. If all this glitz is starting to make you feel important or somehow special, then you could be endangering your position as a Time Rep. And for goodness sake, you can't tell anyone about this in the twenty-first century. Not Zoë, not anyone. It has to remain top secret."

"But…"

Before Geoff could even contemplate finishing this sentence, a footman suddenly opened the car door to let Geoff out. There was a loud cheer from the crowd, the people at the front bulging up against the rope cordon, their arms stretched out with autograph books. Geoff stepped out of the car and took a few steps forward, closely followed by Tim and Eric.

"How am I supposed to ignore this?" Geoff whispered back to Tim. "Everyone's going crazy for me!"

"You've got to try," Tim replied.

"I blame the media," Eric said. "They've been hyping you up all week."

"Hyping me up?" Geoff said.

"Look this way, Geoff!" someone cried.

"Over here!" came another voice.

"Smile for the holotographers," Tim said, placing his hands on Geoff's shoulders and steering him to face a group of journalists. "Just give them a few good shots and head inside. And don't answer any questions."

Geoff did as he was told and smiled. The "holotographers" held up some camera-like devices and flashed away.

"What do you think of the future, Mr. Stamp?" a journalist said, thrusting a microphone forward as far as he could.

"I…"

"Don't answer," Tim said.

"Mr. Stamp!" another journalist shouted. "How do you respond to the allegations that you've been lied to about the…"

"That's enough," Eric said, pulling him back.

"What was that?" Geoff said. "What have I been lied to about?"

Tim and Eric said nothing, hurrying Geoff up the red carpet and through the entrance without saying a word.

NINE

Ruth was waiting for them in the frosted glass lobby, sitting on the edge of her frosted glass desk. Her hair was immaculately styled into a tight bun, her lips were glossed in a subtle pink lipstick, and she wore a tight-fitting red and black dress. Geoff couldn't begin to comprehend the effort that had probably gone into her appearance; after all, he'd had enough trouble just trying to do up his shoelaces in the limousine.

"Good evening gentlemen," she said, standing up. "How are we doing?"

"Fine thanks," Geoff said. "I mean, somebody just tried to shoot a bolt at me, but otherwise I'm doing pretty good."

"Yes, I heard about that," Ruth said. "Don't worry—our best people are trying to figure out what happened, and in the meantime you'll be safe here." She looked at Eric. "You ready for your big moment upstairs?" she asked.

"I guess so," Eric replied.

"Good. Well, everyone else is already upstairs. Shall we join them?"

"How many people are here?" Tim said.

"Couple of hundred," Ruth replied. She adjusted her heels slightly and led them over to the elevator.

"Hold on a minute," Geoff said. "What was that guy saying outside? Something about me being lied to?"

Ruth stopped for a moment.

"You let him talk to the journalists?" she said, looking around at Tim. "After all those rumors about him in the news?"

"Rumors?" Geoff said. "What rumors?"

Tim sighed. "Rumors that you might not be as insignificant as you've been led to believe," he said. "Some journalists think that your position as a Time Rep has been orchestrated as part of a wider conspiracy to change history."

"So these people think I might not be insignificant?"

"Quite the opposite in fact," Tim said. "These people actually think that you're special in some way."

"Special," Geoff said, nodding to himself. "I like that. So, do you think they're onto something?"

"The story is nonsense," Eric snapped. "If the computer really has made a mistake about you—if you really are 'special'—history would have changed the moment we brought you forward in time!"

"Gentlemen, gentlemen," Ruth said, trying to bring the conversation into a more civilized tone. "Can this wait until later? Mr. Knight is waiting for you upstairs before he gives his speech." She held the elevator door open and ushered the three men inside.

"Please state your destination," the lift said in its synthesized female voice.

"Top floor," Ruth replied.

The doors closed, and the elevator began to move.

Eric leaned his walking stick against the corner of the lift and pulled a white handkerchief out of his pocket. "I hope this speech is shorter than last time," he said, dabbing his forehead before arranging the handkerchief to stick out of his breast pocket in a perfect triangle. "Have you had a chance to read it?"

"Don't worry," Ruth replied. "It's only a couple of minutes long."

"And what's the message this year?"

"The usual. There's a bit about how time tourism enlightens humanity, makes people cherish the past…Oh, and a couple of senior politicians are here tonight, so he's going to publicly reassure everyone that time tourism is still safe despite the attempts to abuse it—thanks to you." Ruth patted Eric on the shoulder. "You might even get a mention."

"Can't wait."

"That reminds me," Ruth said, touching Eric's arm. "Mr. Knight wants you to show the Defense Minister those new precautionary measures you're working on. Can you stop by your lab on the way up and collect the paperwork?"

Eric nodded in silence. He looked pale.

"Laboratory," he said, his voice sounding a little weak.

"Thank you," the lift said. "This lift will stop at the laboratory before proceeding to the top floor."

"You've got your own lab here?" Geoff said.

Tim nudged Geoff's arm. "There'll be quite a few other Time Reps here tonight," he said. "You should try to speak to them if you get the chance. They'll be able to give you a few tips about the job that we might not be able to help you with."

Geoff said nothing. He tugged on his bow tie—Tim had done it up a little tight.

"Geoff?"

Silence.

"Geoff. Say something."

"Basement!" Geoff said.

"Thank you," the lift replied. "After this lift reaches the top floor, it will then head down to the basement."

Tim sighed.

"Happy?" he said.

Mr. Knight clinked his wine glass with a spoon.

"Everyone!" he said, sounding a little out of breath. "Can I have your attention please?"

Across the room, people cut short their conversations and looked around at Mr. Knight, who was being helped up onto his desk by Ruth. Presumably this was so people could see him— Mr. Knight didn't come across as the sort of person who would indulge in unruly office behavior for no reason, even at a party. Through the windows behind him, the moonlit London skyline was exactly the same as Geoff remembered it from over one thousand years ago. It really was a very good re-creation.

The top floor, however, had changed considerably since he was here for his interview, no longer being just an empty expanse of open-plan office space with a lone desk in the corner. Today, it looked more like a Roman palace with a shiny marble floor, ornate fountains dotted around the place, and huge stone pillars rising into the ceiling. Geoff tapped on one with his hand. Solid stone. It was hard to believe that this was the same room.

He turned toward Tim, who was sitting on some sort of chez longue. "What's the deal with this décor?" he whispered.

"Oh, it's not always like this," Tim replied, tossing a grape in his mouth. "Each year a Time Rep takes it in turn to provide the food and decoration for the annual inauguration. This year it's the turn of the Time Rep from Ancient Rome."

"Ladies and Gentlemen," Mr. Knight said, looking over the crowd from his desk-cum-pedestal, "welcome to the tenth annual Time Rep inauguration party!"

The guests erupted into a round of applause.

Mr. Knight waited for the noise to die down. "Tonight," he continued, "we are honored to welcome four new Time Reps into the organization, all of whom you will get a chance to meet later. As of today, we are now able to offer holidays to over a hundred different historical time periods from ancient Egypt, to the second Renaissance period, right the way back to prehistoric times. This is a far cry from our roots fifteen years ago when we could only offer holidays to a handful of destinations. Tonight, we are here to celebrate the fantastic growth the time-tourism industry has seen over the past year. We're here to celebrate the increased understanding we are able to offer the world about its past. But most of all, we are here to celebrate you—the Time Reps. The ambassadors for history."

Geoff picked his nose and wiped it on a pillar.

"However," Mr. Knight continued, "a small minority of people out there want to abuse the benefits of time travel. They want to take this new freedom away from us and use it to change history for their own selfish means. In these times of crisis, we mustn't forget those who work tirelessly to protect us from this threat. Let me make this clear: time travel has always been safe, and it remains safe because of the continued effort of one man. Please give a huge round of applause for the double Noble Prize winner, and our Chief Physicist, Dr. Eric Skivinski!!!!"

There was another round of applause, although Geoff noticed one lady standing nearby who wasn't clapping. Instead, she had her arms folded tightly over her chest. He was just close enough to make out her name badge, which read "Jennifer Adams."

"Where is Eric?" Mr. Knight called out, looking out across the party. A few heads began to turn in the crowd, but Eric was nowhere to be seen.

"No matter," Mr. Knight said, looking a little embarrassed at Eric's absence. "I'm sure you'll all get to meet him later. Please, have a drink, get to know your fellow Time Reps, and above all, enjoy yourselves!"

The crowd gave a final, less enthusiastic round of applause, suggesting they were getting a little bit bored with all the applauding. Mr. Knight dropped down from his desk and went over to chat with the nearest group of guests. Around the room, people returned to their conversations.

Geoff wandered over to Tim, who was craning his neck over the crowd.

"What are you doing?" Geoff said.

"Looking for Eric," Tim said. "You seen him? Mr. Knight's going to be pretty pissed if he doesn't show his face tonight."

"What does Mr. Knight actually do?" Geoff said.

"Mr. Knight? He's the president of the company," Tim replied, giving up his search. "Mainly deals with the more political side of the business. He secures funding for us, negotiates with the government over tourism regulations, dictates our corporate responsibilities, and he keeps the shareholders happy. You've got to deal with some very slippery individuals when you're at his level, and he does that very well."

Geoff looked over at Mr. Knight. He was standing in the far corner of the room talking to an overweight, well-dressed gentleman.

"Let's go over and speak to him," Tim said, getting to his feet. "You'll see what I mean."

Geoff picked up a glass of wine from a nearby table and followed Tim across the room, negotiating his way past a number of well-dressed men and women who were making polite conversation with each other in small groups.

"That's David Cartwright, the Defense Minister he's talking to at the moment," Tim said, weaving his way through a group of men wearing togas. "Probably having one of their regular arguments about the danger of the terrorist threat."

The Defense Minister was a large man, probably about the same size as an armchair. He had bulging red cheeks, a weak chin, and a neck that spilled out over the top of his shirt collar. He had short, light brown hair that looked as though it would have the texture of Velcro if you touched it, and a face that seemed to move like he was chewing rubber as he spoke.

As they approached, Geoff began to hear the conversation between him and Mr. Knight.

"…forcing us to shut down until you've caught these terrorists would be a very brave decision for you to make," Mr. Knight said, looking quite relaxed. "A very brave decision."

"But Ernest," the Minister replied, taking a small sip of what looked to be brandy. "We still have serious doubts about the safety of this operation—especially after today. Did you read Eric's report on what happened earlier in 1666? How could someone slip through the supercomputer's checks and be able to fire a bolt at one of your reps?"

"I don't know," Mr. Knight said. "But there really is no need to worry. Dr. Skivinski is on the verge of completing his new algorithm, and I'm told it's flawless."

"And what if he can't complete this work in time? What if someone changes the past before it's ready?"

"Eric will come through," Mr. Knight insisted, his voice unwavering. "He was supposed to be here to show you some of the other precautionary measures we're working on, but unfortunately he seems to have disappeared for the moment. From what I understand though, he's on track to upload the new algorithm into the mainframe by the end of the week. There's absolutely nothing to worry about."

Mr. Knight noticed Tim and Geoff approaching and stepped to one side, motioning them to join the discussion.

"David, this is Timothy Burnell, one of our chief Time Rep recruiters working under Dr. Skivinski. He's the man who finds us our Time Reps. Tim, you know the Defense Minister."

"I do," Tim said, shaking his hand.

"And this is Geoffrey Stamp," Mr. Knight said, placing his hand on Geoff's shoulder. "One of our newest Reps for the twenty-first century. Recruited today, in fact."

Geoff also shook hands with the Defense Minister. It felt a little clammy, like shaking hands with a lump of beef.

"You two are the ones Eric mentioned in his report?" the Defense Minister said. "The ones who chased that man in 1666?"

"We don't know if it was necessarily a man," Tim replied.

"I was shot at!" Geoff said.

"We know, Geoff," Tim said. "We know."

"Very concerning," the Defense Minister muttered. "Very concerning indeed …"

"The Defense Minister still has a few doubts over safety," Mr. Knight said to Tim, not taking his eyes of the Minister. "He's thinking about closing us down."

"I just don't see why you object to being shut down for the next few days," the Minister replied, swirling the brandy around in his glass. "At least until this new algorithm of yours is ready."

Mr. Knight took a moment to pause.

"Shutting down isn't a problem, David," he said, smiling. "Not a problem at all."

"Good. I'm glad we agree on …"

"But think of the message that would send out to the world," he added. "Think what those blasted Varsarians might make of it.

Shutting down now would be admitting defeat. These terrorists need to know that their efforts to disrupt our freedom have been futile. They need to know that they have achieved nothing. If we shut down, we'd be handing them a small victory. We'd be showing them that we're scared. Are you scared, David?"

"Yes," the Minister replied, looking into his glass. "I'm terrified. If something should happen…"

"It won't," Mr. Knight said, pulling a cigar out of his pocket. "You've seen the safety checks we have in place. In fact, both Tim and Geoffrey were there earlier." He turned to face them. "How many people did we turn away today?"

"Sixteen," Tim replied.

"You see? Sixteen." He put the cigar in his mouth and lit it.

"But someone *did* get through today," the Minister said. "The loophole…"

"Is fixable," Mr. Knight insisted through an exhalation of thick smoke. "And even if it wasn't, despite what happened today, the chances of exploiting it are one in a googolplex."

"I'm not sure that's a chance I'm willing to take," the Minister said, finishing the last of his drink. "The slightest change to the space-time continuum could be disastrous."

"No one's going to change anything. I guarantee it."

"Twenty-five years in politics has taught me that there's no such thing as a guarantee," the Minister said.

"Think what you like, David," Mr. Knight said, "but as I said, shutting us down would be very… brave."

"Allowing you to stay operational could be even braver," the Minister countered. "I don't know, Ernest—I need to sleep on this. We'll speak again tomorrow. Now gentlemen, if you'll excuse me…" He handed his glass to a passing waiter and walked away.

Mr. Knight stood there in silence, his eyes fixed on the Minister as he left. He watched him as he passed through the crowd, grabbed his coat, pressed the elevator button, waited for the elevator, stepped into the elevator, and stood inside the elevator as the doors closed behind him. As if that wasn't quite enough staring, he remained staring at the elevator doors for a good few seconds, just for good measure. Geoff thought this was too much staring for his liking until he realized he must have been staring at exactly the same things for him to be able to relay back to himself what Mr. Knight was staring at.

"Find Eric," Mr. Knight said, still staring directly at the elevator doors. He grabbed the Minister's empty glass from the waiter and tapped his ash into it. "He really should be with me when I get stuck in these technical conversations."

"I haven't seen him since we came up here," Tim said. "He's disappeared."

Mr. Knight took a deep puff of his cigar. "Well if you see him, tell him to come find me. We'll need to work on a response to this situation tonight in case they try to shut us down tomorrow morning." He gave them both a brief nod and strolled off, leaving a thick trail of cigar smoke in his wake.

Tim waved his hands in front of his face to disperse the smoke. "I'm going to find Eric," he said, turning to leave.

"Wait," Geoff said, grabbing his arm. "What am I supposed to do while you're gone?"

"What?"

"I haven't been to a party for years. The last one I went to had this game where you had to take your shoes and socks off, put your shoes in one box and your socks in another, then the first person to put their shoes and socks back on won some jelly."

"Jelly? How old were you?"

"Twelve."

"Twelve?" Tim said. "You went to your last party when you were twelve?"

"You've been keeping me indoors playing computer games, remember? What do people do at these things? What am I supposed to do if someone comes over and talks to me?"

"Talk back."

"Talk back?"

"Yes."

"And how do I do that?"

"Wait for someone to finish what they are saying, then say something back."

"I can't do that."

"You're doing it now. That's what people do when they're having a conversation. You'll be fine."

"This is different. We're having an argument, not a conversation."

"Then get into lots of arguments," Tim said. He flashed Geoff a quick smile, released his arm from his grip, and walked off.

Geoff looked around at the other guests, all of whom were happily chatting away. He didn't do chatting—least of all with strangers. Unfortunately, all the people he *did* know were busy in mid-chat: Mr. Knight was chatting to someone, Ruth was chatting to someone, and even William Boyle from the seventeenth century was chatting to someone. Geoff did a double take—how on earth had William managed to get here so quickly?

It didn't take long for Geoff to convince himself that he wasn't really in the mood for a chat. He grabbed a few grapes from a nearby table and retreated into a quiet corner of the room, being sure to stare at the floor the whole time to avoid eye contact with anyone. Hopefully, the other guests would read this body language as saying, "GO AWAY."

"Hey—you Geoffrey Stamp?" a voice said. American accent.

Geoff chewed nervously on a grape and looked up. A man was walking over to him in long strides, dressed in a smart, pinstriped suit. He was tall with not an ounce of fat on his body to speak of.

"You're the slob, right?" The man said.

"The slob?" Geoff said, picking some grape skin out from between his teeth.

"Yeah—the unemployed guy. The one who never leaves the house. That you?"

"Apparently," Geoff said.

"Miles Wentworth," the man said, extending one hand for Geoff to shake and tugging his name badge with the other. "Time Rep for 1930s America."

Geoff shook his hand. Miles certainly had a firm grip. The man must have been in his early forties with a long, clean-shaven face, a jaw that looked as though it had been chiseled from a slab of granite, and sunken cheeks. Flecks of gray hair peeked out from under his trilby, and his eyebrows were so thick they looked as though two small badgers had fallen asleep on his face.

"Yeah, been doing this job four years now," he said, looking around at some other guests. "Big attraction, the Great Depression."

"Really?" Geoff said. "Isn't the Great Depression a bit … well … depressing?"

"That it is, pal, that it is. Unemployment's at an all-time high, people are jumping out of windows on Wall Street, and they reckon there might be another war around the corner. Why would anyone want to go see that?"

"Beats me," Geoff said, eating his last grape. "Same reason people watch reality TV, I suppose."

Miles paused. "You got me there," he said. "Reality TV?"

"Never mind."

"So, first day, huh?" Miles said, changing the subject. "Enjoying it so far?"

Geoff thought about this for a second.

"It's certainly been unusual," he said.

"Unusual? In what way?"

"Let me see … Traveling through time, seeing the Great Fire of London, being shot at, driving through a re-creation of London in a limousine, talking to a man from the 1930s … Little things like that."

"You were shot at?"

"It's a long story. Wasn't your first day unusual?"

"I guess," Miles replied, brushing some fluff off his tie. "Started off the same as any other day, mind; woke up, ate my breakfast, walked to work, sat at my desk, made a few phone calls, you know, usual stuff. Then about lunchtime my boss walks in. Says he's been looking at the shares I've been buying for the last few years, and he's noticed that my investments make no impact on the stock market whatsoever."

"No impact?"

"Yeah, and he was right. He'd been making me work later and later hours to the point where I had no social life whatsoever, but no matter how much overtime I put in doing the research, the stock I bought remained static. Don't get me wrong—it would fluctuate up and down all right, but by the time we were ready to sell, the stock was the exact same value as the price we bought them at. Always bugged me. Thought he'd finally lost it with me when he came in that day. But he was fine. In fact, he wanted to talk to me about investing in this new company that had invented 'earphones'. So he puts a pair on my desk and says that everyone will be buying them someday."

"Earphones?"

"Yeah. So he wants to know my opinion. I say sure, but I want to try them first, so he lets me wear them. Next thing I know I wake up strapped to some damn table, lights flashing in my eyes. You probably know the rest. Turned out my boss of seven years had been working for this place all along. He'd been making me work overtime to remove me from the outside world as much as possible."

"It's the same for everyone apparently," Geoff said. "Today I found out that my only friend was the spy, and that the past seven years have been nothing more than an act. I mean don't get me wrong—it's very exciting to learn about time tourism, but at the same time, I feel a bit of an idiot. You know?"

"What does Ruth say?"

"Ruth? What has Ruth got to do with this?"

"You haven't spoken to Ruth?"

"Ruth … the receptionist?"

"She's no receptionist," Miles laughed, tugging his shirtsleeves out from under the arms of his jacket so they protruded exactly the same length on either side. "She's the brains behind this whole operation, if you ask me. A real whiz kid. You and I wouldn't be here if it wasn't for her, that's for sure."

"We wouldn't?"

"Nope," Miles said, leaning in toward Geoff and lowering his voice to a whisper. "From what I hear, this whole 'Time Rep' thing was her idea."

"You don't say…" Geoff muttered.

It took Geoff a few minutes to find Ruth, who was sitting peacefully on the edge of one of the mock-Roman fountains, staring into her wine glass.

"Allow me to introduce myself," Geoff said, sitting down next to her. "I'm 'the slob'."

Ruth looked up. "The slob?"

"Yep. At least that's what everyone's calling me. 'Hey! You're that slob guy!' 'You're the slob, right?'"

"That's because you *are* a slob."

"I know that. You know that. But why do other Time Reps know that? Why does Colin the thirteenth century turnip farmer know that?"

"You're a Time Rep," Ruth said, placing her wine glass on the floor. "You saw the crowds outside—you're famous here! Everyone knows everything about you."

"And I understand I have you to thank for that."

"For what?"

"For being here. For being a Time Rep."

"Yes, I suppose you do," Ruth replied, leaning back on her hands.

"So this whole thing was your idea?"

"It was my idea to recruit people from different time periods, yes."

"And how did you come up with that?"

"Because we needed something to revitalize the time-tourism industry: something to make it more interesting. You see, when we first started offering holidays to the past, it wasn't actually that popular. It was a real shock—we thought the idea of going back in time would be hugely successful. Thought it would revolutionize everything. And for a while, it did—holidays to the past became as popular as the exotic spaceflight holidays to distant galaxies. By the end of the first few years, however, people got a bit bored of it all, and sales began to decline."

"Bored?" Geoff gasped. "How could people get bored of something so incredible so quickly? That's nearly as bad as when *Firefly* got cancelled after only one season."

"The problem was people didn't really know what to do when they went back to somewhere like 1595," Ruth said. "There were no hotels in most destinations and certainly none of the amenities they were used to. And as the years passed, people stopped going on long breaks—most would just go back in time for a couple of days out of curiosity, check out the scenery, and then come back."

"What's wrong with that?"

"Nothing," Ruth replied, "if you're prepared to lose money on every holiday you sell. It's not cheap sending someone back in time. If you want to make any money at all, you need people to be going back for at least a week. So I thought to myself, why aren't these people exploring the time period properly? Why don't they stay to witness significant historical events or visit all the notable landmarks of the period? Then it dawned on me—these people had no one there to guide them, no one to tell them about all the things they could be doing. Take the time period you are representing. If we want people to spend any significant time in the twenty-first century, we need an expert there: someone who knows all the sites; someone with extensive knowledge of all the customs of the time period; someone on call twenty-four hours a day."

"Or you could just use someone like me," said Geoff. His tone of voice made it sound as though he was joking, but in truth, he wasn't. On call twenty-four hours a day? With no pay? What a deal!

Ruth laughed. She picked her wine glass up off the floor and took a sip.

"So anyway—that's where the idea of having Time Reps came from," she said.

"So I take it from all this that the idea was successful?"

Ruth nodded.

"Like you wouldn't believe. When we told people they could actually speak to people from the past and learn about these time periods properly, sales went ballistic, exceeding even the most optimistic forecasts. Schools starting booking educational trips for entire classes thirty-five tickets at a time, universities would organize massive field trips for their students, and families started to take notice again. Before we knew it, our market value had trebled in a matter of months, and I was hailed as the savior of the company. From that point on, my life totally changed: no longer was I just one of Mr. Knight's many assistants—a girl fresh out of university with a degree in marketing, a head full of ideas, and a dream of making it to the top. I was promoted to being the youngest board member in the company's history—the Director of 'Innovation and Strategy,' no less." She made two little "inverted comma" signs with her fingers as she spoke as if to suggest the title was not to be taken too seriously.

"Is that good?" Geoff asked. Corporate hierarchies weren't really his specialty.

"Yes, it's good—particularly for someone my age. But I'll tell you the most satisfying thing of all—in an environment full of male egos and testosterone flying about the place, it felt damn good coming up with something none of the boys had thought of."

"That sounds great and everything," Geoff said, "but can I ask—don't you ever feel guilty about this at all?" Geoff said.

Ruth paused halfway through her sip and looked at Geoff.

"Guilty?" Ruth said, bringing the glass slowly back down from her mouth. "Why should I feel guilty?"

"Well, you've effectively been playing God with my life for the past seven years, haven't you? You've kept me locked indoors, removed me from the outside world, lied to me, all so you can make the twenty-first century a better place to visit, a place more ..."

"... commercially viable?" Ruth offered.

"And it's not just me," Geoff said. "I've been talking to other Time Reps. Apparently it's the same for everyone. You keep them cocooned away for years before they know what's going on. Don't you feel the slightest bit guilty about the way you're controlling people's lives?"

"If a Time Rep's life was going to otherwise be interesting and fruitful before we stepped in, then yes, I would feel guilty. But you know how this works—you wouldn't have exactly turned out to be a nuclear physicist had we not interfered with your life. Remember—you're all totally insignificant. Would you like to know what you'd be doing right now if we hadn't interfered in your life?" Ruth said.

"Go on."

"At this moment, you'd be unemployed, sitting in front of a computer trying to work out how to program your own computer game. You'd be spending hours sitting in front of the machine, making very little progress, before giving up on your dream and drifting between mundane temp jobs for the rest of your life. Would you rather be doing that than being here?"

Geoff swallowed hard.

"I suppose not," he admitted.

"So you see, I don't feel guilty about how we control the destiny of Time Reps. Not at all. Not when I know how your lives would have turned out otherwise. I actually feel like I'm making a positive difference to somebody. Do you know what Colin the turnip farmer would have been doing had we not recruited him?"

Geoff shook his head.

"He would have been a parsnip farmer."

"I just don't like the fact that I've been deceived," Geoff said, rubbing the back of his neck. "All this time, I thought Tim was my friend. I've always wondered why he put up with my mess, why he didn't mind the fact that I owed him two year's rent. Now it makes sense—he was just some guy who was paid to live with me."

"Listen—you've known each other a long time," Ruth said, touching Geoff's arm. "He wouldn't have stayed assigned to you had he not been enjoying it. Why don't you speak to him?"

"Can't find him," Geoff said. "He's gone off to find Eric."

At that moment, Mr. Knight came over and tossed the stub of his cigar into the fountain.

"Everything all right?" he said.

Ruth stood up abruptly.

"Geoff's trying to find Tim," she said, smoothing her skirt against her legs. "Don't suppose you've seen him anywhere?"

"Tim?" Mr. Knight said. "Yes, as a matter of fact I spoke to him a few moments ago. Said he'd gone downstairs to see if Eric was in his lab."

"So Eric's still missing, is he?" Ruth said, rolling her eyes. Her voice was laced with a hint of sarcasm. "That doesn't surprise me."

Mr. Knight wasn't really paying attention to the way she was speaking. He seemed more interested in a group of people standing in another corner of the room. "I'm sure he'll turn up," he said, peering over Ruth's heads and giving the group of people a wave. "Now, would you please excuse me?"

Geoff turned to Ruth.

"Where's this lab?" he said.

"It's on the floor below," Ruth replied.

"Listen—I'll be back in a minute," Geoff said, getting to his feet. "Now could be a good chance to catch Tim alone."

He was just about to leave when Ruth grabbed him lightly by the wrist.

"Geoff?" she said.

"Yes?"

"Nothing," she said, releasing his arm slowly. "Just—good luck."

TEN

Just as Ruth had said, Eric's laboratory was one floor down from the party, the faint bass of the music and the sound of people's chatter gently reverberating through the ceiling. It certainly wasn't how Geoff had imagined a laboratory to look—he was expecting huge test tubes full of bubbling green liquid, metal spikes conducting surges of blue electricity, and shelves crammed with deformed biological specimens. Instead, all he got were a few rows of humming data banks and a filing cabinet. Eric's desk sat at the back of the room, unoccupied. It was covered in paper.

"Tim?" Geoff called out, wandering over to Eric's desk. "You in here?"

He listened. The data banks continued to hum. The filing cabinet continued to make a noise like a filing cabinet. Tim wasn't here—he must have just missed him.

Geoff sat down at Eric's desk and looked around, drumming his fingers on the surface. In front of him, amongst a scattered mess of paperwork and diagrams (including some old blueprints of a large, doughnut-shaped space station, which Geoff thought looked pretty-cool), he noticed a large file with the name "Geoffrey Stamp" written on the spine and a photo of him stuck on the cover. He picked up the file—it was surprising heavy, bulging with documents, and wrapped with a thick elastic band to hold it all together. Geoff slipped his thumb under the band and pulled it free, allowing the file to expand and breathe. A few documents spilled onto the floor. Rifling through, he found transcripts of conversations, voyeuristic photographs (many of which were of him standing on Tower

Bridge, for some reason), medical details, everything. Someone had certainly been doing their homework on him but in a different way to that time he was bullied in maths class.

He bent down and picked up one of the documents that had fallen on the floor. It was a certificate. It read:

This is to certify that
GEOFFREY STAMP
has passed the third assessment phase.
The subject is now cleared for one to one surveillance.

If he wasn't mistaken, it was dated just a few days before he'd lost his job and moved in with Tim.

Toward the back of the file the documents seemed a little more recent, the paper a little less yellow. He was now getting on to things like psychological case studies, intelligence assessments, and all sorts of random hypotheses about himself that he'd never even considered: Was he prone to violence? What was his favorite color? Why wasn't he ticklish under the arms? Why didn't he like zucchini? The questions were endless.

The last section of the file was totally dedicated to the seagull Eric had mentioned a few hours ago—the one that was looking right instead of left as a result of him being made a Time Rep. There were even a couple of photos of it: one of it looking right, the other of it looking left. Apart from that, the photos were identical. It was standing in the exact same position, in the exact same place on the edge of a small outcrop of rock. Even the clouds in the photos were the same. Geoff turned the photos over. One said "Original Timeline" on it, the other "Modified Timeline."

Continuing through the file, Geoff was amused at how many scientists had taken an interest in this seagull, some choosing to write whole theses on the subject. He skimmed through a few pages. It seemed as though everyone was in agreement that the seagull's decision to look the other way was just an unexplainable, insignificant blip in an otherwise unaltered timeline, and that Geoffrey should be made a Time Rep candidate regardless of such a benign alteration to the space-time continuum. One thesis was even entitled: 'The Geoffrey Stamp Seagull — Who Cares?"

Geoff flicked over the next few pages before stopping again. One scientist it seemed *did* care and had written a report with a very different name: "The Geoffrey Stamp Seagull—Are We *All* Looking the Other Way?" Geoff turned the page and began to read.

For months now, the scientific community has been debating whether or not we should allow Geoffrey Stamp to be given Time Rep candidature. Normally, Time Rep candidates are only approved if history remains totally unchanged as a result of their appointment. In Geoffrey Stamp's case, we are on the verge of making an exception to that rule—a seagull will choose to look right instead of left in one hundred thousand years' time, and we are willing to overlook this apparently insignificant change to make life easier for a holiday company. Friends, I believe we are making a grave mistake, one that could spell disaster for the integrity of the space-time continuum and the future of the human race. This report explores the truth behind the seagull's decision to look the other way and why Geoffrey Stamp should be immediately dropped from the twenty-first century Time Rep shortlist.

Geoff licked his finger and turned the page. It was blank. He flicked on—the rest of the file was blank. Either someone had removed the other pages of this report or the author was some sort of comedian with a penchant for invisible ink.

"Uhh…"

Geoff looked around. Unless he was mistaken, somebody had just said "Uhh…" He closed the file and stood up.

There it was again.

"Uhhhh…"

The voice was very faint. It appeared to be coming from behind the third row of data banks, just barely managing to croak above the dull humming of the machines.

"Hello?" Geoff said, slowly walking in the direction of the voice. "Is anybody there?"

"Geoff?" the voice whispered. "Geoff, is that you?"

"Who is it?" Geoff said. The voice was too weak to recognize.

A fit of coughing came in response. Sounded unpleasant.

"Who is it?" Geoff repeated.

"It's … It's me, Geoff. It's Eric …"

"Eric? We've been looking all over for you! Where have you been?"

"No time …" Eric said. "Help me …"

Geoff walked around the other side of the data banks and stood shock still. Eric was sprawled on the floor in a pool of blood, clutching his stomach.

"Oh, my God!" Geoff said, dropping to his knees. "I've got to get you help!"

"No!" Eric said, clutching Geoff's arm. "There's no time! You need to listen to me!" He pulled on Geoff's arm and hunched himself up against the data bank, coughing profusely. Specks of blood were splattering from his mouth.

"Who did this to you?"

"Remember what I was saying? About someone on the inside leaking my al … algo …"

"Algorithm?"

Eric nodded. "I didn't get time to finish it. I didn't … get time to fix the loophole."

"Eric, please—who did this to you?"

Eric's head drooped. It looked as if he was having serious trouble breathing.

"Who did this to you!?" Geoff shouted, grabbing the lapels of Eric's blood-stained dinner jacket and shaking him.

"The loophole," Eric said, looking up again. "It can be fixed. You … can fix it …"

"Me?"

"It's … it's simple really. I'll tell you … what the secret is. I'll tell you how the computer … can be tricked … Come close …"

"Eric, no! I've got to get you help!"

"No!" Eric shouted, pulling Geoff close to his face. He winced in discomfort, a trickle of blood dripping from his mouth and running through his beard. "I won't let them break my algorithm! I won't let my life's work go to waste! You sit here…and you listen to me!"

Eric whispered into Geoff's ear, explaining exactly how the computer could be tricked. Geoff listened carefully, his eyes widening as Eric spoke. Of course! When you thought about it like that, it was so simple! As Eric finished his explanation, he smiled at Geoff and released his arm, his hand dropping lifelessly to one side.

"You…understand?" Eric said.

Geoff nodded.

"Be quick…" Eric said, clutching his stomach. "These people are on the verge of…of…"

"Of…?" Geoff said.

Before Eric could finish his sentence, he coughed up a mouthful of blood and slumped over, dead.

"Eric?" Geoff said. "Eric!!!"

It was no use. Eric was still dead.

Geoff stared into Eric's vacant eyes and thought seriously about going into a mad panic: the sort of panic where you pull your hair out, eat some of it, then run around the room with your pants on your head screaming. But no—he had to get a grip on himself and speak to Mr. Knight right away. He was now the only person who knew how the supercomputer could be fooled and what needed to be done to fix it. He turned around and froze.

A familiar-looking hooded figure was standing in the doorway, clutching Eric's walking stick, blood dripping from the tip onto the laboratory floor. Geoff's expert powers of deduction led him to believe that this was probably the person who had attacked Eric and perhaps even the person who had fired the bolt at him during the Great Fire of London.

"I know you," Geoff said, rubbing his hands. He took a step back. "I saw you earlier today…"

The hooded figure remained silent and took a step forward.

"And you were in my dream," Geoff said, taking another step back. "You're the person I hooked out of the lake in my dream…"

The masked figure took another step forward, still saying nothing.

"You're going to hit me, aren't you?"

The figure gave a single nod and took another step forward. Geoff tried to compensate for this by taking another step back, but some idiot had decided to put a wall in the way. He was cornered. The figure took another step toward him, lifted the walking stick in the air, and struck him violently over the head with it.

Geoff thought this was pretty bad manners as his skull crunched against the floor.

ELEVEN

Geoff lay face down in the muddy bank of his imaginary lake, his body aching as if it had just been released from a complicated yoga position. He had a splitting headache. He lifted himself up, spat out a dollop of wet dirt, and slowly rolled himself over onto his back, resting his head back down in the mud. Geoff looked up at the sky, trying not to think about the searing pain that ran through his body. The searing pain, however, had other ideas, giving off a sharp pang at every opportunity to remind Geoff that it wasn't going anywhere.

It was nighttime in his imaginary world, the sky clear of clouds and full of stars. What the hell was going on? Who had attacked him? What was happening back in the real world? Was he in a coma? Was he dead?

All of a sudden something caught his eye—a blur of white gliding across the sky. He brought himself up to rest on his elbows and tried to focus on the blur, his arms weak and shaking as they supported the weight of his body. He looked closer.

It was a seagull. A big, white seagull soaring above him, its wings outstretched as it circled gracefully over the lake. Geoff followed it with his eyes as it descended lower—unless he was mistaken, it seemed to be heading straight for him. Within a few seconds, the seagull had slowed to a hover a few feet above Geoff, arched its wings into a landing position, and dropped down in one swift movement, neatly tucking its wings into its body as it planted its feet on his chest.

Geoff lay his head back down in the mud and sighed, his arms too weak to lean on any longer. The seagull pattered closer to Geoff's face and looked down at him. It seemed to be holding something in its beak—a small pen and paper. Brilliant—this day had been weird enough already without him dreaming about a bloody seagull with a pen and paper in its mouth. This was probably the one that looked left instead of right, or up instead of down, or whatever it was.

"Go away," Geoff murmured.

The seagull blinked.

"Scram!" he said, using the last of his strength to try to brush the seagull away.

The seagull opened its beak and dropped the pen and paper on Geoff's chest.

"Stop it!" it said, ducking its head to avoid Geoff's swing. "We haven't got much time!"

Geoff raised his head up and looked at the seagull. Was someone in the real world talking to him? Had a voice manifested itself in his dream as the voice of a seagull, like when Tim was trying to wake him up this morning? Geoff couldn't tell. In any event, he was in too much pain to start debating this anthropomorphic turn of events, so he decided to just accept the talking seagull for what it was and continue with the conversation.

"What are you talking about?" he said.

"Look at the lake," the seagull said, nodding its head in the direction of the water. "They're already coming for you."

Geoff did as he was told. Sure enough, the hooded figure was beginning to emerge from beneath the surface, making its way toward the shore.

"Who's coming for me?" Geoff said.

"The person who attacked you," the seagull said.

Geoff tried to get up, his arms slipping around in the mud, but it was useless—there was no feeling in his legs.

"What do I do?" Geoff said, still looking as the hooded figure got closer and closer. "I can't move!"

"I'm not surprised," the seagull said. "In the real world, you're in pretty bad shape—the back of your head is split open, pouring with blood."

Geoff looked at the seagull and felt the back of his head. It was wet, but he was sure this was just mud.

"No," Geoff said. "It's mud; look." He brought his hand back around to show the seagull, which was indeed brown with mud.

"That's how you've translated the injury into your dream," the seagull said. "Mud is blood. Blood is mud. Get it?"

"You're confusing me now," Geoff said, spitting a bit more mud out of his mouth. "Mud is blood?"

"We don't have time for this," the seagull said, wandering around impatiently on Geoff's torso. "Grab that pen and paper and write down everything Eric told you."

"Why?"

"Because now that Eric's dead, you're the only one who knows how to fix the computer," the seagull replied, "and that person coming out of the lake is going to try to make you forget what you know."

"How can they do that?"

"It doesn't matter. Just write everything down, quickly! You're the only person who can stop them!"

Geoff was in too much pain to write. He rested his head back down in the mud and shut his eyes.

"Hurry!" the seagull said, pecking at Geoff's chest through his t-shirt. "They're almost here! You've got to write down everything you know! If you write it down, it won't matter if they make you forget. Your memory will be preserved on the paper."

This didn't quite make sense. Surely if this was a dream, he wasn't really writing anything down—the paper only existed in his imagination. By now though, the hooded figure was stepping out of the lake and onto the muddy shore. Using the last of his energy, Geoff leaned over, grabbed the pen, and scribbled down everything Eric had told him about the loophole as fast as he could.

"There," Geoff said, slumping back down in the mud in relief. "That's everything."

"Thank God," the seagull said, jumping down to Geoff's side. "I'll look after this until you're ready to remember again." It picked up the piece of paper with its foot and took off, narrowly avoiding a swipe from the hooded figure, who was now standing directly over them.

"Damn," the hooded figure said, looking up at the bird as it disappeared into the night sky. "Almost had it." The voice seemed familiar, but Geoff couldn't quite place it.

"Hello Geoffrey," the figure said, crouching down at Geoff's side. "How are you?"

"Err … Not too great, actually," Geoff said, trying to avoid looking directly at the hooded face. He was scared. "I'm in a bit of pain."

"I know. And there's one more bit of pain I need to inflict on you."

"There is?" Geoff said. He could feel his heart beating faster.

"Yes," the figure said, pulling out a knife. "Hold your hand still."

Unfortunately, holding still wasn't going to be much of a problem. Geoff barely had enough energy to blink at the moment, let alone move his hand.

"What are you going to do?"

The hooded figure said nothing.

"Does it involve that knife you're holding?"

His question was soon answered by the intense pain he felt in his right hand. Looking down his body, he could see that the hooded figure had jammed the knife deep into his right palm, twisting it through to the other side. Geoff screamed out in agony. He would have preferred a simple "Yes."

"Now," the hooded figure said, standing up again. "You're almost ready to wake up. I just need you to forget everything that happened here. Forget everything Dr. Skivinski told you about the loophole in his algorithm. And forget everything about that seagull."

"Why should I?" Geoff said, trying to move his hand. "Why should I forget?"

"Because you're in pain. Your head is bursting with pain, and every memory you have of this evening is the cause; every memory is tearing through your mind like a bolt of lightning. If you forget, the pain will stop."

Geoff's head really did hurt, exactly as the hooded figure had described. It was unbearable. He looked up at the stars and tried to relax, letting the gentle sound of crickets envelop his thoughts as he emptied his mind of all the things that had been bothering him—hooded figures, algorithms, loopholes, seagulls; he let it all drift away into the comforting sound of the night, his head feeling better with every thought he discarded.

"That's it," the hooded figure said. "Can you feel it? Can you feel the pain disappearing?"

"Yes," Geoff said, breathing deeply as he let a soothing wave of amnesia wash over him. "I'm feeling much better…"

"Good," the figure said. "Very good. Now, there's one thing I *do* want you to remember before I go: something very important. Are you ready?"

Geoff nodded submissively.

"Very soon the sky will turn red. When this happens, you will get down on your knees, place your palms on the floor and wait. In time, one of my brethren will appear before you. When he does, you must say these words: 'I bring a message from Tringrall. In the year of Dranculees, you must revert.' Do you understand?"

"What?" Geoff said.

"You heard me! Do you want me to bring the pain back?"

"No!" Geoff said. "No…no please…"

"Then repeat after me: I bring a message from Tringrall. In the year of Dranculees, you must revert."

"I…I bring a message from Tringrall. In the year of Dranculees, you must revert?"

"Good," the hooded figure said.

Geoff remembered what Eric had said about the Varsarians—about certain words and phrases being particularly important to them. Was his person…an alien?

"Who's Tringrall?" Geoff said.

"It doesn't matter."

"It doesn't?"

"No. My brethren will understand. So remember—when the sky turns red, get down on your knees, place your palms on the floor, and wait. My brethren will recognize the ancient position you have adopted and come looking for you when they see it."

"I see," Geoff said, not seeing at all. "Is there anything else? Would you like me to start break-dancing when the sky turns blue again, or something?"

"The sky will not turn blue again for thousands of years," the hooded figure said. "Not until the year of Dranculees."

"Ah." Geoff said.

"So, repeat after me, one last time: I bring a message from Tringrall. In the year of Dranculees, you must revert."

"I bring a message from Tringrall. In the year of Dranculees, you must revert." Geoff said. He knew this was all quite sinister, but he couldn't help but feel a little bit stupid.

"Good. There is one more thing. Once you hear yourself say these words, you will remember everything that has happened here. You'll remember what Eric told you, you'll remember the seagull, and you'll know just how your pathetic race was fooled into extinction. But by then, it will be too late for you to do anything about it. Until that time, you will have no memory of this conversation."

"What conversation?" Geoff said.

There was no answer. Geoff strained his head up to look around. There was no one here. Had he been talking to someone? Confused at why he had randomly chosen to say "what conversation?" Geoff rested his head back down on the ground and stared up at the stars. A seagull was hovering far above, gliding across the night sky like a lazy comet. Relaxed, he shut his eyes and immersed himself once again in the recurring chirp of crickets.

Or was that a recurring beep?

TWELVE

Beep.
　　Beep.

Beep.

After hearing this noise several times at exact two-second intervals for the last few minutes, Geoff had determined that as far as beeping noises went, this was certainly a recurring one.

"How is he?" A voice asked.

"We've hooked him up to a life support machine to monitor his heart rate," another voice answered. Sounded like Tim. "He should be okay from here."

"Can you turn that beeping down?" another voice said. "It's driving me mad." Was that … Mr. Knight?

"Sure," Tim replied. The recurring beep that Geoff had only just begun to notice faded away into the background.

"How long were they operating on him?" the first voice said. Was that Ruth?

"A long time," Tim replied. "He took quite a blow to the head, and his hand's been messed up pretty bad. He won't be able to use it for months."

"Why his *hand*?"

"I don't know—it makes absolutely no sense whatsoever. But there must be a reason."

"That's what we need to find out," Mr. Knight said, sounding a little stressed. "The Defense Minister will be here any minute. What am I supposed to tell him?"

"Why don't you tell him the truth?" Ruth said.

"But he'll shut us down for sure!" Mr. Knight replied.

"I don't really think we have a choice," Ruth said. "A Time Rep has been attacked, Eric is dead, and the loophole in his algorithm will never be fixed."

"Then we're finished."

"Not necessarily," Tim said. "We can try to catch whoever was responsible for this."

"Yes!" Mr. Knight said. "You see Ruth? Why can't you be more positive? Maybe young Geoffrey knows something. He was with Eric just before he died. Can you wake him up?"

"We should probably let him rest," Ruth said. "If you wake him up now, it might be a bit of a shock to his system."

"Waking up is always a shock to his system," Tim said. "But I agree. He was hit pretty hard over the back of the head—his synapses need time to heal properly. If we wake him up now, his brain might not be able to take it. Any questions we ask him now could be met with complete gibberish."

"I'm already awake," Geoff said, opening his eyes. He appeared to be lying in some sort of hospital bed. The sheets felt like plastic, the air smelled like disinfectant, and his pillow was thinner than a water biscuit. Ruth, Tim, and Mr. Knight were all looking down at him.

"Where am I?" Geoff said, sitting up and having a look around. "What happened?"

He appeared to be in a hospital ward. The ward was very long, very beige, and very clean, with a large set of double doors at one end and two windows at the other. A few rubber plants were placed at equal intervals along one wall, presumably to provide some sort of decoration. Other than that, the only other furniture he could see were a number of other beds identical to his. They were all empty though, as if the ward had been reserved just for him.

"You're in hospital," Tim said, picking up a chart from the foot of the bed and making a note on it.

Geoff didn't like hospitals. Horrible places. He always had the suspicion that whoever designed them had a secret vendetta against anyone who needed to visit one. Why were the magazines in the waiting rooms always about bloody golf? Why were toys only provided for children in the waiting rooms? And why were all the notice boards crammed with scary posters, taunting you with all the other illnesses you could get? It was almost as if they were trying to encourage people to start a collection. Geoff had once gone into a hospital with an ingrown toenail only to emerge five hours later worrying about cancer, Alzheimer's disease, whooping cough, and genital warts. He was only six!

"Do you remember anything about last night?" Tim asked, resting his glasses on top of his head and looking up from the chart

"Last night?" Geoff said, looking up and down the ward again. He hadn't noticed it before, but a group of armed guards were standing by the entrance, their weapons drawn. "Am I in some sort of trouble?" he said.

"No, Geoff, you're fine," Tim said, looking over at the guards. "They're here for your protection. Now tell me: Do you remember anything about last night?"

"Of course I remember last night," Geoff said, a little unnerved by the two small plastic tubes he'd just noticed coming out of his nose. They were hooked up to a large gray machine to his left, which had lots of flashing lights and buttons dotted all over it. "There was the party. Roman decorations. All of us were there."

Tim raised his eyebrows in surprise. "This is quite encouraging," he said to the group. "I would have expected him to show at least some signs of mental trauma, but he appears to be ..."

"I like cheese," Geoff said.

"What?" Tim said.

"Cheese," Geoff said. "I like cheese."

"I take that back," Tim said, dropping his glasses back over his eyes and making a note on the chart. "Clearly he needs more time to rest. I'll get something to put him back to sleep."

"Parmesan cheese," Geoff said. "I like that on my spaghetti."

"Wait!" Mr. Knight said, holding his arms out. "At least *some* of the things he is saying appear to make sense. Can't we just ask him a few questions and try to filter out the nonsense?"

"Sir," Ruth said. "I don't think …"

"Geoffrey?" Mr. Knight said. "Look at me, Geoffrey. Tell us: What's the last thing you remember?"

"I remember … talking to Ruth about being Time Rep," Geoff said, struggling to form his words properly. He felt a little drunk. Had he been drugged?

Ruth nodded. "That's true," she said. "We did speak, briefly."

"Anything else?" Mr. Knight said.

"I remember … going down to Eric's lab …"

"Good …"

"… and I remember going up in a hot air balloon."

"A hot air balloon?"

"Yup."

"Before the hot air balloon," Mr. Knight said. "Do you remember anything else about what happened in Eric's lab?"

"I remember—Oh my God! I remember what happened to Eric! He'd been attacked!"

"That's right," Mr. Knight said, looking anxiously at the rest of the group. "Was he alive when you found him?"

"I can't remember. I think I was busy playing baseball at the time. How's your swing these days?"

"Try to think, Geoffrey," Mr. Knight said, giving Tim a concerned look. "Was Eric alive when you found him?"

"I think so," Geoff said, struggling to remember. "I remember him talking to me about something."

"What?" Mr. Knight said, standing up out of his chair. "What did he tell you?"

"He was trying to tell me the recipe for a good potato soup."

Mr. Knight shut his eyes and let out a deep breath. "Please try to remember," he said, sitting back down in his seat. "What did Eric tell you?"

"I … I can't remember," Geoff said. "I can't remember if you're supposed to add the cream before or after the coriander."

"This is hopeless," Mr. Knight said. He took a vial of pills out of his jacket pocket and popped one in his mouth.

"May I ask a question?" Ruth said to Mr. Knight.

"Of course," he replied. "Ask whatever you like."

"Did you see who attacked you?" she asked.

"I've been attacked?"

"Yes," Tim said. "That's why you're here in hospital. You were hit over the back of the head and stabbed through the hand."

"Great," Geoff said, lifting his hand up. It was wrapped in a thick bandage. "How am I supposed to win tomorrow's arm wrestling championships now?"

"Answer Ruth's question," Mr. Knight said. "Did you see who attacked you?"

"I can't remember," Geoff said, closing his eyes. "I…I can't remember anything."

All of a sudden, Geoff could hear a commotion outside the entrance to the ward.

"Out of my way! Out of my way!" A voice boomed from outside the ward. "Where are they? Ernest! Where are you?"

"Here we go," Mr. Knight muttered under his breath, straightening his tie as he got to his feet. "We're in here, David," he shouted back.

The Defense Minister flung the doors to the ward open and marched in. He looked a lot less dignified than he did last night—unshaven, messy hair, and bloodshot eyes.

"Give me an update on everything that happened last night," he said, stopping at the foot of Geoff's bed. He sounded out of breath.

Mr. Knight tugged nervously on one of his cufflinks. Geoff noticed that they had little clocks on them. Cute.

"Last night, Dr. Skivinski was attacked in his laboratory by an unknown assailant. We have reason to believe he was in the final stages of fixing his algorithm when this happened. A few moments after the attack, he was discovered by Geoffrey here, who was then also attacked. Probably by the same person."

"And what is the status of Dr. Skivinski?"

"Eric's dead. He suffered multiple fractures to his rib cage and punctured a lung."

The Defense Minister gulped. "Do we have any idea who could have done this?" he said, crossing his arms protectively across his own chest.

"It had to be someone at the party," Tim said. "No one else would have had access to Eric's lab at that time."

"And who was at the party?"

"Three hundred time-tourists, ninety journalists, sixty-eight politicians, fifty Time Reps, thirty-two junior physicists, twenty caterers, and us."

"So it could have been anyone."

"Yes."

"Did the lifts hear anything suspicious?"

"Basement!" Geoff said.

"Basement?"

"Ignore him," Mr. Knight said. "We checked the logs—nothing."

"What about the murder weapon?"

"His walking stick," Tim said. "We found it at the scene of the crime. It was covered in Eric's and Geoff's blood, so it must have been used to attack them both."

"Did Mr. Stamp discover Dr. Skivinski before he died?"

"Yes," Tim said. "But he can't remember anything beyond that. We've tried talking to him, but as you've already heard, he's feeling a little … confused at the moment."

"Let me try," the Defense Minister said, motioning Tim to step out of the way. He moved around to the side of the bed and sat down.

"I wouldn't …"

"Geoffrey?" he said, ignoring Tim. "Can you hear me?"

"Yes," Geoff said.

"Good. I need you to tell me what happened when you saw Dr. Skivinski. Eric. Did you speak with him?"

Geoff thought long and hard about his answer.

"When are we going to the circus?" he eventually replied.

"You see?" Mr. Knight said. "He's no use to us at the moment. We need to give him more time to recover."

"We don't *have* any time," the Defense Minister said. "With your chief physicist dead, the time-tourism facility is completely vulnerable to attack." He closed his eyes and sighed. "Look, Ernest—I was prepared to entertain the idea of keeping Time Tours open on the proviso that the algorithm would be fixed, but with that out of the window, I'm afraid I have no choice but to shut you down until further notice."

"Now wait a minute, David," Mr. Knight said, looking anxiously at Ruth. "Let's not be too hasty. Surely we could still operate a limited service, increase security checks…"

"I'm sorry," the Defense Minister said, pulling a tie out of his pocket. "I've got a press conference on this incident in twenty minutes and I just can't take that risk. As of this minute, I want all tourists recalled from their holidays, all future trips canceled, and all Time Reps sent back to their native time periods."

"What about Geoff?" Tim said. "He's in no state to go back. He can barely walk."

"His legs are fine," the Defense Minister said, hurriedly feeding his tie through his collar, "and I know the kind of medication you can get these days. By the time you get him back to the departure chamber, he'll be all right. I want you to get him out of here and get him home. Any questions?"

"I have a question," Geoff said, raising his good hand.

"Apart from you," the Defense Minister said, knotting his tie. Geoff watched as his large neck bulged over his collar as he tightened it. "Anyone got any *serious* questions?"

"This *is* a serious question," Geoff said, feeling a little offended.

"Go on then. What is it?"

"Do you have any cheese?"

Thirteen

It was bad enough trying to convince Geoff to get out of bed without the added annoyance of him having a large gash in the back of his head and a broken hand, so you can probably imagine the difficulty Tim had in doing just that. No trail of sweets leading out of the door was going to work this time—that was for sure. In the end he had to resort to administering Geoff with some particularly strong painkillers, powerful enough to relieve almost anything except perhaps paper cuts and stubbed toes, which still hurt like hell no matter what futuristic medicine you took.

"How are you feeling?" Tim said, leading Geoff through the entrance to the departure lounge.

"Surprisingly great, given the circumstances," Geoff replied. "Whatever you gave me to ease the pain certainly did the trick."

They'd picked up a few other Time Reps on their way back, all of whom had been ordered by the Defense Minister to return to their native time periods. Keeping close behind Geoff was a butler from Victorian times called Winterbottom and an unknown Greek philosopher called Nestor who apparently was ignored by everyone in his time period because his philosophy was awful.

It was absolute chaos in the departure lounge. All around, people were either arguing with officials or barging their way through to the exit. Many were just standing still, looking up in disbelief at the departure boards showing that all departures were canceled.

"LADIES AND GENTLEMEN," a voice boomed over the loudspeaker gentle but firm. "WE REGRET TO INFORM YOU THAT HOLIDAYS TO ALL TIME PERIODS HAVE BEEN CANCELED

UNTIL FURTHER NOTICE. THIS IS DUE TO UNFORESEEN CIRCUMSTANCES. PLEASE MAKE YOUR WAY OUT OF THE DEPARTURE LOUNGE AND ONTO THE REPLACEMENT BUS SERVICE. THANK YOU."

"Unforeseen circumstances!" someone shouted. Geoff looked to his right. A woman dressed in chainmail was arguing with an official. "You've got the most powerful computer in the known universe, capable of predicting every eventuality, and you're telling me you're canceling my holiday due to 'unforeseen circumstances'?"

"I'm sorry, miss," the official said. "I don't know much more than you. All I know is that they're stopping all departures until further notice."

"I knew I should have summered in Mars instead!" the woman said, removing her wig and throwing it to the floor.

Geoff and the other two Time Reps stayed close to Tim as they waded against the general flow of the crowd. They appeared to be heading for one of the more distant quarantine chambers.

"This is all your fault," Winterbottom whispered in Geoff's ear. "If you hadn't been attacked, none of this would have happened."

"What are you talking about?" Geoff whispered back. "I didn't exactly have a choice in the matter! I was backed into a corner and hit over the head with a walking stick!"

"Yes, but couldn't you have defended yourself? Couldn't you have fought the attacker off, perhaps even caught him? If you hadn't been such a wimp, we wouldn't be in this situation!"

"Will you two stop arguing?" Nestor said from behind. "We're all friends here, and an argument between friends is like sheep grazing in the wrong field."

"What?" Geoff said. "What has arguing got to do with sheep?"

"It's all right for you," Winterbottom continued, sidling his way past a family dressed as pirates. "You're not going back to my time period. You're not returning to a lifetime of servitude: waking up at four in the morning; preparing the master's breakfast; feeding the horses; polishing the silverware—we don't even have electricity, for goodness sake! How am I expected to just leave all the pleasures of being a Time Rep behind and return to being a mere butler? I'm going to go mad!"

Geoff felt a little sorry for Winterbottom. Clearly this was a man who had become accustomed to a wonderful new lifestyle when he became a Time Rep just as Geoff had become accustomed to a wonderful new lifestyle he discovered squeezy Marmite. Going back wasn't going to be easy for everyone.

Up ahead, hundreds of confused tourists were being ushered out of the quarantine chambers by an overly aggressive group of security guards who were clearly relishing the occasion to use their batons and shout commands into loudspeakers. Most of their days were probably spent reprimanding teenagers for sticking chewing gum to the seats, or stopping people from running with their luggage. Today must have been the day they had all been waiting for—an excuse to hit people over the head and look important.

"Move along!" one guard barked at a man who was awkwardly trying to cradle all of his belongings in his arms. To his left, a weeping mother was struggling to keep hold of her two children. The guards marched on relentlessly, their minds fixed solely on funneling the crowd out of the nearest exit.

"Coming through!" Tim shouted, trying his best to lead the three Time Reps through the oncoming throng of tourists. "Please make way!"

One of the younger-looking security guards stepped in front of them to block their path, his expression displaying such self-importance that if he'd frowned any harder, his face would probably have turned inside out.

"Where do you think you're going?" he said, pushing his baton forcefully into Tim's shoulder. "All quarantine chambers are off limits!"

"Oh well," Winterbottom said, turning around to leave. "You heard the man. All quarantine chambers are off limits. We'll have to come back some other time."

Tim pulled out an identity card and shoved it in the guard's face. "You might want to get out of our way," he said, pushing the baton to one side, "unless you want to explain to the Defense Minister why three of our Time Reps still haven't been sent back to their proper time periods."

The security guard looked nervously at Tim's identification, then even more nervously at Tim, his frown melting away into a more sheepish expression.

"Sorry, sir," the guard said, taking a step back. "Please go right through."

"Come on," Tim said, placing a firm hand on Winterbottom's shoulder and turning him back in the right direction. "You're not getting out of this *that* easily."

The quarantine chamber was eerily silent as the three Time Reps sat on their frosted glass seats waiting for the scan to finish: the sort of silence that usually occurs when someone has just made a faux pas. And we're not talking any old faux pas, like doing a little fart in an elevator and knowing it was just loud enough for everyone to hear; it was so deathly quiet in the quarantine chamber that it felt as if someone had just turned up to the annual Vegetarian Society dinner and dance evening only to complain very loudly that there was no meat on the menu.

"If I know Mr. Knight," Tim said, breaking the silence, "he's working on a way out of this. He's probably got some scheme to get us back up and running. You'll see."

Geoff, Nestor and Winterbottom stared at Tim. None of them looked particularly convinced by his attempt to reassure them.

"Don't believe me?" Tim said. "Trust me—we'll be up and running again in a week. Two at most."

The quarantine chamber flashed green, indicating that they were all safe to travel. Tim got to his feet and held open the door to customs.

Winterbottom stood up reluctantly and led the way. "I wonder what my first chore will be when I get back," he said, walking as slowly as he could down the corridor. "Perhaps I'll be clipping the master's toenails or scrubbing out the latrines."

"Jesus," Tim said. "Will you stop whining? Anyone would think you were going back to the Dark Ages!"

"I am, compared to this," Winterbottom said. "I won't even be able to watch tonight's Hoverball game!"

"Come on, it's not that bad," Tim said, stopping just before the arch that scanned tourists for any prohibited technology. "I told you—Mr. Knight's got this all under control."

"But what if…"

"Look at Nestor," Tim said. "He's being sent back much further than you, and he's fine!"

They turned to look at Nestor, who was staring at the ceiling. He seemed to be in another world.

"Yes, but Nestor's an idiot, isn't he?" Winterbottom said.

"Just calm down," Tim said, standing to one side of the metal arch and motioning the Time Reps to walk through. "Let's get on with this."

Geoff was the first to walk under the arch, giving it a suspicious look as he passed through. He knew he wasn't carrying anything that would make it go off, but he was suspicious anyway—things that were capable of making loud noises often did when he was nearby, like car alarms, dogs, or teenagers. On this occasion, however, he succeeded in passing through without incident.

Nestor was next, dawdling through the scanner like a poodle at a dog show. Again, the arch made no sound.

Winterbottom hesitated for a minute, pacing around nervously. He looked a bit like Geoff psyching himself up to have a shower.

"Well?" Tim said. "Get on with it!"

"Okay, okay, don't rush me," Winterbottom said, positioning himself carefully in front of the arch as if he needed a run-up to get through. He looked at Geoff and Nestor on the other side, took a deep breath, and walked through the scanner briskly. Immediately the alarm went off.

"Hand it over," Tim said, pressing a button on the wall to stop the beeping.

"Hand what over?" Winterbottom said.

"Whatever it is you're carrying. Hand it over."

"I–I don't know what you're talking about," he stammered.

This was embarrassing. Everyone could see Winterbottom was lying. His attempt at looking innocent and confused was about as convincing as the time Geoff had tried to look nonchalant when a power cut made him lose five hours of progress in *Final Fantasy VII* because he hadn't been able to find a save point. Unfortunately, Geoff's pretense was somewhat betrayed by the fact that he'd screamed at the top of his voice and thrown the joypad out of the window.

"Come on," Tim said, holding out his hand. "You're blatantly hiding something."

"And wh-what makes you say that?" Winterbottom said.

"Wh-what makes me say that?" Tim mimicked, trying not to laugh. "Listen to yourself! You can barely get your words out properly! And the way you walked through the arch was just pathetic…"

Winterbottom looked over at Geoff and Nestor, both of whom were nodding in agreement.

"It *was* pretty crap," Geoff concurred.

"Fine!" Winterbottom snapped, reaching into his pocket. "It was only a bloody personal stereo, for goodness sake!" He slapped the stereo into Tim's hand and stormed off toward the paradox-scanning facility.

Geoff had forgotten just how boiling it was in the paradox-scanning facility—it was so hot you probably could have fried bacon in mid-air. He was sweating to such an extent that wiping his brow was fast becoming a futile exercise, like turning on the windscreen wipers after driving your car into a swimming pool. Tim had evidently thought ahead, as he had brought a large bottle of water with him.

"Right, we all know how this works," Tim said, pacing in front of the three Time Reps like some sort of drill sergeant. "Step into the beam of light, wait for it to turn green, and proceed to the departure chamber. Simple as that." Behind him, the thick beam of white light shone down from the ceiling, waiting for its first subject.

"Wait," Winterbottom said. "What happens after we get back? Will we ever hear from you again?"

"Absolutely," Tim said, taking a large gulp of water. "We'll be working around the clock to straighten this out—you can count on that. Who would like to go first?"

"I'll go," Winterbottom volunteered, much to Geoff's surprise. "Might as well get it out of the way." He stepped up into the beam and stood still as the light enveloped his body. A few moments later he was cleared to travel.

"1889, here I come," he said, sounding about as enthusiastic as a child who had just been given a peanut as their main Christmas present. He stepped down from the scanning pedestal and made his way through to the departure chamber.

"You're next, Nestor," Tim said. He motioned the Greek philosopher to step forward, taking another deep swig of water.

"Me?" Nestor said, stepping back. "I was hoping to go last. He who goes last…"

"I want Geoff to go last," he said, interrupting what Geoff assumed to be a sentence most worthy of never being finished.

Nestor reluctantly shuffled forward and stepped into the light. Within seconds the beam turned bright green, as if the computer wanted to get rid of him as quickly as everyone else did.

"So," Tim said, watching as Nestor disappeared down the same corridor as Winterbottom. "I guess it's just you to go, Geoff."

"I guess," Geoff replied, stepping up into the beam of light. As before, the beam was wonderfully cool.

"So, what have you made of your first day?" Tim said, looking at his watch. The scan seemed to be taking a little longer than usual.

"Well, it's certainly turned out differently to how I expected," Geoff shivered. "When I woke up this morning, the only unusual thing I thought I'd be doing was the laundry."

Suddenly Geoff felt very hot again.

The light had turned green.

Time to go home.

FOURTEEN

Geoff had only been back home for a few minutes, but he soon began to realize just how much he'd missed the little quirks of 23 Woodview Gardens, the small comforts of the house that he'd taken for granted. The second he walked through the front door, he was instantly reassured by the faintly nauseating "house smell," he smiled to himself upon noticing the old pair of socks that were inexplicably draped over the banisters, and he even felt a twinge of nostalgia at the familiar sound of the toilet flushing. The future may have had its cheering crowds, fantastic technology and improved quality of life, but did he know exactly where all the creaky floorboards were in the future? No. Could he walk around all day in his bathrobe in the future? No. If the future really wanted to win him over, it was going to have to significantly up its game.

Geoff sat down on the sofa, kicked off his shoes, and stared vacantly at the ceiling for a few moments. It had certainly been one hell of a day: He witnessed the extinction of the dinosaurs, traveled into the future, been treated like a celebrity, spoke to people from as far back as ancient times, been brutally attacked, and lost his memory. More unusual that that, he'd even been for a job interview.

It was normally after a grueling day like this that Geoff liked to reward himself by doing something constructive, something that made him use his brain, something like playing *Space Commando* for ten hours straight. Unfortunately, his right hand had a few objections to this idea, mainly due to the fact that it had just had a large knife thrust through it and could no more hold a joypad than it could a conversation. One thing was for sure—he certainly wouldn't be practicing his skills with the *Death Bringer* today.

This left Geoff with a slight dilemma. What was he supposed to do if he couldn't play computer games? He stared at the ceiling again as if the sight of a bare lightbulb would somehow inspire him to find a new source of amusement. Nothing. He picked up a nearby magazine and flicked through it. There was an article about the top ten superfoods, an interview with someone he'd never heard of, and a pullout section on subwoofers. Geoff tossed the magazine to the floor and thought about the onomatopoeic qualities of the word "woofer" for ten minutes, wondering if there was perhaps a more appropriate word to describe a low-frequency loudspeaker.

Within a couple of hours, Geoff was bored out of his mind. He'd tried to pass the time by making himself tea, watching a bit of television, and even doing some tidying, but it was no good; after everything that had happened in the last twenty-four hours, returning back to the house, pairing all his socks, and watching a repeat of *Deal or No Deal* was somewhat of an anticlimax. And the contestant only won ten quid.

It began to cross Geoff's mind that he may never actually see anyone from the future ever again, despite Tim's assurances to the contrary. What if they really couldn't fix the supercomputer without Eric? What if Mr. Knight couldn't persuade the politicians to let them resume business? He remembered what Ruth had said about what his life would have been like if they hadn't intervened: He'd have been sitting in front of a computer trying to work out how to program his own game before giving up and drifting between mundane temp jobs for the rest of his life. Geoff felt a little weak at the knees at this thought. Having caught a brief glimpse of what it was like to be a Time Rep, was he doomed to being relegated to that way of life? Would he be forced to go back to being the old Geoffrey Stamp? The "insignificant nobody?" The man less important to the world than certain types of mushroom? And which mushrooms were more important than him anyway? Probably those bloody shiitake ones that everyone was going on about these days. He'd have to ask Tim if he ever saw him again.

This was ridiculous. Not only could Geoff feel himself spiraling into an ever more depressing chain of thought, but he was now at the stage where he was getting competitive with shiitake mushrooms. If Fate was going to be kind to him, it needed to provide some sort of interesting distraction at this difficult time, something to help him take his mind off things: a telephone call; a gas explosion; a meteorite falling through the ceiling; anything. Unfortunately for Geoff, Fate must have been off playing pool at that precise moment because there wasn't so much as a fly buzzing around to help him take his mind off things.

The thing that frustrated Geoff most of all was the fact that while he was here in the twenty-first century watching daytime television, he had no way of knowing what was going on in the future, and even if he did know, he would be powerless to help matters. He imagined Tim and Ruth frantically running around at this very moment, trying desperately to piece together what had happened at last night's party. Mr. Knight was probably busy too: managing the media, speaking to senior politicians, and negotiating conditions under which they could get things up and running again. In the meantime, the only problem Geoff needed to deal with was the fact that he was running low on tea bags. Unless the trip to the shops involved some sort of spectacular car chase, it was fairly safe to assume that this problem wasn't going to pose quite the same excitement.

Perhaps he should call Zoë. She'd seemed keen on meeting up again when he'd last spoken to her, and he very much wanted to see a familiar face. Maybe they could wander down to the lake again like they'd used to do in the old days. There was just one problem: whenever she saw him, she always asked him if he'd "found another job yet." What was he supposed to say? He didn't really want to lie and say no because this was what he always said. On the other hand, he couldn't exactly say that he *did* have a job because he'd then have to explain that he couldn't tell her what the job was, and by the way, he may not have it anymore anyway because he was attacked by a group of people trying to change the course of history. No, this would probably sound a little bit crazy to most people, and although Geoff wasn't exactly an expert on women, he was pretty sure that sounding like a lunatic wasn't the best way of endearing himself to anyone.

Geoff picked up the phone and stared at it for a while to the point where it started beeping impatiently. Just as he had plucked up the courage to dial Zoë's number, there was a loud knock at the door. Slightly startled at the interruption, Geoff hung up the phone and went to see who it was. He wasn't expecting anyone.

He opened the door. It was Tim.

"Oh," said Geoff, a little surprised.

"Oh?" said Tim. "What do you mean, 'Oh'?"

"I wasn't expecting … I mean, I didn't …"

"You haven't seen me for two weeks and all you have to say is 'oh?'"

"Two weeks?" Geoff said, stepping aside to let Tim in. "What are you talking about, two weeks?"

"Sorry," Tim said, shrugging off his coat. "I keep forgetting. It hasn't been two weeks for you, has it? I suppose you've only just got back?"

"Yes," Geoff said, shutting the door. "Couple of hours ago."

"I see," Tim replied, walking into the kitchen. "Well, it's been two weeks since *I* last saw *you*. Two very stressful weeks." He filled the kettle with water and turned it on.

"So you managed to sort everything out?" Geoff said. "You caught my attacker, fixed the algorithm, and all that?"

Tim looked at Geoff in silence for a few moments.

"Not exactly," he said.

"Pardon?" Geoff said, blinking a little bit more than necessary in surprise.

"Not exactly," Tim repeated.

Geoff sat down at the kitchen table and thought seriously about banging his head against it.

"By 'not exactly,'" he said, opting to restrain himself, "do you mean, 'no'?"

"We've got a few leads on your attacker, but we still don't know who it was for sure," Tim said, getting the milk out of the fridge. "As for the supercomputer, we haven't been able to fix it. Eric didn't leave any notes on what he was doing in case they fell into the wrong hands, and as far as we know, he didn't manage to explain the loophole to anyone before he died."

"So what the hell are you doing here?" Geoff said. "Isn't it dangerous?"

"Yes and no," Tim said, waiting for the kettle to finish boiling. "We have a plan."

Geoff reconsidered the option of banging his head against the table again. He didn't like plans. In his experience, a plan was just a quick way of describing something that wasn't actually going to happen. When he was thirteen, he'd *planned* to become a rock star. When he was on his paper route, he'd *planned* to ask Zoë out on a date. What he soon discovered was that plans always failed to take into account a certain obstacle that prevented you from achieving the desired result. In the case of him planning to be a rock star, he hadn't considered the fact that most people could get a better song out of a lettuce than he could get out of a musical instrument, and in the case of him asking Zoë out on a date, he hadn't considered the fact that he was a complete coward. No, whether it was best laid plans or worst laid plans, Geoff always found it hard to believe that things would go exactly as expected. He was even suspicious of the plans for next door's conservatory.

"I don't like this," Geoff said. "You know how I feel about plans…"

"That's because your plans are always stupid," Tim said, dropping the last two tea bags into a couple of mugs and adding the milk. "This isn't like the time you planned to become an extra in *Star Wars* by sending George Lucas a photo of you molding your hair into the shape of a Star Destroyer. This plan has actually been *thought through*."

"I still can't believe that didn't work," Geoff said. "I even got the shield generators right…"

Tim topped the mugs up with boiling water, saying nothing. Geoff got the feeling that he wanted to talk about more pressing matters.

"So what's your brilliant plan?" Geoff said. "And does it involve me being in any danger?"

"A bit," Tim said, casually spooning the tea bags out of the mugs and passing one to Geoff.

"Sorry?" Geoff said. "Did you say 'a bit'?"

"The plan is use to you as bait. Flush out the attacker."

"Bait?" Geoff said. He was disappointed that he wasn't sipping his tea at that precise moment because he would have liked to have melodramatically spat a mouthful across the table to demonstrate just how shocked he was at what Tim had said.

"The way we see it, whatever these people are trying to do to change history has something to do with you."

"Me?"

"We don't know what it is, but we know there's a connection: the hooded figure that took a shot at you in 1666, the man who attacked you in Eric's lab—everything seems to revolve around you for some reason."

"I don't understand," Geoff said. "What possible …"

"And another thing," Tim interrupted. "Don't you think it's worrying that you're not dead?"

"No," Geoff said. "In fact, I feel quite good about that—not being dead is excellent."

"I didn't mean it like that. But think about it—for all your attacker knew, Eric could have told you how to fix the algorithm before he died. So why did they risk letting you live? And why did they stab you through the hand?"

"You tell me," Geoff shrugged, making sure to sip his tea this time in case the next part of this plan involved him dangling from a rope or something.

"Well, we have a theory," Tim said, adjusting his glasses. "We think that you were meant to be sent back here as some sort of Trojan horse."

"A Trojan horse?"

Tim nodded. "It's the only thing that would explain why you weren't killed when you discovered Eric. We believe that whoever stabbed you through the hand wanted you alive. They wanted you to come back to the twenty-first century so you could change something for them. Change something without even realizing it."

"But that doesn't make sense," Geoff said. "If I was going to change something, even without realizing it, wouldn't your 'supercomputer' have picked it up? The light went green, remember?"

"Precisely," Tim said. "That's why I'm here. Since history hasn't changed, Mr. Knight has convinced the Defense Minister that whoever these people are, they must still have some unfinished business with you. So we're resuming holidays to all time periods in the hope that we can tempt your attacker to come looking for you in the twenty-first century. When he does, we'll be waiting, and we'll be able to put an end to this fiasco once and for all."

"Well, it's a superb plan," Geoff said. "Truly superb. But I still have a small issue with the part where you use me as bait."

"That's not *part* of the plan," Tim said. "That's the whole plan!"

"Okay then. I have a small issue with … the whole plan."

"Why?"

"Don't you think it's a little dangerous? You're talking about just letting some maniac waltz right up to me and stab me through the other hand, or break my legs, or do whatever it is they should have done to me in the first place!"

"Relax," Tim said. "Everything will be fine."

"Relax?" Geoff said. "How am I supposed to relax? This is the second least-relaxing situation I've ever found myself in!"

"What was the first?"

"Thinking I was about to be hit by a meteorite in 65m years BC. And in case you're interested, the third least relaxing situation I've ever been in was when someone tried to fire a bolt at my in 1666. Spot a theme to all this? I'll give you a clue—they all happened pretty recently, and they're all because I'm now a bloody Time Rep!"

"Look, Geoff—if we're lucky, they won't even make it past the paradox-scanning facility."

"And if we're unlucky, perchance? I only ask because my luck hasn't been particularly great of late…"

"If they get through, I'll be watching you at all times. You'll be reasonably safe."

Geoff took another sip of his tea. He didn't like the use of the word "reasonably" in that last sentence just like he wouldn't have liked it in the sentence 'when you jump out of the plane, there's a reasonably good chance that your parachute won't fail.'"

"I just can't believe that the Defense Minister is really happy about all this," Geoff said. "What does he have to say about using me as bait?"

"Oh, he's totally on board," Tim replied.

"On board what?" Geoff said. "The Titanic?"

"Look, pull yourself together," Tim snapped. "This is our only chance to find out who's behind all this, so stop worrying, finish your tea, and get your coat. We're scheduled to meet the first group of tourists in Trafalgar Square in less than an hour, and your attacker could be one of them. I need you on your toes."

Geoff gulped down the rest of his tea and wiped his mouth clean. He was quite fond of his toes and hoped he'd still have some left when this was all over.

Geoff had never been the biggest fan of tourists. They always seemed to have the urge to get in everyone's way by reading maps at the bottom of escalators, or to waste people's time by asking them for directions to somewhere that didn't exist. Now that one of them could possibly be trying to injure, maim, or even kill him in some bizarre way, he found himself even less enthusiastic at the thought of spending a day with a whole group of them.

The group in question were made up of an average number of men, women and children, all of whom looked like … well, tourists.

They all had their guidebooks, cameras, sunglasses and rucksacks, and were waiting patiently for Geoff and Tim at the foot of Nelson's Column in the middle of Trafalgar Square—a popular tourist destination for anyone visiting London, whether they were from the future or not. Some of the tourists were randomly pointing at double-decker buses and black cabs as if they had just seen an endangered species in a safari park. Others were looking at passersby and whispering excitedly to each other. The children seemed to be entertaining themselves by chasing after the few pigeons that had gathered at their feet in the hope of food. Geoff did a quick headcount and guessed their numbers to be no more than thirty. The tourists that is, not the pigeons.

It was a beautiful day in Trafalgar Square. All the clouds you would normally expect to find over London in November must have been distracted by something good on television because there wasn't a single one in sight. This left the sun to have all the sky to itself, shining so brightly that it appeared to be in Geoff's eyes even when he was looking in the opposite direction.

The tourists quickly seemed to recognize Geoff. As they saw him approach, they immediately stopped what they were doing and gathered together.

"Leave the talking to me for now," Tim whispered, walking ahead and smiling at the group. "Hello everyone!" he beamed.

"Hello!" the group chimed back.

"Welcome to the twenty-first century. For those of you who don't know me, my name is Timothy Burnell, and I am one of Time Tours Inc's recruiters. First off, I'd like to congratulate you all on passing your paradox scans and being the first group to visit this time period. Well done."

Geoff surveyed the group and thought about which person in particular might deserve an extra special congratulation for slipping their violent motives past the supercomputer undetected. Maybe it was the old guy at the back who was dressed entirely in black or the young lady at the front looking at him funny. That said, he didn't like the look of the tall man wearing a sunhat to his right, either. It wasn't an especially suspicious looking sunhat, but then his attacker would have been a bit daft to wear something to arouse suspicion, like a sunhat with knives sticking out of it, or something. Come to think of it, he wouldn't have been surprised if the real attacker turned out to be the most innocent-looking person in the group.

"As I'm sure you all know," Tim said, breaking Geoff's train of thought, "the gentleman standing behind me is Geoffrey Stamp—the man we've just recruited to be the Time Rep for the twenty-first century."

Everyone stared at Geoff, which he didn't like at all. Now that he thought about it, they *all* looked a bit suspicious in their own way. He attempted to stare back at them in some sort of Clint Eastwood "don't mess with me" style but ended up looking as if he had something in his eye.

"I'm sure most of you will be familiar about the role of a Time Rep," Tim continued, "but for those of you who are new to time travel holidays, allow me to explain. Geoffrey will essentially be your tour guide while you are here. He'll show you the sights, teach you a bit more about the culture of the time period, and answer any questions you may have. I know some of you may be a little starstruck to see him in the flesh, especially after all the coverage you would have seen about the attack, but please, don't be shy in asking him anything. He's only too happy to help."

Geoff wouldn't really have chosen to describe himself as being "only too happy to help," and smiled uncomfortably at the group. All of a sudden, one of the children broke free from her parent's grip and ran over to him.

"Mr. Stamp?" she said, tugging at his t-shirt.

"Aggghh!" Geoff screamed, pushing her hand away.

The little girl looked a bit upset.

"Did I do something wrong?"

"Sorry," Geoff said. "I…I thought you were going to hit me."

"No," the girl said, playing with her hair. "I wanted to see if you could take us to the zoo later. I want to see a penguin. They don't exist anymore where I'm from."

"Oh," Geoff said, looking sheepishly at the other tourists. He felt a little embarrassed at the way he had reacted. "I…er…I don't know. I'll ask Tim if it's okay."

"Thank you!" she said, running back to her parents.

"Will you all excuse me for one moment?" Tim said to the group. He put his hands in his pockets and marched over to Geoff.

"What the hell's the matter with you?" Tim whispered.

"Sorry," Geoff replied. "I thought she might be the attacker."

"She's only eight! How could she be the attacker?"

"I don't know," Geoff said, "although I have been attacked by an eight year old before."

"I see," Tim said. "And how old were *you* at the time, dare I ask?"

"Eight," Geoff admitted.

As the day went on, Geoff's paranoia toward the group of tourists had settled down considerably. He'd taken them to London Zoo, shown them Buckingham Palace, walked them around Piccadilly Circus, put them on the London Eye, and even sent them on a pseudo shopping spree down Oxford Street. To preserve the integrity of the space- time continuum, the tourists weren't actually allowed to buy anything—they just went into a few shops, had a browse, picked things up, put things down, and walked out, like children being allowed to run through a department store. After all this, not one of them had made any attempt to hurt him, and by now they'd all certainly had the opportunity. The only brief moment of panic had occurred when one man accidentally trod on his foot in the Apple store, but apart from that, today had been relatively pain free. Yes, Geoff was feeling far more relaxed as the sun began to set and decided to finish the day off by taking them to see Big Ben.

"I guess that wasn't so bad after all," he said to Tim as they led the group along the north bank of the Thames toward Westminster.

"It's not over yet," Tim replied. "Remember—you're looking after these guys for a whole week. One of them may be trying to lull you into a false sense of security—strike when you least expect it."

"Wait a minute," Geoff said, feeling his heart beat a little faster. "I'm not expecting anything to happen to me *now*! Does that mean something's going to happen now?"

"I don't know Geoff," Tim replied, looking out across the river. "All I'm saying is, don't let your guard down."

"But I thought *you* were my guard?" Geoff said, feeling a slight headache coming on. "I mean, you know me! I'm no good in a fight! I'm afraid of moths, for goodness sake!"

"Mr. Stamp?" a voice called from behind. It was one of the girls near the front of the pack. "Can I ask you something?"

"Um…sure," Geoff said, regaining his composure. He flashed a cautious glance at Tim as he turned to look at her. "What is it?"

"I'd really like to know what it's like living in the twenty-first century," she said. "What do people do with their spare time? How do they relax? What do they aspire to be?"

"That's easy," Geoff answered. "In most people's spare time, they watch television. If they want to relax, they watch television. And they aspire to be on television."

"So you're saying everybody is obsessed with television?"

Geoff opened his mouth to respond, but he suddenly found himself being interrupted by an almighty roar from above. The noise was deafening, like the sound of a thousand jet planes flying overhead at once. All around, everyone stopped what they doing and looked up. Geoff was pretty curious about where all the noise was coming from as well, and did the same.

As it happened, the noise appeared to be coming from a large number of flying saucers descending from above. There must have been well over a hundred of them that swooped down over the city and maneuvered themselves through the air like nothing Geoff had ever seen. He got a closer look at one as it banked on its side like an enormous, badly thrown Frisbee and shot over the Thames at an incredible speed, the sheer force of its engines parting the river in two in its wake. Geoff was speechless—these ships were enormous with a perfectly smooth metallic exterior. He began rubbing his hands together nervously—from his extensive experience of watching hundreds of science fiction movies in the past, intimidatingly large flying saucers looming overhead was rarely a good thing. It didn't usually turn out that they'd got lost by mistake or wanted to deliver some flowers; it usually meant they wanted to cause trouble.

He was scared.

This feeling turned out to be completely justified as one ship circled over the Houses of Parliament and fired a bright orange laser beam into the building that effortlessly ripped through its target as if were made of papier-mâché. It was clear that whoever was responsible for designing the Houses of Parliament's structural integrity hadn't taken into account the possibility of an alien ship firing a laser beam into it, and the building promptly exploded in every direction, the few remaining walls collapsing in on themselves in a smoldering cloud of dust with only Big Ben still standing. As more ships descended on the city, the wind began to feel gale force in strength. Behind Geoff, a news vendor was struggling to stop his papers from blowing away, despite the fact that they were now a little out of date. Geoff was no journalist, but in light of recent events he assumed *The London Evening Standard* would be revising its front page for the late edition to cover this invasion, unless the Beckhams split up in the meantime, of course.

"Wow!" one of the tourists shouted at Geoff over the noise. "You didn't tell us this would be part of the tour!" It was the man Geoff had earlier thought was wearing a suspicious sunhat, which by now had blown clean off his head. He lifted up his camera and took a picture of one of the flying saucers as it sliced through Big Ben and sent the spire crashing to the ground, the clock faces shattering across the road like plates being smashed in a gigantic Greek restaurant. Geoff recognized the angle from which they were looking at Big Ben. Unless he was mistaken, the photo that had just been taken would look exactly like the one he had seen on the poster the other day, if they ever lived to see it being developed.

"Oh my God!" Tim screamed, running over to Geoff. "It's the Varsarians! It's the bloody Varsarians! And they're two hundred bloody years early! Do you know what this means?"

"We're going to die, aren't we?" Geoff said, watching in horror as one of the spacecraft did a swift barrel roll and tore through a gridlocked Westminster Bridge, sending the vehicles tumbling into the river below. This was now the second time he had watched London being burned to the ground, but this time he doubted if the Lord Mayor would turn up and declare that a "woman could piss it out."

"They must be the ones who cracked the algorithm!" Tim shouted, grabbing Geoff's arm and running for cover. "You must have changed something without realizing it after all! We're doomed! We're doomed!"

Geoff agreed. They were indeed doomed.

He started rubbing his hands again.

"Think!" Tim said, looking desperately around for somewhere to hide. "This must have something to do with your hand! What could you have changed?"

Apart from having picked his nose a little less than usual, Geoff couldn't think of anything he'd done differently.

"You're supposed to be one of the most insignificant human beings that's ever lived! What possible influence could you have had over the timing of the Varsarian invasion? And why didn't that stupid computer spot it?"

That was quite a difficult question, and right now Geoff was a little bit preoccupied with not being killed to give it much thought.

All of a sudden, one of the Varsarian ships roared through the sky above, the blistering force of its engines flinging cars and buses up into the air.

"Look out!" Tim said, pushing Geoff clear of a Ford Fiesta that was pirouetting toward them.

Geoff felt himself violently lunge out of the way, the oncoming vehicle narrowly brushing behind him and crashing across the pavement. He looked around. Tim had been completely crushed.

His lifeless body lay still, barely recognizable under the car's twisted metal chassis.

It was at this point that most of the tourists began to realize that the alien invasion they were witnessing might not have been part of the tour after all, and that perhaps something might have gone a tad wrong. Everyone was now running around screaming and climbing over each other to get away, the less fortunate ones being vaporized by the bursts of laser fire from above. Geoff looked up at the sky again. There were spaceships everywhere, firing lasers at anything that moved. A wave of jet fighters appeared to have been scrambled by the Air Force in a futile attempt to defend the city, but their rockets and missiles had no effect, disintegrating into dust whenever they struck the hull of an attacking ship. With no means of defending themselves, the fighters were soon shot down, spiraling destructively into a row of tower blocks below.

All of a sudden, the spaceships stopped firing and slowed to a quiet hover, the roar of their engines dying down to a low hum. Those that were still alive on the ground stopped running around and looked confusedly up at the sky to see what was happening. Geoff did the same. What he saw was incredible: the ships were slowly maneuvering themselves into a giant circular formation that rotated clockwise high up in the sky. Ship after ship joined the circle, each one glowing bright red as if they were all powering up to collectively fire some sort of massive weapon. As the last ship completed the circle, the sky changed color, going from pale blue to bright red itself. At this sight, Geoff felt compelled to get down on his knees and place his palms on the floor.

"Oh please," a man said nearby. "It's a bit late to get down on your knees and start praying, don't you think? Haven't you heard? This is happening all over the world! You don't really think God can save us now, do you?"

"I don't know," Geoff said. "I ... I don't know why I'm doing this."

Almost immediately, one of the ships shone a spotlight directly down on Geoff's position and broke free from the formation, swooping down at an incredible speed. Within seconds, it had slowed to a halt a few feet in front of him and repositioned its engines to point downwards. As it lowered itself toward the ground, it became clear just how big these ships really were—the hull spreading itself not just across the road but right across the rubble of demolished buildings to Geoff's right, and the river to his left. As it descended the last few meters, the downward thrust of the ship's engines cushioned its landing, instantly melting the tarmac of the road down into a sticky black mush and vaporizing part of the river.

The ship's engines powered down, and a small door in the lower section of the hull slid open a few feet from the ground. All around, people fell silent and motioned forward to see what would happen. The optimists in the crowd were probably hoping that some prankster television presenter from your typical "aren't the general public a bunch of morons" show was going to jump out and shout, "Gotcha!" but somehow this seemed unlikely.

Geoff waited. He couldn't understand why he had chosen to kneel on the floor with his hands on the ground and why he felt compelled to wait here, of all places, for something to happen. Under normal circumstances, he would have been more compelled to run away and hide up a tree. It was almost as if he'd been hypnotized into doing this or something.

Within moments, a strange-looking creature appeared at the door, crouching down slowly to look at Geoff. Geoff in turn looked back up at it. The creature must have been about six feet tall with two arms and two legs, and generally the same body structure as that of a human being. Its appearance, however, was a little more animalistic—its skin was green and leathery like that of a crocodile's, and its eyes were small and black, with burning red pupils in the center. So this was a Varsarian. It opened its mouth to speak

"We recognize the ancient position of Granbleen you have adopted," the creature hissed. "You have something you wish to say?"

Geoff didn't think he had, but suddenly found himself saying, "I bring a message from Tringrall. In the year of Dranculees, you must revert."

After saying these words, Geoff frowned at himself, as if he had just burped without expecting it.

The alien nodded.

"Thank you, human," it said, getting to its feet. "We will remember." The door closed again, leaving Geoff to look at his own stupid reflection in the hull of the ship. He wondered how the alien was able to understand what he'd said and respond back in plain English. Perhaps they'd stopped off at a service station on their way to Earth and picked up a phrase book?

As the spaceship powered up its engines, the alien's parting words echoed around in Geoff's mind. "We will remember?" It was *Geoff* who was beginning to remember something at that moment, something important, something about the algorithm … That was it! He *had* spoken to Eric before he died! He *had* been told how to fix the loophole! Unfortunately, just as Geoff was having this revelation, the spaceship switched its engines to full power, angled its thrust directly toward him, and burned his body to a crisp as it rejoined the circular formation of flying saucers high up in the blood-red sky.

So Geoff was dead. And he *still* hadn't managed to ask Tim what type of mushroom was more important than him. Perhaps the computer had meant mushroom *clouds*, which were about to envelop every city on the planet.

Fifteen

It wasn't a pleasant thing watching human civilization being wiped off the face of the Earth before your very eyes, even if it was just a video simulation. Tim was so shocked at what the supercomputer had just shown him that he had to sit down on the floor.

"Holy crap, Geoff!" he said, shaking nervously. "Did you see that? It's a good thing we double-checked what would have happened before sending you back the twenty-first century! If you'd have gone back now, the Varsarians would have invaded two hundred years earlier than they should have! We'd have all been killed!"

Geoff said nothing.

"I've got to think," Tim said, standing up again to pace up and down. "This doesn't make any sense. Why did the light turn green? Why did the computer clear you for travel? An alien invasion is a pretty big thing for it to miss, wouldn't you say?"

Still Geoff said nothing.

"Geoff?"

Tim stopped pacing and looked around. Geoff had collapsed on the floor of the paradox-scanning facility, unconscious.

Typical, Tim thought.

Was it something he'd said?

Sixteen

As a matter of fact it was something Geoff had heard *himself* say on that video simulation that had caused him to pass out: "I bring a message from Tringrall. In the year of Dranculees, you must revert." These words must have triggered something powerful in his mind because he immediately found himself lying in a rickety old rowboat, drifting peacefully in the middle of his imaginary lake. This was getting a little ridiculous now; he'd been back here so many times in the past couple of days that he was surprised his imagination wasn't charging him rent.

There was something slightly different about this latest visit though: something Geoff couldn't put his finger on. On the surface, everything certainly looked very familiar—his bench was where it should have been, the air smelled the same, and all the trees were pointing in the right direction, but somehow, Geoff sensed that something had changed, something he couldn't describe.

Geoff sat up in the boat and stretched his legs. It must have been the beginning of a new day in his imaginary world, the bright orange sun just beginning to peek over the hills in the distance. This wasn't any old sunrise mind, like the generic ones often used as logos for morning television; this was something quite glorious, the bright orange glow of the sun dissipating into a patchwork quilt of pink and blue cirrus cloud. Indeed, it was almost romantic—Geoff could well imagine young couples playing to stereotype and sitting in front of this sunrise on a beach before realizing how bloody cold it is outside on the coast at six thirty in the morning.

The only blemish to this magnificent view was a little dot gliding across the sky, like someone flashing a laser pen on the screen at the cinema. Geoff looked closer. It appeared to be a seagull circling high above the lake.

"Blimey—that was quick!" a voice shouted. "You back already?"

Geoff looked around. Where had that voice come from? There was certainly no one in the boat with him, and as far as he could tell, there was no one standing on the edge of the lake.

"Up here!" came the voice again.

Geoff looked up. The seagull seemed to be getting lower and lower.

"That's right!" it shouted. "It's me!"

Great. First a talking fish, now a talking seagull. Geoff was a little unnerved by the number of talking animals populating his imagination. He really needed to cut down on watching so many cartoons.

The seagull swooped down over Geoff's head, arched its wings into a landing position, and perched itself on the end of the boat. It appeared to be holding a piece of paper in its left foot.

"Remember me?" the seagull said, tucking its wings back into its body and adjusting its footing.

"Erm … no." Geoff said. "Sorry."

"Don't worry. Didn't think you would. Those gits made you forget everything, didn't they?"

"What?"

"The Varsarian who attacked you—he made you forget everything. Eric's murder, what he told you about fixing the algorithm, everything."

"Eric told me how to fix the algorithm?"

"Yep."

"And this … Varsarian made me forget?"

"That's right."

"But … how?"

"I don't know for sure. You must have been in a semi-lucid state after you were attacked, which meant that everything you experienced here was a mixture of the real world and your imaginary world. That would explain how they were able to talk to you in your dream, hypnotize you into forgetting everything, and why the injury to your hand was both real and imagined."

Geoff considered himself to be quite lucky. There probably weren't many seagulls in the world that were capable of putting together such an eloquent, psychoanalytical hypothesis for everything that had happened to him today. In his experience, the only things most seagulls were capable of doing were eating small fish, pooing on cars, and if they were feeling really adventurous, standing on one leg.

"Who *are* you?" Geoff said. "Are you real?"

"Am I real?"

"Yeah. Are you someone talking to me in the real world?"

"What?" the seagull said. "Am I someone talking to you in the real world? That's the most ridiculous thing I've ever heard!"

"Who are you then?"

"I'm a seagull."

"But you're talking!"

"Yes, I'm a talking seagull. Well spotted. And I don't mean that *I'm* well spotted by the way because there's no such thing as a well spotted seagull."

Geoff was really confused now.

"Sorry—birdwatching joke," it said.

"So you're a talking seagull. Is that not more ridiculous than being someone in the real world talking to me?"

"Hey! I'm not just any old seagull! I'm a herring gull! We're pretty smart birds, let me tell you!"

Geoff didn't need convincing of that. This talking herring gull was probably so smart that it could beat him at chess using only the top hat from *Monopoly*.

"Funny thing is," the seagull continued, "I'm actually a part of your subconscious. I'm you."

"What do you mean you're me? You're a seagull."

"Let me ask you something," the seagull said, edging its way around the rim of the boat toward Geoff. "How did you feel when those people from the future told you that you were totally insignificant?"

Geoff leaned against the back of the boat and let out a deep breath.

"Not brilliant," he said, looking up at the sky. "Bit crap actually."

"Not brilliant?" the seagull replied. "You were angry. Deep inside, you resented the fact that you'd been conditioned to live a life of obscurity for all those years—that your life wasn't allowed to follow its natural course. These people had stopped you from trying to better yourself, kept you indoors playing computer games, and even restricted your contact with other people. They'd placed you in a carefully controlled artificial environment to turn you into the person they needed you to be—someone society considers as being useless, an "insignificant nobody." But you're so much more than that."

"I am?"

"Oh yes," the seagull said. "Trust me Geoff—you are capable of great things."

"I don't know," Geoff said, shaking his head. "For as long as I can remember, I've wondered what I was really looking for in life— what contribution I could make to the world. But I always ended up drawing a blank. The fact of the matter is—I don't have any real skills to apply to anything. In fact, the only thing I'm great at is playing computer games, and that's not exactly the most worthwhile of pursuits, wouldn't you say?"

"That's the conditioning speaking again Geoff," the seagull said. "Don't you see? You're mind has been suppressed by these people for so long, all you're capable of these days is self-doubt. But think about it again—*why* are you so good at computer games?"

"I don't know," Geoff said. "I guess I've got pretty fast reactions…"

"Go on…"

"And I'm good at finding an enemy's weak spot. Noticing patterns in the way they attack. Anticipating what they might do next."

"That's it!" The seagull began jumping up and down. "What else? Don't stop now!"

"Also," Geoff said, sitting up in the boat, "when I play online with a group of others, I'm usually the one everyone wants to take charge of the situation—I'm good at formulating a strategy, problem solving, and telling everyone their role in the mission…You know, that sort of thing…"

"There you go!"

"But…that's just in the world of computer games," Geoff said, sinking back down again into his seat. "It's all just make-believe, isn't it?"

"True," the seagull said. "But is there any reason why those sorts of skills can't be applied to real life?"

"I guess not," Geoff admitted, dangling his arm over the edge of the boat and dipping his hand through the silky surface of the lake. "But I don't really find myself in any real life situations that require that sort of strategic thinking."

"And whose fault is that?" the seagull asked.

Geoff looked at the seagull in silence for a moment, feeling the cool water trickle round his fingers.

"I suppose I've never really been given the chance to show what I can do," he said, "now that you mention it."

"That's right—you haven't. What's worse, being identified by that supercomputer as someone worthless to society was almost a self-fulfilling prophecy. So tell me—how did you feel when you found out that the supercomputer might not have been so super after all? That there might have been some sort of mistake in its calculations?"

"I don't know," Geoff said. "Relieved?"

"No, no, no. It was more than that. The moment you found out there was a flaw in the algorithm, something woke up inside you— something that had been dormant for a long time."

"You're right," Geoff said. "Now that you mention it, I did feel something stir inside me. But I thought it was that lasagne Tim made the other day. He always puts bloody zucchini in it."

"This wasn't Tim's lasagne," the seagull said. "Remember why Mr. Knight hired you to be a Time Rep? He hired you because you had absolutely no aspirations. No desire to better yourself. But all that changed when you discovered you might not be worthless after all. You became determined to prove that you weren't just some insignificant nobody."

"I did?"

"Yes. You might not have realized it, but you did. And that's where I come in."

"You?" Geoff said.

The seagull nodded. At least Geoff thought it looked like a nod. He wasn't particularly experienced at talking to seagulls and wasn't quite sure if he'd translated the gesture properly.

"I am the symbol your subconscious has chosen to embody all the confidence these people have been trying to take away from you, all your resistance to the idea of being an "insignificant nobody," and all your desires to show them what you are truly capable of."

"A seagull?" Geoff said. "Wouldn't it have been better for me to choose a massive robot with rocket launchers for eyes or a big tank with loads of guns? You know—something bastard hard?"

The seagull let out a little seagull sigh. "Robots and tanks may be pretty cool, but they don't mean anything to you Geoff," it said, looking out across the lake. "The seagull, on the other hand, is *hugely* symbolic. To most people, it may be just a stupid bird that chose to look right instead of left, but to you, it represents so much more. It's the thing that proves you *do* make a difference; it reassures you that you're not the same as all the other Time Reps—that you're not just another turnip farmer or failed philosopher. But more than that, it's something you believe will one day reveal your true influence on the course of history—something that will give you a chance to show these people what you're really capable of."

"That does sound pretty important, now that you mention it," Geoff said.

"Oh believe me, there's more to that bird than meets the eye, Geoff," the seagull said, jumping down onto the wooden seat in front of him. "Much more. Figure out the mystery behind why it chose to look right instead of left, and you'll reveal your true significance to the world—significance far greater than anyone could ever imagine."

"And how exactly am I supposed to do that?" Geoff said. "I have enough trouble trying to figure out the mystery of how many *Nectar* points I've got."

"With this," the seagull said, releasing the piece of paper in its foot and nudging it toward Geoff. "That's everything Eric told you about the loophole in his algorithm before he died, and how to fix it. You wrote it all down just before your attacker hypnotized you into forgetting everything."

"I wrote it all down?" Geoff said, picking the piece of paper up. It was folded in half.

"Well, not literally. You *imagined* writing everything down as a way of protecting the information in the back of your mind."

"I see," Geoff said. "So you're saying that once I read this, I'll know how that stupid computer can be tricked?"

"Correct. And once you know that, you'll be able to figure out why that seagull chose to look the other way."

Geoff couldn't think of a better incentive to open the piece of paper and read it, which he did immediately. When he'd finished, he leaned against the back of the boat, looked up in the sky, and laughed out loud—underneath the explanation behind how Eric's algorithm could be fooled, he'd also written down quite a funny joke he'd heard the other day in case he'd forgotten that as well.

SEVENTEEN

"Geoff?"

"Hee hee hee…"

"Geoff!"

"Hee hee…wha…"

"Geoff, wake up!"

"Mnnn…?"

"Stop mumbling and wake up!"

Geoff opened his eyes, only to be greeted by a large, freeze-framed image of his own death—not the most pleasant sight to wake up to after a nice nap. In fact, now that he thought about it, Tim was developing a nasty habit of waking him up in a variety of bad ways: blinding him by opening the curtains, strapping him to a table, putting tubes up his nose, and now tormenting him with a high-resolution image of his body being toasted in a spaceship's fiery backwash. One of these days he'd have to get his own back—perhaps by tying Tim's foot to a passing truck while he slept.

"Agghhh!" Geoff yelped, shielding his gaze. "Turn it off! Turn it off!"

"Sorry," Tim said. "I watched it through again while you were unconscious. Computer, please turn off the screen."

On command, the screen disappeared in a flash of vapor, a bit like Geoff's body had done in the simulation, as it happened.

"It's gone," Tim said, helping Geoff to his feet. "You can look."

Geoff brought his hand back down from his eyes and sat on the scanning pedestal in the middle of the room. He was sweating.

"You feeling okay?" Tim said.

"Oh I'm just spiffing," Geoff replied. "I've been stabbed through the hand, I've watched London being destroyed by an alien invasion, and I've seen my own death being simulated in glorious widescreen. Things couldn't be better. Is there anyone nearby who could kick me in the bollocks just to round the day off?"

Tim sighed.

"Yes, it looks like we've got a bit of a problem on our hands here," he said, sitting down next to Geoff. "Maybe the papers were right about you, after all."

"What?"

"The newspapers. Remember what that journalist said to you before the party?"

"The one who said I might have been lied to about your insignificance?"

"Yes. Maybe he was right."

"You think?" Geoff said, giving Tim a sarcastic look.

"The question is: how the hell did we miss it?"

"I can tell you how."

Tim removed his glasses for a moment and rubbed his eyes.

"You can?"

Geoff nodded. "Eric told me how the computer could be tricked before he died."

"What?" Tim said, leaping to his feet. "I thought you couldn't remember anything!"

"I couldn't, until now," Geoff said, leaning back on his hands. "Listen—you're not going to believe this, but the person who attacked me also hypnotized me. They hypnotized me into delivering that message about Tringrall and Dranculees to the aliens, and they hypnotized me into forgetting what Eric told me before he died. But I remember now. He *did* explain the loophole to me."

"So how come you remember?"

"Because I heard myself say all that crap about Tringrall and Dranculees," Geoff said. "That was the trigger I was given to restore my memory."

"What? But why did they want you to remember at all?"

"A cruel trick, I guess. Whoever's behind all this must have known I was going to die seconds after I said those words. They wanted me to remember how they'd changed history—how they'd managed to finally wipe out the human race—but only when it was too late to stop them. They wanted me to suffer one final moment of torment before my death."

"But they didn't think we'd double-check the paradox scan before you went back," Tim said, smiling. "They didn't reckon you'd hear those words in a simulation."

"No. But it still counts though," Geoff said. He got to his feet and walked toward Tim. "The condition to getting my memory back was hearing myself say the words: 'I bring a message from Tringrall. In the year of Dranculees, you must revert.' No one said anything about hearing those words in a *simulation*."

"So what do you think it means?" Tim said.

"Not sure. Tringrall must be the person who killed Eric and attacked me because that was the person who gave me the message. As for the rest, I've got no idea."

"But that would mean 'Tringrall' is the person on the inside who leaked the algorithm!" Tim said. "You mean to tell me that the mole in the organization is a Varsarian?"

"What are you talking about?"

"Tringrall is trying to change the course of history so that the alien invasion succeeds, right?

"Right…"

"Don't you get it? Tringrall must be a descendant of the Varsarian crew that crash-landed on Earth all those years ago— the crew who molecularly rearranged themselves to look like human beings! Remember? Someone high up in this business is an alien!"

"Oh dear," Geoff said.

"Did you recognize who it was?"

"No—they were wearing a hooded cape. In fact, I think it might have been the same person who took a shot at me during the Great Fire of London."

"What about their voice? You said they hypnotized you. Did you hear their voice? Did they sound familiar?"

"They *did* sound familiar now that you mention it," Geoff said. "But I can't quite remember."

"Was the voice male … or female?" Tim said.

"I don't know," Geoff replied. "Who do you think it could be?"

"Who knows?" Tim said. "It could be Ruth, it could be Mr. Knight … It could even be me, for all you know …"

"I doubt that," Geoff said, "Besides—you were the one who chased Tringrall in 1666, remember?"

"I know. But time travel *does* allow you to be in two places at once."

"No, it can't be you," Geoff reasoned. "Unless of course you like thwarting your own plans for fun."

"I suppose you have a point there."

"What about the Defense Minister? Could it be the Defense Minister?"

"I don't know," Tim said. "I just don't know."

Tim began pacing up and down. "So are you going to tell me how this Varsarian bastard tricked the algorithm, or are you just going to stand there and look pleased with yourself?"

"I'd quite like to stand here and look pleased with myself a bit longer, if that's okay," Geoff said. "I don't get to do it very often."

"I'd rather you didn't," Tim said. "Aren't you feeling a slight sense of urgency to all this?"

"I suppose," Geoff replied. "Okay—bring up the final nanosecond of the supercomputer's simulation, one hundred thousand years in the future, and I'll show you how they did it."

"I don't get it," Tim said, rubbing the back of his head. "Everything looks fine."

Everything did indeed look fine. The planet was exactly as it should have been: peaceful, green, blue skies—returned to Mother

Nature. The only difference was the seagull in Brighton, which was still insisting on looking right instead of left.

"This is the final nanosecond of time that the computer can predict," Geoff said, looking up at the simulation. "Remember what Eric said the last time we were here? If there are any changes to this moment in time, even at the most infinitesimally small molecular level, the computer detects that the space-time continuum has been altered and stops anyone from traveling."

"I still don't get it," Tim said, looking closely at the screen in case he'd missed something. "If the Varsarians managed to invade Earth in the twenty-first century and wipe out humanity, how can everything still be the same?"

"Let me ask you a question," Geoff said. "What if you could change the course of history, but only so it took a *diversion*?"

"What do you mean?"

"I mean, what if you could change history in such a way that everything returned exactly back to normal at a certain point?"

Tim laughed.

"That's impossible," he said.

"Eric didn't think it was. In fact, that was the loophole in his algorithm. If the final nanosecond in the new simulation remains the same as the original one in the computer's memory banks, the computer assumes that the course of history hasn't changed. Only when there is a *difference* between the two versions does it know to go back through its calculations and raise the alarm. But if someone worked out how to *divert* the course of history rather than *change* it completely, the computer would happily allow that person to travel back in time. After all, as far as the computer's concerned, its job is done. If the final nanosecond looks the same, it can go home early and catch the last ten minutes of *Eastenders*."

"But *no one* could work out how to do that," Tim said. "You'd need to be some sort of mathematical super genius."

"You're absolutely right. No one is that smart."

"Well there you go."

"You'd need to have access to a supercomputer 'powerful enough to predict the vibration of every molecule on the planet for the next one hundred thousand years,' as Eric put it, to make those sorts of calculations. A bit like the one we're standing in."

"You mean … someone could manipulate the supercomputer to work out how to cheat its own algorithm?" Tim said.

Geoff nodded.

"But only someone with access," he said. "That's the reason Eric thought it was an inside job. It had to be someone with high-level access. Remember when we were driving to the party? Eric told us that the computer's own powers of prediction could be used against itself—that someone had hacked into the mainframe and modeled a scenario in which the computer could be tricked. That was what he was worried about—someone was using the predictive powers of the computer to tell them how to alter history in such a way that it would return back to normal by the time it reached the final nanosecond. Once they'd worked out how to do that, he knew they'd be able to walk straight through the paradox scan undetected."

"Or get someone else to do it for them," Tim said.

"Exactly. And that someone turned out to be me."

"That's quite unbelievable," Tim said, "This alien—Tringrall, or whatever his name is—has basically used the computer to work out how to completely change the course of history and then return it back to normal?"

"Well, I'm only telling you what Eric told me," Geoff said. "Shall we work our way back from the final nanosecond and see if he was right?"

Tim and Geoff didn't have to work their way back for very long to find out what had happened. In fact, they only had to go back by one hour to see how the supercomputer had been tricked into almost allowing Geoff to go back and change everything.

The loophole had been exploited exactly as Eric had predicted. If the computer had had a face, there wouldn't just be egg on it— there'd be bacon, sausages, beans, waffles, and maybe another egg for good measure. And a pancake.

Tim and Geoff watched the screen. A huge Varsarian fleet was sweeping from one side of the planet to the other, each ship firing some sort of particle beam at the Earth's surface. As the beam passed over the ground, the landscape was instantly transformed: one minute there were huge, sprawling metallic cities, evidence of thousands of years of alien occupation; the next minute there was nothing but green fields, thick forests, and beautiful mountain ranges. Even the sky was turning back from blood red to pale blue as the ships sailed through it, purging any evidence that the aliens had ever invaded the planet.

"I'm guessing this is the year of Dranculees," Geoff said.

"And that must be reverting," Tim said, pointing at one of the ships on the screen as it transformed a whole city into a forest. "They must have their own way of knowing what the planet should have looked like if they hadn't invaded! They're using their molecular rearrangement beams to turn everything back to how it should have been!"

"This is crazy," Geoff said. "How can they possibly transform a whole planet?"

"If we managed to use that technology to recreate London exactly as it was," Tim said, "then there's no reason why they can't do it on a much bigger scale. That's why the final nanosecond looked so perfect, right down to the last molecule."

Geoff felt like he was watching a sinister version of one of those horrible home-makeover shows. Then again, home-makeover shows were pretty sinister themselves—at least the aliens weren't barging into someone's lounge and painting the skirting boards green. In the end, he couldn't decide which was worse.

Within a few minutes, the entire planet was almost completely back to normal, with most of the ships making a few finishing touches here and there with their molecular rearrangement beams.

Some were taking great care over recreating the rainforests; others were repositioning every single grain of sand on the world's coastlines. One ship over Brighton had the thankless task of recreating all the seagulls, making sure they were in exactly the same position as they would have been before. When it had finished creating the final seagull on the end of a small outcrop of rock, the spaceship switched its engines to full power and ascended into the sky, its molecular rearrangement beam following closely behind. As it blasted out of the Earth's atmosphere, the seagull on the rock looked around as the molecular rearrangement beam retracted into space, repositioning all the clouds into their original size, shape, and color. It even removed the ship's ionisation trail.

"Well, that explains a lot," Tim said, turning his attention to Geoff as the simulation ended.

"It certainly explains why that bloody seagull was looking the other way," Geoff added, "and why everything else in the simulation looked exactly the same."

"Okay," Tim said, standing up. "'Tringrall' must have worked out that the only way to get you through the paradox scan and change history was if he made sure you told the aliens to put things right again, one hundred thousand years in the future—'In the year of Dranculees, you must revert.' If he didn't, the computer wouldn't have let you go back to the twenty-first century to change whatever it is you changed to let the Varsarians invade in the first place."

"I still don't understand what all this has got to do with me," Geoff said. "How could my hand possibly be responsible for changing the date of an alien invasion?"

"I have no idea," Tim said, scratching his head. "The only way we're ever going to find out is if we can work out who this 'Tringrall' really is. He must have used the computer to work out what he needed to do, and somehow, it involved your right hand. We've *got* to try to figure out who he is, but it's not going to be easy—this 'Tringrall' has managed to keep his true identity hidden for years and years."

Geoff sat in silence for a moment.

"I think I may have just had a brilliant idea," he said.

Tim looked at Geoff skeptically. The last "brilliant idea" Geoff had come up with was tea ice lollies.

"Can't we use the computer to simulate last night's party?" Geoff suggested. "If we can, we might be able to see Eric's murder and find out who the killer was."

"That *is* a pretty good idea actually," Tim said in surprise, making some quick adjustments to the computer. "I'll just tell it that you're not going back in time anymore—otherwise, all we'll see is some horrible, alien-infested version of Earth."

The screen popped up again but didn't look like it was showing them much of a party. Instead, it showed them a horrible, alien-infested version of Earth. All around, the world was covered in twisting alien architecture with swarms of leathery-skinned Varsarians living under a blood-red sky. If it *was* showing them a party, it must have been some sort of fancy dress party where everyone had decided to go dressed as a Varsarian. Either that, or the computer was still showing them a version of the space-time continuum where the alien invasion had succeeded and the human race had been wiped out.

"I don't understand," Geoff said. "Shouldn't it be showing us the party from yesterday? I thought you told the computer I wasn't going back in time anymore."

"I did." Tim said, checking a computer panel on the wall and looking back up at the screen.

"You did?"

"Yes."

Geoff looked at Tim in silence for a few moments.

"Honest?"

"What do you mean, 'honest'? Do you really think I'd pick this, of all times, to lie?"

"So…why are there still aliens everywhere?" Geoff said.

"There's only one explanation," Tim said, sitting down on the floor and putting his head between his knees. "History must now be changed whether we choose to send you back or not."

"Meaning, what?" Geoff said, raising his eyebrows. "Does this mean that this has nothing to do with me after all?"

"I don't know, Geoff!" Tim sighed, crossing his hands over the back of his head. "I need to think!"

"Okay, okay. It's just that…if history's changed, why are we still here?"

"What?"

"I mean, shouldn't we be dead? Are we going to disappear?" He held up his hand and looked at it for a few seconds to make sure it wasn't going transparent.

"It doesn't work like that," Tim said. "The computer is showing us what will happen if history continues to run along its present course. But two timelines can exist alongside each other as long as there's still a way to change things back."

"So…what do we do?"

"I have an idea," Tim said, getting to his feet. "But we'll need to speak to the Defense Minister."

"The Defense Minister?" Geoff replied. "But I thought…what if he's really a Varsarian in human form? What if he's 'Tringrall'?"

"Unless you know someone else with military connections, I think that's a risk we're going to have to take."

Geoff used to know a guy in the police, but he wasn't sure how effective pepper spray and a baton would be at destroying a fleet of invading alien warships. That might take a while, and they'd have to keep still.

"Right, we'd better get going," Tim said, switching off the computer simulation.

"Where?" Geoff asked.

"Where do you normally find government ministers?" Tim said.

"I don't know," Geoff said. "Down the pub?"

"Possibly," Tim replied, "but I was thinking of the Houses of Parliament. We should call Ruth and Mr. Knight. Get them to meet us there."

"Good idea."

"I have to say, Geoff—that was some good work you just did there. You've changed. Even Eric couldn't get to the bottom of this plot, and you've just cracked it in the space of a few minutes. I never knew you had it in you."

"Thanks," Geoff said, "although there's still one thing I don't understand."

"What's that?"

"When we were in the car earlier, Eric said he had already witnessed the scenario we'd just seen—he just didn't tell us what it was. So here's my question—if he already knew what the aliens were planning, why didn't he say anything? Why didn't he try to put a stop to all this?"

Tim stopped walking and thought about what Geoff had just said.

"I have absolutely no idea," he replied.

Eighteen

The Houses of Parliament were quite impressive when they weren't being blown up by a Varsarian spaceship. As the sky turned to dusk, the tall, gothic architecture was lit up by a golden array of floodlights, the building casting a beautiful reflection across the River Thames. And although Geoff knew it was only a reconstruction, he was amazed at how similar it was to the Houses of Parliament of the twenty-first century—every detail was perfect, from the honey-colored stonework right down to the fact that Big Ben was still running two minutes slow. The only real difference he could see was a shimmering dome of light that stretched over the building, which apparently acted as a protective shield against laser beams, hijacked spaceships full of explosives, and bird droppings. Other than that, everything was practically identical.

After making their way through several security checks and explaining why they were here, Geoff and Tim were conducted through a large set of double doors into the Defense Minister's private office, where they were told to sit and wait. Or stand and wait. Either way, they had to wait.

"He's locked away in some budget meeting," they were informed by the office junior who had acted as their escort. He had greasy hair, wore a suit two sizes too big for him, and smelled faintly of egg mayonnaise. "Shouldn't be long."

"Tell him it's urgent," Tim said. "We must speak to him right away."

The office junior nodded and left, closing the large double doors behind him with a click.

The Defense Minister's private office was one of the most ostentatious old-fashioned examples of interior design that Geoff had ever seen, with a broad oak desk, a thick red carpet, and a ceiling so high it was a wonder the room hadn't formed its own weather system. A set of arched windows offered a stunning view across the River Thames, and along the left wall stood a row of enormous bookcases, which were neatly stacked with shelves and shelves of pristine, leather-bound literature. None of the books looked as though they'd ever been read. Geoff picked one off the shelf and flicked through it to make sure it actually *was* a book and not one of those stupid video cases people used to buy to make themselves look more studious than they actually were. Satisfied that the book in question was genuine and not actually hiding a copy of *Police Academy 3*, Geoff replaced it on the shelf and strolled over to one of the tall windows with his head in the air and his arms behind his back, much like the way people walk around in modern art galleries when they feel a little out of their depth and want to disguise the fact that they have no idea what to make of some flowers sprouting out of a ceramic female bottom.

Tim sat down in a squeaky, high-backed leather chair and looked up at a huge painting of the Defense Minister, which hung above a large open fireplace on the far wall of the office. It depicted the Minister in full robes, standing in the middle of the House of Commons with an ornamental mace in his right hand. The attention to detail in the picture was quite magnificent—you could make out every individual hair on his head, every crease in his clothing, and even get a feel for the texture of his skin. In the bottom corner it was signed *Adobe Photoshop version 145.7b*. Geoff's eyes wandered down from the painting to the fireplace below. Unless he was mistaken, it looked as though someone had been burning some papers recently—the crumbly black remains of some sort of document lay smoldering across the glowing pile of logs.

Before Geoff had a chance to look at the papers any closer, the doors to the Defense Minister's private office opened, and Mr. Knight walked in, followed closely by Ruth. They were both dressed a little more casually than Geoff had seen them in the past—Ruth wore blue jeans and a gray jumper, and Mr. Knight was wearing jeans and a black polo sweater with a suit blazer over the top—the kind of clothing you'd wear if you were about to present *Top Gear.*

"We got here as quickly as we could," Mr. Knight huffed, taking off his blazer and throwing it over the arm of the nearest chair. "Are you going to tell us what's going on?"

"We'd better wait for the Defense Minister," Tim said, picking nervously at the leather stitching on his seat. "I think he should hear this as well."

As if on cue, the Defense Minister suddenly burst into the room carrying a large folder under his arm.

"Right, what's all this about?" he said, sitting down behind his desk and tossing the folder to one side. "I'm supposed to be on Holovision in half an hour to give an interview about this bloody Time Rep fiasco, and the Prime Minister's just bawled me out over my defense budget for the next year. This better be good."

"I'm afraid it's *not* good actually," Tim said, getting to his feet.

"What the hell is *he* doing here!?" the Defense Minister said, suddenly noticing Geoff standing by the window. "I thought I told you to send all Time Reps back to their native time periods!"

"Geoff's the reason we're here," Tim said quietly, walking over to the desk. "Listen Minister—I think we may have a bit of a problem."

"Problem?" the Defense Minister said, snapping his head back in Tim's direction. "What sort of problem?"

"Well, there's no easy way of saying this," Tim said, "but we think someone has succeeded in cheating Eric's algorithm."

"What?"

"We think someone has changed the space-time continuum."

"But…but…" the Defense Minister stammered, looking at Mr. Knight, "you told me it was impossible to cheat that computer! You told me the chances were one in a googolplex!"

"David, I…"

The Defense Minister held his hand up to silence Mr. Knight.

"How bad are we talking?"

"How bad?"

"Yes. Quite bad? Reasonably bad?"

"I'd say this is disastrously bad," Tim said. "This is so bad that we might all disappear from existence any minute."

The Defense Minister blinked.

"In that case, you won't mind if I pour myself a drink," he said, reaching into his bottom desk drawer and pulling out a bottle of brandy. "Start from the beginning."

Geoff sighed. The beginning? That was going to take ages...

The Defense Minister unscrewed the bottle cap and poured himself a large glass of brown liquid. Geoff could smell the drink from where he was standing—it was so strong he was surprised the paint on the windowsill next to him wasn't starting to peel.

"Tell me what's happened," the Minister said.

It took Tim quite a while to successfully explain everything to the Defense Minister: how the loophole had been exploited, the mystery of how Geoff had unwittingly brought an invasion forward by two hundred years, and how a Varsarian called "Tringrall" was possibly behind it all, secretly hiding in human form.

"There's still something I don't understand," the Defense Minister said, taking another small sip of his drink. "You're telling me that if we send Geoffrey back in time with a broken hand, the Varsarians invade two hundred years early?"

"Correct," Tim sighed.

"And yet if we *don't* send him back at all, they *still* invade two hundred years early?"

"That's... what the computer thinks."

"But how is that possible?" Mr. Knight interjected. "If Geoff is somehow responsible for bringing forward the date of an alien invasion, why do they still invade the Earth even if we *don't* send him back? Surely he won't be there to change anything! Shouldn't everything go back to normal?"

"I think I might have an explanation, sir," Ruth said, closing her eyes in concentration. The rest of the room looked at her in silence.

"Well, let's hear it," Mr. Knight said impatiently.

Ruth opened her eyes again.

"It's simple," she said. "We must be looking at this the wrong way around."

"Carry on …"

"Think about it. Up until now, we've all been talking about Geoff changing something that brought *forward* the date of the invasion. Isn't that right, Geoff?"

"That's right," Geoff said.

"But what if it's the other way around?" Ruth continued. "What if the Varsarians had always planned to invade Earth in the twenty-first century, and that Geoff was originally responsible for somehow *delaying* them?"

"But how?" Mr. Knight said, scrunching his face up like he'd just eaten a fly. He didn't seem to buy this theory.

"You'd have to ask 'Tringrall'," Ruth said, "but I'm guessing he worked out that it had something to do with Geoff's right hand."

Geoff looked down at his injured hand in the hope that something would click in the back of his mind. It baffled him how this simple appendage could be responsible for postponing the invasion plans of an entire alien race. How on Earth could his hand have been involved in changing the course of history, when he had enough trouble using it to change his pillow covers?

"So let me get this straight," the Defense Minister said, finishing his drink and placing the glass down on the desk. "You're saying that this 'Tringrall' character discovered that Geoff did something that was responsible for *postponing* the Varsarian invasion, which was originally planned for the twenty-first century?"

"Correct," Ruth said. "And more than that, he must have discovered that it had something to do with Geoff's hand. That's why he tried to shoot at it during the Great Fire of London, and why he stabbed Geoff while he was unconscious—he wanted us to send him back to the twenty-first century in a state where he was unable to do whatever it was he originally did that stopped them."

"It's a good theory," Mr. Knight said. "But it still doesn't really help us, does it? I mean, without details, how are we supposed to know how to change things back?"

"It does make a lot of sense though," Tim said, stepping forward in Ruth's defense. "If what she's saying is true, it would explain why the computer is predicting an invasion even if we *don't* send Geoff back. After all, if Geoff was the only reason the aliens delayed their invasion by two hundred years, not sending him back would be just as bad as sending him back with an injured hand—on the one hand, he's not going to be able to stop them, and on the other hand, he won't even *be* there to stop them."

"Stop talking about hands!" Geoff said.

"Okay, so answer me this," Mr. Knight said. "Why didn't this 'Tringrall' just kill Geoffrey?" His voice used the word 'kill' a little too casually for Geoff's liking. "Wouldn't that have been easier?"

"Not at all," Tim said. "Killing Geoff was the *last* thing he could do."

"And why's that exactly?"

"Because the key to this whole plot has been to prevent any changes from registering on the supercomputer, from the moment we were considering Geoff as a Time Rep candidate seven years ago, to the moment we were supposed to send him back to the twenty-first century this afternoon. Tringrall needed to make sure that the computer wouldn't alert us to Geoff's true significance, and for that to happen, he needed to exploit the loophole in Eric's algorithm and keep the final nanosecond looking *exactly* the same. That's why he couldn't kill Geoff—his whole plan hinged on Geoff delivering the message about 'reverting' the Earth back to normal at a certain point in time. If that message didn't get through to the aliens, his plot to change history would have been unraveled the moment the computer calculated the consequences of making Geoff a Time Rep."

Everyone looked at Geoff for a reaction.

"Told you I wasn't insignificant," Geoff said.

"Tringrall must have worked out how to cheat the algorithm a long time ago," Ruth continued, turning back to the group, "and if that's true, we have to consider the possibility that he's quite a senior figure at Time Tours, someone with access to the supercomputer, and someone who has successfully concealed their true identity for years. I hate to say it, but it could even be someone in this room."

Everyone fell silent and looked awkwardly at each other.

Tim looked at Ruth.

Ruth looked at Mr. Knight.

Mr. Knight looked at the Defense Minister.

The Defense Minister looked at Ruth.

Geoff could sense an air of tension a room, even worse than the time he last went to a board game convention and someone announced that they thought *Settlers of Catan* was rubbish. He decided to step forward to see if he could diffuse the situation.

"Hey guys," he said, holding his hands up, "let's not jump to any conclusions about each other, okay? Right now, we need to be working together, not fighting. After all, for all we know—this 'Tringrall' could be someone else, okay?"

Mr. Knight looked around and raised his eyebrows.

"Have you had some sort of personality transplant?" he said. "You seem to be uncharacteristically level-headed."

"No transplant," Geoff replied. "I've just…woken up."

"Geoff's right," Tim said, bringing them back on the subject. "We have to trust each other, but we also need to be very careful. Tringrall is obviously a very dangerous person and obviously very smart. As far as the computer's concerned, he's already succeeded in changing the course of history, so whether he's standing in this room or not as we speak, we're still in a *very* precarious situation."

"So why are we still here?" the Defense Minister said, looking around as if he was suddenly going to disappear. "If history has changed, shouldn't we be dead?"

"The reason we are all still standing here talking to each other is because there is still a chance to change things back," Tim said.

"You see, two paradoxical timelines can exist alongside each other as long as there is a way to correct things, but if we miss the opportunity to undo whatever it is Tringrall did, the timelines will instantly converge, we will cease to exist, and the Varsarians will win."

"So what do you suggest we do?" the Defense Minister said, leaning back in his chair.

"I was hoping you could tell me."

"Me?"

"You're the Defense Minister," Tim said. "Since it's now inevitable that the aliens are going to invade Earth in the twenty-first century whether we choose to send Geoff back or not, I think we've got to take the military option."

"By which you mean …?"

"I mean our only hope is for you to send Earth's battle cruisers back in time to confront the Varsarian fleet before they get a chance to attack. We need to go back to the twenty-first century and destroy them before they get a chance to begin their invasion."

"Are you insane?" the Defense Minister said, standing up out of his chair. "I can't just mobilize the battle fleet with a click of my fingers! I'd need to run it by the Prime Minister, consult Parliament, hold a ballot…"

"There's no time for a bloody ballot!" Tim shouted. "Don't you have some sort of emergency powers for situations like this?"

The Defense Minister slumped back down in his chair and rested his head in his hands.

"What you're asking of me is very difficult," he said.

Tim said nothing. Presumably he felt it was best to give the Defense Minister a quiet moment to think.

"Call me stupid," Geoff chirped, "but couldn't we just wait for my hand to get better and then send me back?"

The Defense Minister looked up.

"That's a pretty good idea, actually," he said.

"Yes, but it's still a risk," Tim said. "Even if we send Geoff back in time once his hand has healed, there's no guarantee that he'll behave in the same way. We still don't know exactly what he did to delay the invasion, and for all we know, he might do things differently this time. Besides, this is our chance to wipe the aliens out once and for all. And even if Geoff *did* succeed in postponing the invasion again, we'll just be back to square one—Tringrall will live to try to change history some other time, and we may never find out who was really behind all this. No—we've got to go back and destroy them."

"You're right," the Defense Minister sighed. He stood up and walked over to the doorway. "This is our chance to end this, isn't it?"

"I'm glad you see it that way," Tim said.

"And it certainly helps me justify my defense budget to the PM," he added. "When I tell him I needed the cash to help prevent the human race from being erased from existence, he's hardly going to ask me how much it cost, is he?"

"That all depends on whether you can convince him we couldn't have thwarted the invasion by a cheaper means, like running an aggressive leaflet campaign," Geoff said. "Politicians love a good leaflet campaign…"

"We're not going to defeat an alien invasion by running a leaflet campaign," Tim said.

"I know that," Geoff replied. "Just trying to lighten the mood."

"I'll lighten your mood in a minute…"

"Right—follow me," the Defense Minister said, leading everyone out into the corridor. "We'll need to take the Ministerial space shuttle into orbit and rendezvous with the fleet."

Geoff looked at Tim uneasily.

"Did he say 'space shuttle'?"

NINETEEN

Much to Geoff's amazement, the Ministerial space shuttle was housed vertically *inside* the clock tower of Big Ben, which looked as though it had been reconstructed to conceal some sort of launch chamber. From the outside, a casual observer wouldn't have been able to tell any difference to the Houses of Parliament of the twenty-first century, but nonetheless, Geoff assumed that this was probably a new addition to the building, unless the government of the twenty-first century was in the habit of keeping secrets from the general public, perish the thought.

The shuttle itself was quite a remarkable piece of engineering, no bigger than two double-decker buses placed side by side. It had a sleek metallic exterior, a cluster of engines at the base, and a row of windows dotted along either side, leading toward a rounded cockpit at the front. Plumes of steam were being discharged from two smaller engines on the wings, which stuck out like little fins at the rear.

Geoff hesitantly joined the others on an elevation platform and gripped the safety rail as tightly as he could as they hovered up to a hatchway on the side of the shuttle. He didn't like heights. Down below, various people in brightly colored overalls were preparing for takeoff. A few engineers were making adjustments to the engines, others were running through diagnostics on a huge bank of monitors, and some were snaking across the launch chamber with a large refueling pipe cradled in their arms. In many ways, Geoff felt like he was watching an IndyCar pit stop team in action, except this was hardly comparable to the sensation of watching a race from the comfort of his living room sofa. And even if he *had* been watching this from the comfort of his living room sofa, he still would have been a bit disturbed by the fact that he was hovering thirty feet in the air, wondering what on Earth a piece of furniture from his house was doing here in the first place.

They were greeted at the hatchway by the ship's pilot—a middle-aged woman with short blonde hair, thin lips, and a no-nonsense look in her eyes. She stood at just over six feet tall, wore no makeup, and her brilliant white uniform was so pristine it looked as though it was dry-cleaned every six hours. With her in it.

"Welcome aboard, sir," she said, saluting the Defense Minister as he stepped inside the shuttle. "I have to say this is most unexpected—I didn't think we had any trips scheduled for today."

"We didn't," the Defense Minister said, climbing into his seat. "An emergency situation has developed. I need you to take us into orbit to rendezvous with the battle fleet immediately."

"Very good," the pilot said, offering her hand to the others and helping them into the craft. "We should be ready to launch in a few minutes."

Everyone had a little difficulty getting into their seats, as the shuttle was pointing up in the air, and by the time Geoff had finally managed to lay back in his seat with his legs in the air, he couldn't help but feel that he looked like someone who had just fallen down the stairs after a heavy night out.

The pilot closed the hatch and climbed into her seat at the front of the ship.

"Everyone okay?" she said, pressing a couple of buttons to her side and looking back at the group.

Tim, Ruth, Mr. Knight, and the Defense Minister all nodded.

Geoff raised his hand.

"What is it?" she said.

"Are we really going into space?" he asked.

"Ignore him," Tim said, pulling Geoff's arm down again. "He's new to all this."

Ruth sat down alongside Geoff and looked at him.

"You worried?" she whispered.

"I don't know," Geoff replied. "It's just—I've never been into space before, you know? I'm kind of a little nervous."

"Well don't be," she said, fastening her seatbelt. "Everything will be fine. Going into space is as easy as catching a bus these days."

That was all very well, unless Ruth was talking about catching a bus that someone had actually thrown at him. He lay back in his seat, took a deep breath, and tried to relax. Unfortunately, his current position gave him a direct view through the cockpit window and up the length of the launch chamber, which wasn't exactly helping him take his mind off things. And while it looked as though Big Ben's belfry had thankfully been removed to make way for the shuttle's launch path, the roof of the spire still appeared to be blocking the top of the chamber, which was slightly disconcerting to say the least. He didn't like this at all—in fact, the only way this situation could possibly get any worse would be if he were to discover zucchini were on the in-flight menu.

Geoff dug his fingernails into the armrests.

"Erm … what's the deal with that roof?" he said.

"Oh, don't worry about that," the Defense Minister said.

"Don't worry about it?" Geoff said. "What, is it made of tissue paper?"

"No, no," the Defense Minister replied. "Just relax. Everything's under control."

"I need everyone to take a few moments to watch this safety video," the pilot said, pressing a small button in front of her.

Geoff looked up as a wafer-thin television screen folded down from the ceiling and flickered to life. A well-dressed gentleman appeared on the screen and stood next to a computer-generated image of the shuttle. In the background, some soft, cheesy lounge music began to play.

"Hello, and welcome aboard this Boeing 74447 light transport shuttle," the man said, gesturing toward the image next to him as if the viewer was somehow too stupid to understand which shuttle he was talking about. "Please pay attention to the following procedures, which are designed with your safety and comfort in mind."

Geoff normally ignored these sorts of videos when he was on a plane, but right now, it had his complete attention.

"As we are about to take off," the man continued, "please ensure that your seatbelt is securely fastened. To fasten your seatbelt, push the two metal ends together until they click, and tighten the belt around your hips. To unfasten the seatbelt, simply lift the buckle and pull the ends apart."

"I don't think they're going into enough detail about the seatbelts," Geoff said, adopting a sarcastic tone to try to disguise his nervousness. "Can we rewind it just to make sure I understand?"

Everyone ignored him.

"Should additional oxygen be required, a mask will drop down in front of you. Pull the mask toward your face—this activates the oxygen supply."

On the screen, a woman demonstrated how to wear the mask, looking remarkably calm for someone who was supposed to be suffocating in a depressurised cabin.

"In the event of an emergency landing, you must use the 'brace' position to help prevent injury. Place both feet on the floor, with one hand over the other on the back of your head. Lean forward, tucking your elbows outside your knees. If possible, rest your head on the seat in front of you."

The woman demonstrated the "brace" position on the screen. Once again, her face was as calm and unemotional. It was as if she was just practicing some yoga rather than crashing to her death. Presumably all the good actors in the world weren't really interested in starring in a low-budget flight safety video.

"Should the shuttle suffer a power failure in outer space, spacesuits are located under your seat. To put the spacesuit on quickly, step into the legs first, then pull the suit up to your waist. Next, place your arms in both sleeves and fasten the airtight zip. Your captain will pass around helmets and oxygen tanks when all passengers are ready to disembark the craft."

Geoff felt under his seat. There was indeed a spacesuit packed away underneath it, although he wasn't sure if this made him feel better or worse.

"Finally, please remember that your safety is our number one priority, and your pilot is there if you do not understand any of these procedures. Thank you for listening."

The screen went blank and folded back into the ceiling.

"Well, that certainly made me feel better," Geoff said. "I had no idea there were so many things that could go wrong, but now I know about power failures, emergency landings, oxygen shortages—thanks a lot."

"I think we're just about ready," the pilot said, pulling a small portable radio out from the dashboard. "I just need clearance from Space Traffic Control, and we can be on our way."

"Make it quick," the Defense Minister said. "We've got no time to lose."

The captain nodded.

"Space Traffic Control, Space Traffic Control, this is *Black Rod 1*," she said, holding the radio to her mouth. "We are prepped and ready for launch, requesting clearance for departure. Do you read?"

Geoff never understood the point of asking someone if they read in these radio communications. What was "Space Traffic Control" going to say back? "Thanks for asking *Black Rod 1*. We're quite partial to a bit of T S Elliot, as it happens"?

"*Black Rod 1*, this is Space Traffic Control," came a voice over the loudspeaker. "We read you. You are clear for launch. Repeat—you are clear for launch."

"Roger Space Traffic Control," the pilot said. "Please open the launch bay doors. I repeat—please open the launch bay doors."

This was another quirk of radio communication that really annoyed Geoff—why did everyone always insist on repeating everything? You didn't walk into a shop and say, "Can I have a packet of salt and vinegar chips? I repeat—can I have a packet of salt and vinegar chips?" Why did you have to ask for everything twice over a radio?

His annoyance was soon replaced by a feeling of relief as he noticed the roof splitting open down the middle and opening up like a huge mechanical crocodile's mouth, revealing a clear starry night above. Unfortunately, this was soon replaced again by a feeling of panic when he realized this probably meant they were going to take off soon.

"Everything checks out okay," the pilot said, replacing the radio back in its holder on the dashboard and gripping the flight stick with both hands. "Ready when you are."

"Excellent," the Defense Minister said, placing a hand on the pilot's shoulder. "Shall we have a countdown?"

"Good idea," Geoff said, digging his fingernails deeper into the arm rests. "How about we start from a million?"

"Five," the pilot said, checking an instrument on the dashboard.

"Five?" Geoff said. "Five's far too small! Can't we start higher?"

"Four."

"Four? Where did four come from? You said 'five' a second ago! Can't we stick with five?"

"Three."

"Wait a minute—are we counting down already?"

"Ignition."

"Ignition!?" Geoff yelled over the sudden roar of the engines as the ship began to vibrate violently around him. "That's cheating! You missed out 'two!'"

"One!"

"Hang on a second!" Geoff cried, desperately trying to think of a final reason for delaying the launch, "I think I might have left my wallet downstairs!"

"Lift off!" the pilot shouted. "We have lift off!"

And with that, the shuttle began to shudder more violently, the engines roaring so loud it was like listening to a rock concert through a stethoscope. Geoff really wanted to close his eyes as the shuttle accelerated out of the launch chamber and into the night sky, but the force of the takeoff was so powerful that the g-force was pulling his eyelids back as far as they could go. Resigned to the fact that he had no choice but to keep his eyes open, Geoff strained his head to the left to avoid looking at the intimidating expanse of space ahead. Unfortunately, this new position was even worse, giving him a dizzying perspective through the side window of the city below, the streets of London spiraling farther and farther away from him.

Fortunately, he felt much better as the shuttle continued to climb; the street lights and buildings of the city below blurring into less recognizable splashes of yellow and orange. Indeed, the more Geoff watched, the more the view became pretty awe-inspiring—at this altitude, he could already see across the whole of the British Isles, and in the black of the night the country actually looked quite beautiful, as if the land was coated in a glittering spider's web of electric light. The shuttle continued to climb higher and higher into the sky, and soon enough, he was able to see the whole of Europe, the sun just peeking over the curvature of the Earth on the horizon.

"I don't suppose anyone has any sweets?" Geoff said as the shuttle broke free from the Earth's atmosphere and began to level off. "My ears are popping."

TWENTY

The sight of the Earth from outer space was unlike anything Geoff had ever seen before, unless of course you counted all the photos he'd seen of the planet, all the television programs he'd watched, and all the computer games he had played where he'd commanded fleets of spaceships in various space battles around Earth's orbit. In fact, if you wanted to be pedantic, you could argue that seeing the Earth from outer space should not have been something wholly unfamiliar to him.

Nevertheless, seeing it for real was quite different. By now, the shuttle's engines had died down to a quiet hum, and from space everything looked remarkably peaceful. Entire continents looked as though they were made of a soft brown fabric, with mountain ranges giving off a rough texture on the surface of the Earth. Huge swirls of cloud circled over the land as if someone had taken a spoon and stirred them around like the cream in a cup of coffee. Oceans looked like syrup, wrapping around the planet like a thick blue blanket. It was the sort of view that would normally be described as "taking someone's breath away," but since in Geoff's case this would have meant the cabin had depressurized, it was more reassuring to say that it didn't.

"You can take your seatbelt off now if you want, Geoff," Tim said. "The shuttle has leveled off."

"Are you sure?" Geoff said, still gripping the armrests of his chair. "I'm not going to float around, am I?"

"You're not going to float around."

"I don't need magnetic boots."

"There's no such thing as magnetic boots."

"There isn't?"

"No. That's just something you made up. The shuttle generates its own gravitational field. It's perfectly safe."

Geoff hesitantly unfastened his seatbelt but remained seated. He was only too wary of standing up before he was ready—particularly after a bad night's sleep, which usually ended in disaster.

The Defense Minister walked over to the cockpit and sat next to the pilot.

"How long before we rendezvous with the fleet?" he said.

"Not long," the pilot said, looking down at some of the instruments in front of her. "The fleet is currently in geosynchronous orbit on the other side of the Earth. Shouldn't take more than half an hour to reach them."

Geoff stood up. His knees felt a little weak, his hands were shaking, and his ears were still recovering from the sound of the engines during takeoff, but otherwise he felt okay. He made his way over to the other side of the shuttle, peered out of one of the windows facing away from the Earth, and gasped. His gaze was filled with a dazzling array of stars sprawled across the inky blackness of space in a brilliant patchwork of light. Sure, he'd looked up at the night sky before, but through London's night pollution he could only ever make out a handful of stars, as if God was having trouble paying his electricity bill and kept switching stars off to save money. From here, however, outer space was really quite beautiful.

Geoff moved over to another window. Just as he had suspected—more stars. Millions of them, in fact. Then suddenly, in the corner of his eye, he could make out a few flashes of light. He looked closer. In the distance, a few spaceships were darting around, firing quick bursts of laser beams at each other.

"Look at this!" Geoff said, watching as one of the ships exploded. "There's some kind of battle going on over there!"

"That's not a real battle," Ruth said, joining Geoff at the window. "That's just a film set."

"A film set?"

"You can see the camera ships if you look carefully," she said, pointing out one of the stationary craft. "It's nothing to get excited about."

"So they film in space for *real* these days?" Geoff said. "It's not computer generated or anything?"

"Of course it isn't," Ruth replied, losing interest in the view and returning to her seat. "What's the point of doing it on a computer if you can do it for real?"

"I don't know. It just seems like a lot of effort."

"Not these days. Filming in space is just as easy as filming a car chase. And besides, audiences can easily tell the difference. Try watching *Star Trek 2* alongside *Star Trek 200* and you'll see what I mean."

Although the journey was supposed to last half an hour, it wasn't long before they could see the battle fleet in the distance, just on the other side of the moon. Normally at this point in a flight, Geoff would be rummaging around in his pocket to see if he had enough loose change to play a rudimentary game of *Connect 4*, but in this case the view was so spectacular, his nerves from earlier had completely vanished, and he found himself completely mesmerized by what he saw. There must have been hundreds, if not thousands, of ships up ahead, in all different shapes and sizes, orbiting the Earth in a precise formation. The larger ships were incomprehensibly enormous, perhaps bigger than some of the world's major cities, and even the smaller ones had an intimidating presence about them, looking at least as big as the world's tallest skyscrapers laid on their sides. Each ship was beautifully ergonomic in design, with a sleek metallic shell wrapped over a curved black underbelly, and if this was the fleet that the Defense Minister was going to send back in time to defend the Earth, Geoff couldn't help feeling that the Varsarians were in serious trouble.

"Welcome to the fleet," the Defense Minister said, watching closely as the pilot maneuvered the shuttle past a medium-sized cruiser. "What do you think, Geoff?"

"I don't know what to say," Geoff said, looking through the cockpit window as a wave of fighter craft formed an escort around the shuttle. "I wasn't expecting anything like this!"

The pilot steered the shuttle to face a large ship at the front of the fleet and pulled the radio out from the dashboard.

"*Concordia*, this is *Black Rod 1*," she said, weaving the shuttle between two neighboring capital ships. "We are on approach and request clearance to dock. Do you read?"

"*Concordia?*" Geoff said, raising an eyebrow.

"It means 'with heart'," Tim replied, peering through the cockpit window as they passed by a convoy of frigates. "Or something."

"*Black Rod 1*, this is *Concordia*," came a reply over the loudspeaker. We do not have you scheduled for arrival today. Repeat, we do not have you scheduled for arrival. Clearance to dock is denied. Repeat…"

"Give me that," the Defense Minister said, snatching the radio from the pilot.

"*Concordia*, this is Defense Minister David Cartwright," he said, interrupting the ship's transmission. "We have an emergency situation. Please execute priority override four-seven-niner-bravo. Do you read? Please execute priority override four-seven-niner-bravo."

The radio went silent for a few moments.

"*Black Rod 1*, we read you loud and clear. Priority override sour-seven-niner-bravo has been executed. We have you on approach vector three-zero-seven. Deploying tractor beam to bring you in. Hold tight."

"No way!" Geoff said. "You have tractor beams?"

"Thank you, *Concordia*," the Defense Minister said.

The shuttle shook momentarily as a pale red light engulfed the craft. To either side of them, the fighter escorts broke away from their positions and went off to do something else.

"I guess this is out of my hands now," the pilot said, letting go of the flight stick.

"Priority override four-seven-niner-bravo?" Tim said.

"It's a military code reserved for high ranking officers," the Defense Minister said, handing the radio back to the pilot. "It basically means 'do as I say.'"

"Does it work on other things?" Geoff said.

"Other things?" the Defense Minister said. "Like what?"

"Well, say you wanted to go to the cinema, but they wouldn't let you in because the screen was full."

"I think I know where this is going, and the answer is no. It only works in military communications."

"A military cinema, maybe?"

The tractor beam began to pull the shuttle toward the *Concordia*, but the ship was so big that it didn't seem to be getting any closer in the distance.

"How many ships are there in this fleet, anyway?" Geoff said, admiring the sleek aesthetics of a nearby cruiser as they overtook it. If you tilted your head and squinted, it actually looked a little bit like a big, metallic armadillo.

"Let me see," the Defense Minister said, looking up in the air as if the answer was written on the ceiling. "At the last count, I believe there were 258 medical frigates, 584 assault cruisers, 817 heavy artillery ships, 900 capital ships, 2590 support fighters, and of course, the *Concordia*—the pride of the fleet."

"Just don't ask him how much it cost to build," Tim said.

"Why?" Geoff said, leaning forward to try to get a better look at the flagship in the distance. It was so big, it still didn't seem to be getting any closer, despite the fact that the tractor beam was now pulling them toward it at quite a high speed. "Was it expensive?"

"You could say that," Tim said. "The cost of building the *Concordia* makes that 'rare' copy of *Keio Flying Squadron* for the Sega CD you bought off eBay look like an absolute bargain."

Twenty-One

Under normal circumstances, Geoff would have immediately rushed to defend his decision to purchase *Keio Flying Squadron* for the ridiculous amount of money he paid for it. He would have argued about how rare it was, even though deep down, he knew it wasn't *that* rare, and that he'd been stung by an unscrupulous seller and a lack of research on his part.

But Geoff didn't say a word. Didn't respond to Tim's taunt. There were bigger things to worry about as far as he was concerned, and right now he was marveling at the mothership of Earth's battle fleet—the *Concordia*.

The thing that struck most people when they first saw the *Concordia* was just how bloody big it was. And we're not talking "big" in the conventional sense, like saying, "Those pants are a bit big for you," or, "My meal was so big I couldn't finish it." This was in a different league of big. This was a ship big enough to eclipse the sun when it was orbiting the Earth—a ship big enough to warrant its own currency. Just to put things in perspective, the bottle of champagne used to christen it on its maiden voyage was the size of a block of flats.

The second thing most people noticed about the *Concordia* was its elegant design. Like most of the other ships in the fleet, the *Concordia* was almost tortoise-like in its appearance with a sleek, reflective shell arching over a black, angular hull. Upon closer inspection, it was clear that there were actually several ridges and grooves stretching widthways across the shell, as if it could some-how fold back on itself like the roof of a convertible, if say the weather was nice. In reality, however, the shell had no such capability—it had just been decided in a preliminary construction meeting that a few ridges here and there would save a few million tons of titanium, which was pretty expensive stuff to come by at the best of times.

Of course, something as big as the *Concordia* needed some serious horsepower if it wanted to go anywhere—preferably in the form of an engine, since using actual horses to pull a ship the size of a city across the vacuum of space would have proven to be a bit of a logistical nightmare for obvious reasons. Fortunately, the *Concordia* was well equipped in this department, sporting not one engine but twenty. Each engine protruded from the rear of the craft like some sort of bulbous, metallic growth, and the amount of heat and energy they generated was quite staggering—at full power, the *Concordia* could toast a marshmallow two thousand miles away, although why a marshmallow would be floating around in deep space was anyone's guess.

The shuttle glided peacefully into the *Concordia*'s enormous hangar bay, touching down gently on one of the many raised parking platforms.

The pilot unbuckled her seatbelt and stood up.

"We've arrived," she said, as if no one had noticed.

Geoff peered out of the cockpit window and watched as the red glow of the tractor beam faded away.

"Please make sure you take all your personal belongings with you," the pilot said, flicking a few switches over her head, "and I hope you had a pleasant flight."

Everyone got to their feet and stood impatiently by the hatchway for a few moments.

"So … what happens now?" Geoff said.

"We wait," the Defense Minister replied.

"For what?"

"The valet service."

"There's a valet service?" Geoff said. "On a spaceship?"

"What's wrong with that?" the Defense Minister said.

"I don't know," Geoff said. "I just thought a valet service was something you usually got in hotels and restaurants. Places like that."

The pilot began to adjust all the seats back into their upright position.

"Parking on the *Concordia* is a real nightmare—especially in the evening," she said, plumping up one of the headrests. "You've *got* to use the valet service, otherwise it's impossible to find a space."

The shuttle's hatchway was soon opened up from the outside by a tall, well-dressed attendant, who offered his arm as support for everyone to jump down onto the rubbery hangar bay floor. Geoff couldn't believe his eyes: the guy was wearing what looked like a morning suit, a waistcoat—even a top hat.

"Welcome to the *Concordia*," the attendant said, handing the pilot a valet ticket. "Do you have any baggage?"

"Only of the emotional kind," the Defense Minister said.

"In that case," the attendant said, gripping both sides of the hatchway and hoisting himself up into the shuttle, "if you'd like to make your way over to the check-in desk at the far side of the hangar, the concierge will be with you in a moment."

"There's a concierge as well?" Geoff said.

"Thank you," the Defense Minister said, reaching into his pocket and handing the attendant a small tip.

The attendant crouched down at the hatchway to take the tip from the Defense Minister and in turn tipped his hat. That is to say, he lifted the hat slightly from his forehead as a gesture of thanks—in no way was there some sort of bizarre tipping hierarchy whereby the hat received a percentage of the money the Defense Minister had given the attendant, because that would have been ridiculous.

"Shall we?" the Defense Minister said, leading the group over to the check-in desk on the other side of the hangar bay.

"BLACK ROD ONE NOW DEPARTING TO PARKING LEVEL SEVEN," a voice echoed over the loudspeaker. "PLEASE STAND CLEAR OF LANDING BAY FIVE."

Geoff looked back as the valet attendant fired up the shuttle's secondary engines and piloted the craft swiftly down one of the many passages leading deeper into the *Concordia*.

"ICARUS TWELVE NOW CLEAR FOR LANDING," came the voice again. "COULD A VALET PLEASE MAKE THEIR WAY OVER TO LANDING BAY FIVE."

Almost immediately, another shuttle glided in and landed where their shuttle had just been sitting. As instructed over the loudspeaker, a valet attendant rushed over to meet the ship as the encompassing tractor beam evaporating into thin air.

Not that the air was thin in here. Despite the fact that the entrance to the hangar bay seemed to be exposed to the cold vacuum of space, the air was just as clean and plentiful as it was in Geoff's own home, unless you were talking about one of the many days when Geoff had let the laundry pile up, in which case the atmosphere in the hangar bay was actually a marked improvement. Presumably there must have been some sort of invisible force field that prevented the air from escaping into deep space, which was quite handy really, as anyone not strapped to the floor might have otherwise been in a bit of a pickle.

The fact that you could walk around without suffocating wasn't the only good thing the hangar bay had going for it. It was warm, brightly lit, and spacious enough to accommodate several landing craft at once. As the group followed the Defense Minister over to the check-in desk in the far corner, there must have been at least twenty or thirty shuttles flying in and out at once: some landing, some taking off, and others just passing through. It was like watching a well-choreographed dance routine.

The Defense Minister approached the check-in desk and rang a small bell. A girl came out of a side door and walked over to meet them. She wore a similar styled uniform to the valet, with a knee-length shirt, a gray jacket, and a small hat on her head.

"Good evening, Minister," she said, looking a little surprised. "Is everything all right? We weren't expecting…"

"I need to speak to Captain Holland urgently," the Defense Minister said, cutting the girl short.

"The captain?" The girl said. "You…you want to speak to the captain?"

"Yes, the captain," the Defense Minister repeated.

"Now?"

"Yes, now!" the Defense Minister said impatiently, "Tell him to come down and meet me as quickly as he can."

"Of…of course," the girl said nervously, opening up a large book on the desk and handing the Defense Minister a pen. "If you'd just like to sign in, I'll contact the bridge."

Captain Holland didn't seem too happy about being called down to the hangar bay at such short notice, stepping out of the lift in a huff and striding aggressively over to the Defense Minister. He must have been in his late fifties, perhaps even early sixties, but his body language belied his age—the way he walked toward them looked more like a petulant teenager who'd been called into the kitchen to help with the washing up. For a man of his age he looked to be in good shape, with a broad set of shoulders and a muscular neck. He had a broad mouth, his skin was tanned, and his eyes had a certain intensity to them that suggested his was always on alert.

"What's all this about, David?" he said, running his fingers through his distinguished gray hair and flicking a speck of dirt off his otherwise immaculate uniform. "I heard you flew in on a priority override four-seven-niner-bravo?"

"That's correct," the Defense Minister said.

"May I ask why?"

"I need you to mobilize the fleet."

The captain laughed.

"You must be joking."

"I wish I was."

Captain Holland looked at the Defense Minister in silence for a few moments, the smile on his face beginning to think about sitting this one out.

"This is a drill, right?" he said, looking hesitantly at the rest of the group. "You've come here to test us?"

"This isn't a test," the Defense Minister replied. "This is the real thing. I need you to mobilize the fleet immediately."

"David, you know the rules," the captain said, shutting his eyes. "Article seven, sub paragraph B states that unless the planet is in imminent danger, the military are to receive two weeks notice for things like this. Two weeks notice, minimum."

"I'm well aware of the rules," the Defense Minister said.

The captain frowned.

"You mean … the planet *is* in imminent danger?"

"I'm afraid so. Look—I don't have time to explain everything," the Defense Minister said, "but we have reason to believe that history has been changed."

"Changed? Changed in what way?"

The Defense Minister took a deep breath.

"Remember the Varsarian invasion of 2181?"

"Of course," the captain said. "It's one of the first things I studied at the academy. The fleet was sent through a temporal vortex and destroyed six hundred years later."

"Not anymore," the Defense Minister said. "It now seems that the aliens will invade Earth in the twenty-first century, two hundred years before the human race is technologically advanced enough to create temporal vortexes. If our calculations are correct, humanity is about to be wiped out, just over a thousand years in the past."

The captain's eyes widened.

"But … how is that possible?" he said.

"Someone worked out how to cheat the supercomputer," Mr. Knight said, interjecting from behind.

Captain Holland moved a little closer to the Defense Minister.

"Who are these people?" he whispered, looking over the Defense Minister's shoulder at them all.

"They work for Time Tours," the Defense Minister replied, looking back at the group.

"Time Tours?" the Captain replied. "You mean—the holiday company?"

"That's right. These are the people who discovered the plot to change history and brought it to my attention."

"I see," the captain said, giving a brief nod to everyone in the way people do when they can't be bothered to say "hello." Everyone nodded back.

"So, what do you need from me?" he said, leading them over to the elevator and pressing a small button on the wall.

"As I said before," the Defense Minister said, standing to one side as the elevator doors slid open. "I need you to mobilize the fleet. We have to go back to the twenty-first century and destroy the Varsarian fleet before they get the chance to invade."

The captain sighed.

"What you're asking isn't going to be easy," he said, motioning everyone to step inside the lift. "Unfortunately, your little surprise visit has caught us in the middle of shore leave. Most of the ships are either completely empty or operating on a skeleton crew. We're in no state to go back and defeat an alien invasion."

"Can't you call back your personnel?" the Defense Minister said. "This is an emergency!"

"There's no time," the captain replied. "A full recall could take days, and if what you're saying is true, we need to get going immediately."

"So what do we do?"

"The only thing we *can* do."

"Which is?"

"Please state your destination," the lift said. Geoff recognized the voice. Familiarly calm, synthesized, female. Weren't there any male lifts in the future? How were they supposed to make any baby lifts?

"Take us to the remote operations deck," the captain said.

Twenty-Two

"This is madness," the Defense Minister said, pacing up and down nervously as the lift maneuvered its way through the ship. "Are you seriously suggesting we hand over control of the entire fleet to the ship's computer?"

Captain Holland steadied himself as the lift abruptly changed direction. Much to Geoff's surprise, this lift didn't just go up and down—it could move side to side, forward and backward, and even diagonally if it really wanted to show off. It was also capable of moving at quite a high speed, jerking its passengers around uncomfortably with every erratic change of direction. It reminded Geoff of the last time he'd taken a driving lesson.

"I don't see any other option," Captain Holland said, lurching against the wall as the lift violently changed direction again. "As I said before, we've got hundreds of thousands of personnel away on shore leave at the moment. If you want to confront the Varsarians with a full fleet, and you want to do it now, you're going to have to let me relinquish control of every empty ship over to the computer."

The Defense Minister sighed.

"I don't know," he said. "We've already been let down by one computer today. I'm a little nervous at the prospect of being let down by another."

"There's really nothing to worry about," the captain said. "Mai is more than capable of coordinating the fleet in battle."

"Mai?" Geoff said.

"It stands for Military Artificial Intelligence," Tim whispered in Geoff's ear. "She's the ship's computer."

"She?" Geoff said. "You mean you actually give computers a gender in real life as well? And why are they all female?"

"Mai is programed to adapt to every possible attack scenario," the captain said, "and she's never let us down in the past. If you ask me, we're almost better off in her hands."

"So how exactly does this work?" Mr. Knight said. "You mean to tell me the computer will have complete control over every ship in the fleet?"

"Every *empty* ship," the captain said, holding up a corrective finger. "She'll be able to control propulsion, weapons systems, shields, everything. With Mai in command, there's no need for a ship to have its own crew."

"How many ships are we talking about?" Ruth said.

"Oh, I'd say about 90 percent of the fleet," the captain replied. "Couple of thousand, maybe?"

"Interesting," Ruth said.

"Sounds to me like we're putting all our eggs in one basket," the Defense Minister said. "Can this computer cope? What if something goes wrong?"

"Relax," the captain said. "Mai won't let us down. And I think you forget—this fleet is far superior to the one that defeated the alien invasion in 2781. Considering the technological advances we've made since then, this operation shouldn't pose too much of a problem."

"I still don't like this," the Defense Minister said.

"It doesn't matter whether you like it or not," the captain said. "The fact of the matter is we've got no choice. It's either Mai, or a four day wait."

"Then I guess it's in the hands of the computer," the Defense Minister said, a slight hesitancy creeping into his voice as he edged back into the corner of the lift and drummed his fingers on the wall.

Once again, Geoff could sense a feeling of tension in the air and decided to try to diffuse the situation by changing the subject. He'd done such a good job at it in the Defense Minister's office earlier, after all.

"Have you ever wondered," he said, "why people in supermarkets feel uncomfortable about putting their shopping behind someone else's on the conveyor belt if there isn't one of those little plastic separators?"

Everyone looked at Geoff blankly for a few moments.

"Funny, isn't it?"

"Nice to know you haven't changed *too* much," Tim said.

"Good evening, Captain," said a sultry female voice as they all staggered out of the lift, their limbs shaking as if they'd just stepped off a roller coaster.

Geoff looked around to see who had just spoken. There didn't seem to be anyone here, save a couple of male technicians sitting at a control terminal, who certainly didn't look capable of speaking in a female voice, sultry or otherwise. In front of them, a huge grid of square glass pillars towered upwards toward a distant white ceiling, each one glowing in a relaxing pale blue light. There must have been well over a hundred of these pillars equally spaced apart, each one geometrically identical, perhaps a little wider than a person with their arms outstretched.

"Good evening, Mai," the captain replied. "How are you feeling?"

"I feel fine, captain," came a reply. As the computer spoke, a different cluster of pillars pulsated in time with each syllable, like a giant musical instrument. "I think I've just worked out a way to improve the fleet's engine efficiency by 20 percent."

"That's excellent, Mai," the captain said. "Excellent."

"This is Mai?" Geoff said, walking over to the front of the grid to get a closer look. He reached out and touched the nearest pillar. The surface was cool and smooth but felt ever so slightly wet, as if it were coated in a thick, transparent liquid. He pulled his hand back and sniffed it—it smelled like soap. Perhaps this was some sort of futuristic cooling gel designed to stop the computer from overheating or a superconductive liquid that could carry information within its molecular structure.

"Do you mind?" Mai said. "I've just been cleaned."

"Sorry," Geoff said, wiping his hand on his pants. "I didn't think you'd mind being touched."

"Do you mind being touched?"

"Well that depends," Geoff said. "Look, I'm really sorry—I didn't think you could feel anything."

"I feel everything on this ship," Mai said. "I can feel your feet on the floor, your breath in the air—I even felt that thing you flicked onto the wall earlier when you thought no one was looking."

"You felt that?" Geoff said. She was referring to a piece of fluff he'd found stuck to his elbow which he thought he'd disposed of quite discretely.

The computer said nothing.

Captain Holland stepped forward.

"Mai, we need your help," he said.

"I know," Mai replied. "You want me to take control of the fleet so you can go back to the twenty-first century and defeat an alien invasion."

"Wow," Geoff said. "Can you read minds?"

"No," Mai replied. "I've been following your conversation since the captain met up with you in the hangar bay."

The captain smiled.

"Can you help us?"

"I've already begun to make the necessary preparations," Mai said, her glass pillars looking as though they were flashing in excitement with every word. "I've set up a remote uplink with every vacant ship in the fleet, and I'm in the process of performing a pre-battle diagnostic check. All manned ships are on standby awaiting your orders."

"Thank you, Mai," the captain said. "Sometimes, I don't know what I'd do without you."

"I've also taken the liberty of analyzing the historical archives from the original battle of 2781 to formulate an attack strategy,"

Mai continued. "According to my records, the alien fleet consisted of one thousand light saucers with an accompanying armada of fifty capital ships flying alongside. When we attack, the fleet should split into fifty separate waves with twenty standard saucers forming a protective shield around one capital ship. If the aliens use this same strategy, I would recommend that we use attack approach Delta-341. This would allow us to exploit the weaknesses at the top and bottom of this protective formation."

"Sounds like you know what you're doing," the captain said, turning to face the Defense Minister. "Still feel uncomfortable about leaving this to the computer?"

"I'm not convinced," the Defense Minister said, shaking his head. "If you ask me, this all sounds too good to be true."

"I listened to your reservations about my ability to control the fleet while you were in the lift," Mai said, her voice flat and unemotional despite the Defense Minister's criticism. "Can I just assure you that…"

"Let me guess," the Defense Minister interrupted. "Nothing can go wrong? You're incapable of making mistakes?"

"Not at all," Mai replied. "In fact, I sense that's what bothers you. You don't like it when things are too perfect, and I was going to assure you that I probably *will* make a few mistakes."

"You will?"

"Of course," Mai said. "While I'm more than capable of controlling this fleet and reacting to different battle conditions, I won't always make the right decision. Some things will take me by surprise. Ships will be lost. And I know there's no guarantee that we will win. I may be one of the most powerful computers in existence, but I know I'm not perfect."

"I like this computer," Geoff said.

"So do I," the Defense Minister said, looking up at Mai's tall glowing pillars with a new look of understanding on his face. "At least it's got a bit of humility."

The Defense Minister turned to the captain and smiled for the first time since, well, since Geoff had met him, come to think of it.

"What is it?" the captain said.

"I don't know," the Defense Minister replied. "For some reason, I don't feel quite so nervous anymore. This computer of yours is more human than I thought."

"Well that's settled then," the captain said, walking back over to the lift and pressing the call button. "Mai?"

"Yes, Captain."

"Fire up all auxiliary thrusters and move the fleet away from the Earth. If you need us, we'll be on the bridge."

Just as captain Holland had ordered, thousands of engines simultaneously roared to life and began to propel the battle fleet out of the Earth's orbit. Within a few minutes, each ship had slowly built up a determined momentum, displaying both the grace of a ballerina gliding across a stage and the force of a rhinoceroses breaking into a stampede. This is not to say you could mix these metaphors and liken each ship to a rhinoceros in mid-chassé, as no one would have been able to take the fleet seriously.

The bridge of the *Concordia* was about the same size as a large lecture hall, situated right at the nose of the ship. At the very front, a huge reinforced window gave a magnificent view of the space ahead, with the captain's chair positioned a suitable distance away so he didn't have to crick his neck to see where they were going. The walls and floor of the bridge were an off-white color, almost exactly the same neutral shade that people paint their walls when they want to try to sell their house, and all around, banks of monitors and rows of control terminals displayed reams of incomprehensible numbers, fluctuating line charts, and cross-sectional diagrams of the ship. The whole place was bustling with various crew members: some stationed attentively at their posts, others wandering purposely between different terminals and typing things into their small handheld computers. It all looked very exciting.

Tim, Ruth, and Mr. Knight stood at the back of the room, with Geoff sitting next to them in an annoyingly high swivel chair. He thought about fiddling with a few buttons on the armrest to try to make things more comfortable but remembered he had enough trouble adjusting chairs in his own time, let alone a futuristic chair on a the bridge of a spaceship with more controls than those toilets you only found in Japanese hotels. Too embarrassed to get down from the chair so soon after deciding to sit in it, Geoff shifted his body weight as best he could to minimize the discomfort and watched as Captain Holland and the Defense Minister walked to the front of the bridge to address the crew.

"Everyone!" the captain said, holding up his hands. "Can I have your attention please?"

The room quieted down. Everyone stopped what they were doing and looked around.

"Mai," the captain said, looking up at the ceiling, "can you please open a channel to the fleet?"

"Channel open," Mai said.

The captain cleared his throat.

"Everyone, this is your captain," he said, his voice sounding firm and authoritative as it echoed over the loudspeaker. "I'm afraid I come to you today with some very bad news. A serious situation has developed in the twenty-first century, one that could threaten the very survival of the human race. To brief you on the situation, I am handing you over to the Defense Minister, David Cartwright."

A few of the younger-looking crew members glanced at each other with widened eyes. One man even dropped his little portable computer thingy, although he picked it up again in one swift movement as if nothing had happened, much like the way a cat always tries to style things out when they accidentally fall off the back of a sofa.

"Good evening everyone," the Defense Minister said, looking around the room to catch as many people's eyes as possible. "We don't have much time, so I'll make this quick: Earlier today, a Varsarian hiding in human form successfully managed to exploit the time-tourism industry—they managed to change the course of history."

A few people gasped, which Geoff thought was understandable—an alien impostor changing the course of history wasn't the sort of thing that happened every day, and the odd gasp was probably more restrained than what his reaction would have been, had he not heard this story twenty times already. The Defense Minister stood firm in front of everyone, waiting for silence to return before continuing.

"The human race is now in danger of becoming the victim of a vicious plot—a plot to change the outcome of the failed Varsarian invasion in the twenty-second century. If history is allowed to run along its new course, these bastards will succeed in wiping out mankind two hundred years earlier, before we had developed the technology to banish the invading fleet safely through a temporal vortex."

The Defense Minister must have thought this was a good moment for a dramatic pause because he executed one with all the consummate professionalism you would expect from an experienced public speaker, drawing on the silence to create a sense of tension. Obviously, the political fiber of his being couldn't resist the opportunity to make himself look good.

"But we're not going to let that happen," he continued, his voice getting louder with emotion as he spoke. "We're going back in time to the twenty-first century, and we're going to defend our planet. We're going to show these Varsarians the true power of the human race and the true force of its wrath. That is why I believe today will go down in history. Not as the day when we finally wiped out the Varsarians once and for all, and not as the day when we fought for the future of the human race. Today will go down in history as the day we stood together as once race and fought for its past!"

"Yeah!" the crew cheered collectively.

"Are we ready?!" the Defense Minister shouted, his voice bursting with either genuine or well-manufactured passion.

"Yeah!" the crew cheered again, anxiously poised at their stations to go into battle.

"Then let's fight for our past!" the Defense Minister exclaimed.

All around, people punched the air aggressively and cheered again, as if they were auditioning for a part in *Top Gun*. Even those who had previously looked as though they wished they'd called in sick today were standing up straight with their heads held high, a surge of optimism apparently flowing through their veins thanks to the Defense Minister's rousing speech. Geoff had to hand it to the man—he obviously knew how to work up a crowd.

"How are we doing, Mai?" the captain said, patting the Defense Minister on the back for his speech and sitting down in his seat.

"The fleet is armed and ready," Mai replied, her calm female voice providing a welcome antidote to the sea of testosterone Geoff felt like he was drowning in. "My remote uplink with all empty ships is stable, and all systems are fully functional."

"Then let's get this over with," the captain said, leaning forward in his chair and staring intently through the window. "Calibrate a temporal vortex for the twenty-first century, and project it straight ahead."

TWENTY-THREE

Geoff waited on his stupid chair as the fleet continued to drift through space.

Nothing appeared to be happening.

"What's going on?" Geoff said. "Did everyone change their mind about this whole battle thing?"

"What?" Tim said. "What makes you think that?"

"I thought we were going back to the twenty-first century," Geoff said. "Weren't we going to project a temporal whatsit into space and fly through it?"

"A temporal whatsit?"

"Yeah, you know—a temporal whatsit."

"You mean a temporal vortex?"

"That's it—one of them."

"That was ten minutes ago," Tim said. "We're already in the twenty-first century."

"We are?"

"Can't you tell?"

Geoff swiveled around in his chair and looked out of the main window. To be honest, everything looked pretty similar to him, although he guessed there weren't many telltale signs of twenty-first century-ness in outer space, like flat-screen TVs or smart phones floating around.

"You sure this is the twenty-first century?" Geoff said, giving Tim a skeptical look. "I didn't see anything happen."

"You wouldn't have," Tim said. "Traveling through a temporal vortex is instantaneous, and they're invisible to the naked eye.

That's why the aliens didn't realize that they'd flown through one in the twenty-second century, remember? That's why we were able to take them by surprise when they appeared in 2781."

Captain Holland stood up from his chair and walked over to an officer hunched over a computer terminal.

"Bring the ship around 180 degrees," he said. "I want to be facing the Earth."

"Yes, sir," the officer replied.

"Mai, can you do the same for the rest of the fleet?"

"Yes, captain," Mai said.

Geoff watched as the stars streaked across the window in a blur of light as the ship turned on its axis to face the Earth. He looked closer at the planet as it came into view—from here, it looked exactly the same as the Earth of the future, although he presumed that at a glance, planets didn't really change much over the years like people did, say by putting on a bit of weight or getting a new haircut.

The captain sat back down in his chair and looked over his shoulder at a female officer leaning over a radar display.

"Report," he said. "Do you see anything?"

"Nothing as yet," the officer replied.

"Keep looking. I want…"

"Wait," the officer interrupted, pointing at some little green dots that had just appeared on the radar screen. "I think I've got something…"

"What is it?"

"An unidentified swarm of vessels bearing 3-4-0 mark 2-1-5. They're heading straight for Earth."

"How many?" the captain said, leaping out of his chair and rushing over to the radar station.

"Five hundred," the officer replied. "No, wait," she said, looking closer, "Seven hundred. No—over a thousand! We have over a thousand ships on a direct course for Earth!"

The captain smiled.

"They're gonna get the fright of their lives when they see us," he said, not taking his eyes off the radar screen. "They're expecting no more resistance than fighter jets and nuclear missiles. Everyone into position! Mai—plot an intercept course on attack approach Delta-314."

"Yes, captain," Mai replied.

Geoff lurched back in his chair as the *Concordia* suddenly began to accelerate toward the invading fleet. Through the window, he could see a shimmering cluster of gray specks in the distance, screaming relentlessly toward the Earth like an angry swarm of giant bees. In space.

"Recommend we maintain radio silence from now on," Mai said. "According to my historical records, the aliens almost gained the upper hand in the original battle by monitoring our communications. By listening in to what we were saying, they were momentarily able to anticipate our attack strategy."

"Very well," the captain said, returning to the middle of the bridge and leaning on the back of his chair. "It's up to you now, Mai. Maintain radio silence."

"They've seen us!" the radar officer said, looking up from her screen and pointing at the window. The gray specks seemed to be getting a lot larger, revealing a generic, saucer-like appearance to each craft. Geoff could now see that most of the ships looked exactly the same size and shape with the exception of a few larger capital ships, which seemed to be a lot chunkier and heavily armored in their construction. All at once, the ships broke off from their original course and headed straight toward the *Concordia*.

"They're coming around to bearing 5-7-1 mark 3-6-4!"

The captain narrowed his eyes.

"Lock on to all available targets and open fire," he said, his voice unwavering.

Under Mai's control, a few hundred of the more nimble ships in the fleet accelerated past the *Concordia* and engaged the first layer of flying saucers, firing all manner of multicolored laser beams and missiles into their path. Many of the missiles shot harmlessly in between the oncoming craft, but when one connected with a flying saucer that wasn't paying enough attention, the damage inflicted was severe, causing the ship to explode in a dazzling shower of molten metal and yellow sparks. As the first few ships were destroyed, the crew on the bridge applauded, as if they were merely spectators at a football match.

Just as Mai had predicted, the swarm of incoming craft split off into separate waves, with twenty or so flying saucers each forming a protective shield around the larger, more menacing capital ships. Geoff watched as Mai split the fleet off to pursue separate formations. In the background, the Earth looked calm and peaceful, its inhabitants blissfully unaware of the huge battle taking place on its doorstep.

"Bring us around to bearing 8-7-4 mark 2-1-5," the captain barked, snapping Geoff back into reality. "We'll take on the nearest wave!"

Geoff grabbed hold of his chair as the ship lurched over to face a tight cluster of flying saucers, which were somehow managing to keep to a perfect formation around a capital ship as it swung around with incredible maneuverability to take on the *Concordia*.

"Fire!" the captain said.

The bridge vibrated as the *Concordia* unleashed a thick barrage of laser fire, which obliterated over half of the oncoming wave of flying saucers. The aliens quickly spaced their remaining ships equally around the central craft and fired back. A few of the lasers struck the nose of the *Concordia*, but the damage inflicted didn't seem to be anything worth losing sleep over.

"They're making a second pass across the port bow!" the captain cried out. "Aim all turrets directly ahead of their flight path and wait for my mark!"

The captain watched closely as the flying saucers flew back into view.

"Now!" he said.

The bridge vibrated again as the *Concordia* unleashed a second scatter of laser fire. Impressively, the captain scored another direct hit, taking out another five or six ships with one well-directed shot.

The remaining few ships in the protective formation began to spin around the capital ship, acting as a moving barrier to prevent a clear shot from getting through.

"I'm fed up of this," the captain said, narrowing his eyes. "Let's see if we can't take down the main ship. Aim for the weaker external ships and hit them so they take out the middle one."

"I like it," Geoff whispered to Tim. "He's going for a weak spot."

"A weak spot?" Tim replied.

"Yeah, you know—like in a computer game."

"Transfer all energy from the rear shields into the weapons systems," the captain said, his eyes completely focused on the giant screen in front of him. "Let's see if we can take out the rest of this wave with an extra-powerful blast."

"Brilliant!" Geoff said. "He's adjusting the power ratios just like you have to do in *X-Wing*!"

"Rear shields powering down," an officer said, looking up from his terminal at the captain. "Weapons now operating at 150 percent strength."

"Let them have it," the captain ordered.

The bridge shook violently as the *Concordia* fired a painfully bright shower of laser beams at the weakened formation. Upon impact, the few remaining escort ships careened uncontrollably into the capital ship, rupturing its hull and causing it to blow up in a spectacular flash of light, the shockwave from the explosion rocking the bridge as it passed through the *Concordia*.

"Yes!" the captain shouted, shaking his fist. "Well done, everyone!"

Geoff stared through the main window in wonderment as the battle continued to rage on in front of them. Capital ships were darting in and out of view pursued by smaller fighter craft, laser beams were streaming relentlessly across the stars, and colossal explosions continuously lit up the blackness of space, throwing a shower of flaming debris in every direction. It was like watching the most amazing firework display imaginable, except there was no one around selling those ridiculously expensive glow sticks that fizzle out after ten minutes.

"Give me an update, Mai," the captain said, sitting down in his chair and wiping his brow. "How are we doing?"

"We're doing well, captain," Mai said, her voice still sounding calm and understated over the loudspeaker. "According to my calculations, we've already destroyed over a quarter of the alien fleet."

"What about losses on our side?"

"Minimal," Mai replied. "We've only lost the *Intrepid*, the *Lancer*, and the *Tesla*. All…other…shipppssss….arrrrrrreeee fully func-func…function…Function…"

"Functional?" Geoff said, getting impatient.

"Quiet," Tim whispered.

The lights on the bridge flickered momentarily.

"Mai?" the captain said hesitantly.

"Func…func…func…Func…" Mai stammered, her voice slowing down to deep, synthesized drawl.

The loudspeaker went dead.

"Mai?!" the captain shouted. "Mai, can you hear me? Please respond!"

"Should we call the concierge?" Geoff said.

Before Tim had the chance to explain this problem might be beyond the remit of someone employed to take your coat when you come on board and let you know where the washrooms are, the bridge was rocked by an almighty explosion from directly ahead, the blast obscuring the main window in a brilliant flash of light. Geoff was expecting a very loud noise to accompany this spectacle, but because they were in space, it was totally silent. Everyone shielded their eyes as the light faded to reveal the charred remnants of a battle cruiser drifting lifelessly across the battlefield.

"Report," the captain said. "Was that one of ours?"

"Afraid so," an officer said, checking a few details on his screen. "The *Galileo*, sir. Must have been shot down."

"No, no. I recognize that explosion," the captain said. "Did you see? It came from inside. That ship wasn't shot down. It self-destructed."

Geoff stood up from his seat and took a few steps forward.

"Erm … was that meant to happen?" he whispered to Tim.

"I don't think so, no …" Tim replied.

All of a sudden, another ship exploded in the same way, the silence of the blast belying the scale of destruction.

"That was the *Slipstream*, sir," the officer said, his voice weakening. "Looks like you were right—there were no enemy ships nearby when it exploded. It must have self-destructed."

"What's going on?" the captain said, watching as another ship blew itself up of its own accord in the distance. "Why are all our ships destroying themselves?"

"They're not just blowing themselves up, sir," the radar officer said, pointing off the starboard bow. "Look!"

Everyone watched in horror as two battle cruisers seemed to deliberately crash into each other, the impact splitting both space-ships in two, right along the join between the sleek metallic shell on top and the black, angular hull underneath.

"Wait a minute," the captain said, running over to an officer sitting at the back of the bridge. "Were those ships being controlled by Mai?"

"Yes, sir," the officer said, frantically typing something into his terminal.

"What about the *Galileo* and the *Slipstream*?"

"Those too," the officer said. "She has control of 90 percent of the fleet!"

"Shit," the captain said, watching in desperation as a group of fighter craft began to open fire on each other. "Shit, shit, shit, shit, shit …"

Unfortunately, the aliens seemed to be cottoning on to the fact that something wasn't quite the ticket with their opponents and decided that now was probably a good time to step up their attacks on the confused fleet.

"I know this sounds impossible, sir," the officer said, still hammering away at his keyboard, "but could Mai have malfunctioned?"

"Mai doesn't malfunction," the captain said, running over to consult another terminal. "The only way something like this could happen was if someone went down to the remote operations deck and ..."

He stopped still.

"Is anyone missing?" he said

Geoff looked around the bridge.

"Erm ... I think we do appear to be missing somebody, as it happens," he said, his voice trembling.

"Who?" the captain said.

"Tringrall," Geoff replied.

TWENTY-FOUR

"How could we have let this happen?" the captain snapped as they rode the lift down to the remote operations deck, accompanied by a large contingent of armed security guards. "If you all thought one of you might have been this 'Tringrall' character, why didn't you say anything? Why weren't you keeping an eye on each other when you were on the bridge?"

"I got distracted," Geoff shrugged. "There were lots of big explosions outside."

"Well, now there's even more big explosions outside!" the captain barked, grabbing a spare rifle from one of the guards and snapping a clip of ammunition into it. "If we don't stop this 'Tringrall' and undo whatever damage he's done to Mai, the whole fleet will be destroyed!"

"I have a small confession to make," Geoff said, turning to the Defense Minister. "I thought it was you. I thought you were Tringrall."

"Me?" the Defense Minister said. "Why did you think it was me?"

"Just a hunch," Geoff said. "Plus—there were those suspicious papers in your office."

"Suspicious papers?" the Defense Minister said. "What suspicious papers?"

"The ones you burned in your fireplace."

"That was a shopping list!"

"Oh."

"You thought I was an alien because I'd burned a shopping list?"

"I didn't know it was a shopping list!" Geoff said. "I thought it might have been orders from another Varsarian or something, you know? If it was a shopping list, why didn't you tear it up and throw it in the bin like a normal person?"

"I have a confession to make as well," Tim said, giving Ruth a sorrowful look. "I thought it was you. I thought you were Tringrall."

"Me?" Ruth said. "You thought *I* was Tringrall?"

Tim nodded.

"Why? What did I do?"

"Think about it—*everything* points toward you."

"It does?"

"This has been something that has been planned from the start, correct?" Tim said. "And *you* were the one who thought up the whole Time Rep scheme in the first place weren't you?"

"So what?" Ruth said, steadying herself as the lift lurched to the right.

"For a while," Tim continued, "I thought that maybe your idea of recruiting people from different time periods had nothing to do with time tourism at all. I thought you might have devised it as some sort of elaborate means of getting to Geoff. But since we now know that Mr. Knight is really the alien impostor, I guess I was mistaken."

Ruth said nothing—in fact, she was beginning to look a little pale.

"You all right?" Tim said, resting his hand on her shoulder.

"It wasn't my idea," Ruth said quietly.

"What?"

"The Time Rep scheme—it wasn't my idea," she repeated. "It was … It was Mr. Knight's."

"But I thought…" Tim trailed off. "Didn't the Time Rep scheme get you on the board?"

"It did, but it was Mr. Knight's idea all the same," Ruth said, stroking her hair. "He came up with it one night when we were both working late. Told me I could take the credit."

"Wait a minute," Geoff said, feeling his stomach go funny as the lift changed direction again. "Does this mean what I think it means?"

"It does," Tim said. "It means that the whole point of the Time Rep scheme was nothing more than a deception from day one. It was never devised with the intention of improving the time-tourism industry—Mr. Knight thought it up purely as an elaborate way of getting to *you.* ”

Geoff didn't know whether to feel horrified or flattered. He opted for a combination of both, which made him look a bit confused.

“And if Ruth hadn't stolen the idea,” Tim added, “we might have been able to make the connection to Mr. Knight sooner.”

“Hey! I did not ‘steal’ the idea!” Ruth protested. “I tried to convince him to take the credit, but he insisted! He said he had nothing to gain, that I deserved a reward for all the hard work I'd put in over the years.”

“And you believed him?” Tim said.

“Of course I did!” Ruth replied. “Who would have thought he was a bloody Varsarian, for Christ's sake!”

“But when Geoff was attacked, why didn't you say anything? Didn't you see the connection? He let you take the credit for the Time Rep idea because he didn't want anyone to link it back to him when he started to abuse it!”

“I didn't mention it because … because …”

“Because what?”

“I can't say. But trust me—I just … couldn't mention it.”

“Did Mr. Knight … threaten you?”

“No, no … nothing like that. It's just—there was too much at stake.”

“You don't mean … your career? You kept this a secret to protect your career?”

Ruth paused a moment. She seemed to be thinking.

“That's right,” she admitted eventually. “It was my career. I suppose … I've always been afraid of people finding out it wasn't my idea. I've got too much to lose.”

“And I'm sure that's the way Mr. Knight planned it,” Tim said. “With all the success you gained, he knew you'd keep your mouth shut.”

“So … does this mean Mr. Knight killed Eric?” Geoff said.

"So it would seem," Ruth said, looking down at the floor. "That must be why he made me ask Eric to go to the lab before the party—when we were in the lift, remember? Mr. Knight must have been waiting for him there. He must have killed Eric, hidden the body behind the data banks, and run upstairs quickly to give his speech! No wonder he was so out of breath!"

"So all that stuff about asking us to find Eric must have been an act," Geoff said. "He knew exactly where he was all along!"

"Certainly looks like it," Tim said.

"So it was Mr. Knight who took that shot at me during the Great Fire of London," Geoff said, slowly joining the dots in his mind. "He's the one who attacked me in Eric's lab, hypnotized me and broke my hand!"

"Yes," Ruth said. "And that makes sense if you think about it—remember the night of the party, when you were looking for Tim? He was the one who told you that he'd gone down to Eric's lab. That's how he knew where you'd be, and that's how he knew you'd be alone."

"Mr. Knight told you I'd gone down to Eric's lab?" Tim said, standing back in surprise.

"Yup," Geoff replied.

"That lying bastard," Tim said. "I told him I'd already checked the lab. I told him I was going to look elsewhere."

"You'd already checked the lab?" Geoff said. "But...if that's true, why didn't you see Eric's body?"

"I was in a hurry," Tim said. "I just poked my head around the door and called out his name. There was no reply, so I moved on."

Everyone lurched to the left as the lift changed direction again. Geoff couldn't believe it—there were more twists and turns on the route down to the remote operations deck than there were in Mr. Knight's plot.

"Right, we're almost there," the captain said, checking his rifle. "When the doors open, keep low, and watch your fire—we don't want to damage Mai. I'm assuming this guy is armed and dangerous, so if you get a clear shot at the target, shoot to kill."

"Wait," Geoff said, putting his bandaged hand over the end of the captain's rifle and pushing the barrel toward the floor. "Don't kill him."

"Don't kill him?" the captain said. "Are you mad? This guy has already destroyed half the fleet! What do you want us to do—slap him on the wrist and tell him not to do it again?"

"I need to ask him a few questions."

"Questions?!" the captain said. "This is no time for…"

"*Important* questions," Geoff said, looking down at his hand.

"I don't care how…"

"Wait," Tim said, interrupting the captain. "Geoff's right—he's more use to us alive than dead."

"And may I ask why?"

"Because believe it or not, the reason these aliens are invading two hundred years early has something to do with Geoff's hand," Tim said, "and he's the only person who knows why."

"What?"

"It's a little complicated," Tim said, "but when Mr. Knight broke Geoff's hand, history changed in some way that allowed these aliens to invade two hundred years earlier than before. If we could somehow trick him into telling us why, we might be able to use the information to our advantage."

"Plus, if I don't find out, it's really going to bug me," Geoff said.

The captain thought about this for a moment in silence.

"Fine," he said, tugging the end of his rifle free from Geoff's grip and pulling out another clip of ammunition. He turned to the other guards. "Everyone change over to stun rounds," he ordered. "If you get a clear shot, aim for the legs to immobilize the target—these two want to ask our friend a few questions before we kill him."

"Erm…what are you supposed to do if you haven't got a gun?" Geoff said, suddenly noticing that everyone had a weapon of some description apart from him.

"If you haven't got a gun, stick close to me," the captain said. "I'll cover you."

"That's a great plan," Geoff said. "Or—and here's another great plan—how about I get a gun too?"

The captain looked at Geoff.

"Are you right or left handed?" he said.

"Erm … right handed."

"The hand in the bandage?"

"Left handed," Geoff said, correcting himself. "I'm left handed."

"And what's your accuracy rating with a Heavy Assault Laser Rifle?"

"My what?"

"Your accuracy rating."

"Erm … twelve?" Geoff guessed.

"Twelve?" the captain said. "The rating's measured in letters! Have you even *fired* a gun before?"

"Of course," he said.

"You have?"

Tim looked at Geoff and raised his eyebrows. "Playing *Time Crisis* in the arcades doesn't count," he said.

"Okay, so I've never fired a gun," Geoff said. "But I still think I should get one."

"Sorry—it's just too risky," the captain said. "Just stay close to me, and try not to get shot."

"Good advice," Geoff said, already standing a little closer to the captain than was socially acceptable in normal circumstances. "I'll do my best."

"Right, let's get ready," the captain said.

"Now arriving at the remote operations deck," the lift announced.

TWENTY-FIVE

The first things that grabbed Geoff's attention as the lift doors slid open were two twitching bodies, each lying in pools of their own blood and clutching their stomachs much the same way as Eric had done the night he was killed. Looking closer, he recognized them as the two technicians he'd seen in here earlier. This was not a good sign—Mr. Knight was obviously quite adept at killing people by breaking their ribs and puncturing their lungs. Geoff crossed his arms protectively over his chest and took a deep breath.

Captain Holland crouched down on the floor and scuttled out of the lift as quietly as he could, closely followed by everyone else. The place was eerily silent—so much so that you could have heard a pin drop, although there seemed to be an unspoken agreement between everyone that this was neither the time nor the place to start going around dropping pins, unless they were planning on catching Mr. Knight in some sort of hilarious *Home Alone*-style booby trap.

The group quickly dived for shelter behind a nearby terminal and took a brief moment to look around. Mai's towering glass pillars looked cold and empty, the flashes of pale blue light now reduced to a dark, lifeless gray. Over to the left, a row of data banks and monitors were smashed to pieces, a thick carpet of broken glass, wires and microchips splashed across the surrounding floor.

A stray shard of glass cracked under the Defense Minister's feet as he leaned back on his heels, the sound announcing the group's presence as it pierced through the silence and echoed loudly down the rows of pillars. The Defense Minister shut his eyes and winced.

"Aha!" Mr. Knight called out, his voice booming from some-where inside Mai's maze of glass. "Is that my welcoming party I hear?"

Everyone chose not to respond, perhaps in the vain hope that Mr. Knight might dismiss the noise as a stray cat running into a milk bottle or something.

"I know you're there!" Mr. Knight shouted. "It's no use pretending!"

There was something a little different about Mr. Knight's voice, as if some sort of vocal mask had slipped. It sounded more strained, more slithery, with a distinct hiss wrapped around every word. In many ways, he sounded much like the alien Geoff had spoken to in the simulated invasion of London he'd watched with Tim earlier.

"I assume you're here to try to fix your stupid computer," Mr. Knight called out, "and if that's the case, I'm afraid I have some bad news for you—I forced those two technicians to reprogram it before I killed them, then I destroyed all the voice recognition data banks. So unless one of you is exceptionally good at jigsaws, I don't think you'll have much luck fixing her before your entire fleet is destroyed!"

The captain made a few hand signals at his guards, presumably giving them orders on how to proceed. Some of these orders were fairly easy to decipher—when the captain pointed at a guard and then pointed down a row of pillars, this must have meant he wanted that particular person to head in that particular direction. Other orders, however, were a little more complicated to understand and involved the captain pointing at his nose, interlocking his hands, and drawing circles in the air with his index finger. At least, Geoff assumed they were orders—for all he knew, the captain could have been pretending to be a bookie communicating the odds at a horse race. Unlikely though.

Fortunately, the guards seemed to understand the captain's bizarre hand gestures and split off in various directions to look for Mr. Knight. Some began to make their way cautiously into the grid of glass pillars, guns at the ready, while others tiptoed their way around the perimeter. Geoff and the others stayed with the captain, who was still sheltered behind the terminal, listening intently to the quiet footsteps of his men.

All of a sudden, a mild tremor shook the room, the glass pillars rattling gently as they absorbed the vibrations.

"You feel that?" Mr. Knight shouted. "That's another one of your ships being blown to smithereens! Are you keeping count? Nearly half of your pathetic fleet has gone already!"

"Let's get this Varsarian bastard," the captain said, breaking his silence. Obviously there wasn't a hand signal to convey that particular order.

Geoff followed the captain as he rushed over to the nearest pillar and sidled up against it, peering around the corner to see if the coast was clear. Tim, Ruth and the Defense Minister split off in separate directions.

"Looks okay," the captain said. "Follow me."

They began to edge tentatively into Mai's labyrinth of glass, being sure to look left and right every time they approached a crossroads in their path. Occasionally, they would jump in false alarm when they came across a guard, who in turn would jerk his rifle up in surprise before lowering his weapon again in relief. From the inside, it was very difficult to see what was going on—the glass pillars had a nasty habit of playing tricks with the light and reflecting people in all directions.

"I see you've brought young Geoffrey with you," Mr. Knight said, his voice sounding much closer than before. "How very interesting! How did you like my little plan, Geoff? Quite ingenious, don't you think?"

The captain spun around to check the area behind them. Could he see them? Mr. Knight's reflection was drifting from pillar to pillar, but it was difficult to tell exactly where he was.

"I don't know," Geoff said aloud, suddenly sensing an opportunity. "It didn't seem that brilliant to me, really."

"What the hell are you doing?" the captain whispered. "Keep quiet!"

"Wait," Geoff said. "We may have just found…a weak spot."

"A weak spot?!" the captain said, struggling to keep his voice down.

"So it didn't seem that brilliant to you?" Mr. Knight replied, his voice sounding a little agitated. "That's because you don't understand. You don't understand your involvement in all this. *That's* the clever part."

"Then tell me," Geoff said. "Tell me how you…"

"He's here!" one of the guards shouted. "Lower your weapon and…"

Unfortunately, the rest of the sentence was obscured by a very loud burst of laser fire. And some screaming. A bright streak of red light reflected through the towers of glass, momentarily lighting up the room in a flash of color.

"Hitchford?" the captain said, wiping some sweat off his forehead and giving Geoff an uncertain look. "Did you get him?"

No answer.

"Hitchford, respond!"

"Hitchford would love to respond," Mr. Knight called out from somewhere, "but I'm afraid his head isn't quite attached to the rest of his body at the moment. Can he get back to you?"

The captain shut his eyes and shook his head as the remote operations deck echoed to the sound of a piercing, high-pitched laugh.

The room shook again, but much more noticeably than before. Geoff watched as a few hairline cracks appeared in some of the glass pillars, which clearly weren't designed to take this kind of strain.

"That was a big one, wasn't it?" Mr. Knight teased. "Whatever ship just exploded must have been pretty close! Anyway, where were we Geoffrey? You were going to ask me something?"

"Yes," Geoff said, staying close to the captain as they made their way deeper into the computer. "What's all this got to do with me? What did I do to bring forward the date of the invasion? And why did you break my hand?"

Mr. Knight laughed again.

"That's a lot of questions," he said, "but since you're about to die anyway, I might as well start from the beginning." There was almost a childlike excitement to his voice as it echoed across the room, as if he'd been waiting to tell someone this story for years.

"He's taken the bait," Geoff whispered to the captain. "We need to listen to what he's about to say *very* carefully."

The captain nodded.

"We'd always planned on invading the Earth in the early twenty-first century," Mr. Knight said, his reflection fading in and out of view like some strange kaleidoscopic effect. "The human race was so primitive back then, so basic. You didn't deserve to live on that planet, wasting all those natural resources on powering your motor vehicles and microwave ovens. It was a crime. So we decided to take it from you by force. We thought it was going to be easy enough—according to our research, the most advanced weapon you'd developed at that stage was the nuclear bomb, which, to be honest, we could protect ourselves against with a simple face cream. On paper, the invasion looked as though it was going to be a complete walkover."

"So what happened?" Geoff said. "What went wrong?"

"I was just getting to that," Mr. Knight said impatiently. "Having decided that we were going to invade, the battle fleet travelled fifty-eight thousand light-years across the galaxy, arriving in your solar system exactly on schedule. The Earth looked as harmless and primitive up close as we'd thought, aimlessly revolving around the sun like some stupid kid sitting on a carousel. It was almost too good to be true. So everything was set. The entire fleet readied its weapons, moved into attack formation, and accelerated toward the Earth, monitoring all communications on approach. However, just as we were about to break through the atmosphere and reap destruction across the planet, we picked up a transmission."

Mr. Knight went silent.

"A…transmission?" Geoff said, trying to prompt Mr. Knight into continuing his story.

"It was very faint," Mr. Knight continued, "but we could just make out the words: 'I see you stupid aliens, and the Death Bringer is coming your way!' As we later found out, that transmission came from you, playing your blasted computer games. You were talking to another human being over the 'Internet'."

"Please," Geoff said, struggling not to laugh. "Are you telling me you thought I was talking to you?"

"We didn't know what to think," Mr. Knight said. "For a start, we thought we'd gone undetected, and second of all, we'd encountered a weapon that translated as a 'Death Bringer' before, when we tried to invade another planet several centuries earlier. It was a devastating weapon, capable of taking out every ship with one strike, and when we heard the name again, there was a moment of panic. Was our research correct? Everything we thought we knew about the human race suggested you wouldn't be able to detect us until it was too late, yet here was this message. If we'd somehow underestimated your technological ability to detect the battle fleet, had we also underestimated your military capabilities as well?"

"So you broke off your attack?" Geoff said. "You broke off your attack … because I was playing *Space Commando*?"

"Yes," Mr. Knight said. "As a precaution, the fleet did an immediate about-face and retreated back across the galaxy to reassess the situation. The Varsarian high command was very unnerved by your message, and they wanted to double-check the accuracy of their intelligence."

"So I was right!" Ruth called out from somewhere, apparently listening to the conversation as well. "Geoff was originally responsible for delaying the whole invasion!"

"Yes, my dear," Mr. Knight said. "It's terribly embarrassing, isn't it?"

Geoff laughed out loud.

"You travelled fifty-eight thousand light-years across the galaxy," he said, wiping his eyes, "and you had to travel all the way back again because I was playing a computer game? That's hilarious!"

"Indeed. So you can imagine how stupid we felt when, two hundred years later, we discovered the mention of a 'Death Bringer' was just an amazing coincidence, uttered by some stupid kid, sitting in his pajamas, totally oblivious to the invasion. The Varsarians were the laughing stock of the galactic community."

"So when you realized your mistake," Geoff said, "you came all the way back again?"

"We did. In the two hundred-odd years that had passed, Earth was still an easy target. Your planet had been ravaged by a couple of big wars, and you'd developed a few more fancy weapons, but it was nothing we couldn't handle. So the decision was made to go back and finish the job."

"So that was back in 2181," Geoff said. "The twenty-second century."

"Correct," Mr. Knight replied, "and our intelligence was correct—your military capabilities were still no match for ours. So we began destroying your cities from space, one by one—London, New York, Beijing…"

"Basingstoke," Geoff said.

"Yes, Basingstoke," Mr. Knight said. "The battle was even easier than we'd predicted. However, we didn't count on one silly little university in Malta coming to the rescue, firing that temporal vortex into the path of the fleet. Because they'd kept the technology a secret from the world, we had no idea you'd developed it. And while it wasn't principally designed for military use, it was ultimately responsible for our near annihilation."

"So the temporal vortex transported your fleet six hundred years into the future," Geoff said.

"Indeed it did," Mr. Knight replied. "And because the trip was instantaneous, we didn't realize anything had happened. So when we arrived in the year 2781, we carried on attacking. So you can imagine our surprise when, all of a sudden, an enormous battle fleet appeared out of nowhere, firing back at us with weaponry far beyond our expectations—in a split second, we were faced with quite a formidable opponent. You know the rest of the story—our fleet was all but destroyed in that battle, save for one lone ship that crash-landed on the Earth. That ship belonged to my ancestors. Fortunately, it was equipped with a prototype molecular re-arranger, which allowed them to change form into human beings and blend into society. To this day, there are hundreds of us roaming your planet, each one plotting to get into a position of control: politicians, media barons, chat show hosts, scientists, and me—the President of Time Tours."

"There are Varsarians posing as chat show hosts?" Geoff said.

The room shuddered again, this time quite violently. Another ship must have exploded outside, and this time, it must have been much closer than any ship that had exploded before. This appeared to be a little bit too much shuddering for one day, as a few of Mai's pillars couldn't take it any longer, shattering into millions of tiny shards and coating the floor in a crunchy, snow-like layer of glass. As if that wasn't enough to worry about, parts of the ceiling were also showing signs of strain, collapsing all around them in a thick cloud of dust.

"We're running out of time," Captain Holland whispered to Geoff. "I don't know how much longer the shop can maintain structural integrity."

"Please," Geoff said. "I need just a little longer."

"From the moment I started running that company," Mr. Knight shouted over the crash of falling debris, "I began to think about how I could use the technology to change the course of history; how I could change the past to make sure our original invasion in the twenty-first century would succeed. Using the supercomputer, I played back the events surrounding that date and discovered it was *you* who sent us that stupid message—it was *you* who sent us fleeing back home. So I began to think about how I could get to you. At first, I thought about just going back and killing you, but with Eric's blasted safeguards popping up everywhere, I knew I'd be found out, and I'd come too far to take such a stupid risk. I needed to be smarter."

"Which is where the Time Rep idea came in," Geoff said, brushing some glass from his shoulder.

"Exactly. The more I found out about you, the more I was amazed at how insignificant you were, and I began to wonder if

I could use this to my advantage. You were less important to the world than certain types of mushroom, for goodness sake."

"Which mushrooms?" Geoff said. In spite of everything that was happening around him, he was dying to know.

"Shiitake, mainly," Mr. Knight said. "But only because some world leader or other choked to death on one in 2054."

"I knew it," Geoff said. "Bloody shiitake mushrooms."

"So that was when I came up with the idea for Time Reps—using insignificant people to act as tour guides for each time period. And it was perfect—the time-tourism industry was on its knees, crying out for innovation, and while I couldn't get to you, this scheme would bring you straight to me. Everyone was happy. Of course, I needed to cover my tracks in case anyone started asking questions, so I let Ruth take the credit for the idea and got her promoted to the board. With all the success she gained from it, I knew she wouldn't be able to tell anyone that the Time Rep idea was actually mine."

"You bastard!" Ruth shouted out. "You used me!"

"The next stage," Mr. Knight said, ignoring Ruth, "was to work out how to change history but in such a way that it wouldn't register on the paradox scan. That was where I used the help of a few 'friends'—fellow aliens posing as scientists. So I leaked the algorithm to them. It wasn't long before they figured out a loophole—one that would allow me to interfere with the space-time continuum in such a way that the computer wouldn't realize. All I had to do was make sure that the final nanosecond remained the same as the one in its data banks, and I could make as many changes as I liked!"

"But Eric was on to you."

"Eric was never on to me," Mr. Knight said. "He knew there was a problem with his double-Nobel Prize-winning code, and he knew someone on the inside had leaked it, but he had no idea it was me. Nevertheless, he was on the verge of ironing out the loophole, and I couldn't let that happen. His new and improved algorithm would have made changing history far too difficult, if not impossible."

"So you killed him."

"That's right—on the night of the party. After that, the final part of the plan was easy—in fact, the supercomputer was very helpful in showing me exactly how to keep the future the same while still fulfilling certain 'parameters': Firstly, I had to stop you playing that stupid game on the day of the invasion. After all, if you weren't playing it, you wouldn't be able to send out that message. So I tracked your movements from the moment you arrived in the future and broke your hand at the first opportunity."

"So it *was* you who tried to shoot that bolt at my hand during the Great Fire of London!" Geoff said. "You were the man wearing the hooded cape!"

"Indeed I was, Geoffrey, indeed I was. I wasn't the best shot with the crossbow unfortunately, but once I'd stabbed you in the hand in Eric's lab, I had to make sure I could sneak you back to the past again without anyone realizing what had happened. That was where the hypnosis came in—if you were able to pass a message on to my fellow Varsarians telling them to 'revert' the planet back to normal at a certain time, the computer would allow you to travel back to the twenty-first century under the misapprehension that everything was going to remain the same."

"But you didn't count on Tim double-checking the paradox scan even though it cleared me for travel," Geoff said.

"I knew it was a possibility," Mr. Knight said, "but the way I saw it, it was a win-win situation. If he didn't double-check the scan and sent you back, our original invasion would succeed. On the other hand, if he *did* double-check the scan and *didn't* send you back, our original invasion would *still* succeed because you still wouldn't be there to play your game; you wouldn't be there to send that message. I'll admit—I didn't anticipate the fact that history wouldn't change immediately and that you'd be in a position to go back and defend the Earth, but given the fact that your fleet is about to be destroyed, it looks like my little gamble paid off, wouldn't you say?"

"Not yet," the captain said, piping up. "We've still got the *Concordia* and a few other ships out there that weren't under Mai's control. We can still put up a good fight!"

"Don't make me laugh," Mr. Knight said. "By the time all the computer-controlled ships have destroyed themselves, you'll be down to less than two hundred vessels! Face it—you're outgunned, and you're outnumbered."

"I don't care," the captain said. "We've got some brave people on these ships, and we'll fight to the death if necessary. What have you got? You're nothing more than a bunch of cowards who run away when they hear a stupid message from a kid playing a computer game!"

"We are not a bunch of cowards!" Mr. Knight shouted. "The Varsarian high command might have decided to flee when they heard that message, but I'll have you know—my ancestors were the only ones who had to be ordered to break off their attack when we thought humanity had a Death Bringer! Ordered! They still wanted to fight!"

"Oh my God!" Geoff whispered to the captain. "Did you hear that? We've got him!"

"What are you talking about?" the captain said.

"You've got to get me back to the bridge," Geoff said.

"But what about Mr. Knight?" the captain said.

"Leave him to play around in this stupid maze," Geoff replied. "If what he's just told us is true, we can still win this fight…"

Twenty-Six

Geoff paced up and down in the elevator as it made its way back up to the bridge. He could definitely tell the *Concordia* was starting to take a serious amount of damage now, the lift juddering uncomfortably as it headed for its destination. He was accompanied by Captain Holland and a contingent of five armed guards whom the captain had called away from the remote operations deck to act as their protection. Tim, Ruth, and the Defense Minister had remained downstairs to deal with Mr. Knight.

"This plan of yours," Captain Holland said. "It's crazy, but at the same time, it might just work…"

"It's got to work," Geoff said, his heart beating faster as the lift swerved from one direction to another. "It's our only chance."

"WARNING," came an automated male voice. "SHIELDS AT 10% CAPACITY."

Geoff raised his eyebrows. A male computer!

"Who is this man, Captain?" one of the armed guards asked. "I haven't seen him on board before."

"Is he from military intelligence?" another guard asked.

Geoff was about to answer when the captain interrupted.

"That's right," he said, holding up a hand to stop Geoff from speaking "He's one of our key strategists on this mission."

Geoff kept quiet and flashed the captain a quizzical look. A strategist?

The captain let out a deep breath.

"I just hope we can get back in time," he sighed. "I don't think the ship can take much more damage."

"How much farther?" Geoff said.

"Only a few more floors. We should…"

But before the captain had a chance to finish his sentence, the lift came to a grinding halt, sending everyone crashing into each other. The lights above began to flicker uncontrollably, the walls began to buckle, and the control panel to the side of the doors started to smoke.

"What was that?" Geoff shouted. He coughed violently.

"The elevator shaft must be damaged!" the captain replied, fanning the smoke away from his face. "Everyone, get out!"

Two of the armed guards rushed forward and prised their weapons in between the elevator doors, heaving them open as wide as they could. Fortunately, the lift had stopped just above a deck, and there was enough space to crawl between the doors and jump down to the floor.

The lift began to creak.

"Jump!" the captain shouted, pushing Geoff through the gap first.

Geoff fell onto the hard gray floor feet first and cried out in pain, keeling over against a nearby wall. It felt like he'd twisted a muscle. He tried to stand up straight and looked around—he was in a long corridor with metallic walls, a high ceiling, and a long, silver handrail running along one side. The corridor was bathed in a pulsating red light.

"WARNING," came the automated voice again. "SHIELDS NOW AT CRITICAL LEVELS. HULL BREACH IMMINENT."

Geoff watched as the captain exited the lift, jumping down a little more gracefully than Geoff had managed to do. The five armed guards came next, each one throwing their guns down to the floor first before lowering themselves out of the lift and collecting their weapons again once they were safe.

Just as the last guard managed to jump clear, the elevator groaned under the strain of its own weight and plummeted back down into the depths of the ship.

"That was close," the captain said, leaning on Geoff's shoulder as he caught his breath. "You all right?"

"I'm fine," Geoff said, wiping his brow, "But we've got to get to that bridge! Is there another way?"

"We're only three decks below it," the captain said. He let go of Geoff's shoulder. "Follow me!"

But just as the captain began to run, a huge explosion rocked the ship, the tremors causing him to stumble straight into a wall. All around them, the corridor began to tear itself apart, the sound of shearing metal filling their ears like a steam train grinding to a halt. The floor and ceiling split completely in two, the walls cracked open, and the two ends of the corridor began to list away from each other like two halves of a sinking ship, separating Geoff and the armed guards from their commanding officer. Through falling debris and grit in his eyes, Geoff edged toward the gap. He thought about trying to jump it, but the other side was too far away, and it was certainly too far to fall.

The captain staggered to his feet and looked at them from the other side of the newly created crevice.

"Captain!" one of the armed guards shouted. "Are you okay?"

"I'm fine!" the captain called back. "But the ship's falling apart! We need to …"

All of a sudden, a loud hum began to fill the air. The captain stopped talking and looked behind him—a thin line of molten metal had started to appear on the far wall. It began to trace the outline of a large circle—big enough for someone to climb through.

"My God!" the captain said, unholstering his weapon. "That's an outer bulkhead! The Varsarians are trying to cut their way through! They must have their ships locked against the hull! We're being boarded!"

The captain appeared to be trapped—it was too far for him to jump across to where Geoff and his men were, and it didn't look as though he had enough time to make it past the Varsarians before they came aboard.

"What are your orders, Captain?" One of the armed guards shouted.

The captain stood there for a moment saying nothing, just watching the circle of molten metal as it grew closer to completing itself.

"Sir, your orders!"

"Get that man to the bridge!" the captain said, pointing at Geoff. "He's your commanding officer now! Protect him with your lives! Mr. Stamp—you're our last hope of winning this fight—you know what to do!"

The guards all immediately turned to Geoff.

"This way, sir!" one shouted, leading him the opposite way down the corridor. "We'll take the service stairs!"

The other four guards formed a protective escort around Geoff and began to run, but they only made it a few meters before two Varsarians ran out from around a corner up ahead, their lizard-like bodies dressed in full armor and protective headwear. The aliens stopped in their tracks, pulled out their weapons, and began firing brightly colored laser beams toward them.

"Get down!" one of the guards said, pushing Geoff to the ground.

Geoff looked back at the captain as the guards returned fire, shielding his face as the Varsarians' lasers scorched the walls around him. The captain appeared to be speaking into panel on the wall next to him. Behind him, the molten circle of metal fell from the wall with a loud clang, and more Varsarian soldiers began to pour out.

"Crew, this is the Captain," his voice announced, booming over the loudspeakers. "I hereby relinquish command of this vessel over to Geoffrey Stamp. I repeat—I hereby relinquish command of this vessel over to Geoffrey Stamp." The captain looked back at the approaching swarm of Varsarians and straightened his neck. "He is now the only person on board who can win this fight for us, and you will obey every order he gives without question. This is Captain Holland … signing out."

Geoff tried not think about what Tim must have been thought when he'd heard that announcement. Probably something along the lines of "we're doomed."

But for once in his life, Geoff knew exactly what he had to do—he had the right skills, and he had the right experience.

Now he just needed to get to that bridge…

TWENTY-SEVEN

"Report," Geoff said, remembering the language the captain had used when speaking to his crew. He had only managed to return to the bridge with three remaining armed guards—two of the group had given up their lives in order to protect him from the Varsarian boarding parties. "How are we doing?"

If the state of the bridge was anything to go by, Geoff didn't really need a report to tell him how they were doing. Computer terminals were on fire, support beams had collapsed from the ceiling, scorch marks were running up the walls, and a disconcertingly large crack had appeared on the main window. The *Concordia* had obviously taken quite a hammering while they'd been trying to find Mr. Knight, and the bridge seemed to have lost a number of crew members as a result—the dead bodies of various officers were either slumped over their damaged stations or sprawled across the floor, limbs snapped back into painfully unnatural positions. In fact, looking around, there only seemed to be one officer left, sitting in the captain's seat with his head in his hands.

"It's not looking good, sir," the officer said, wiping a streak of ash from his forehead and relinquishing the seat for Geoff. "Almost all of the fleet has been destroyed. The *Concordia* is running on auxiliary power, and all weapons systems are down. The ships that weren't being controlled by Mai are putting up a good fight, but they're heavily outnumbered."

Geoff limped over to the captain's chair and sat down, looking up at the giant screen in front of him. The battlefield was like a spaceship graveyard, with the charred wreckages of hundreds of Earth cruisers drifting all around, scorched debris hanging in the vacuum, and the bodies of countless servicemen and women drifting in every direction. He winced as another battle cruiser ruptured from the inside and exploded. The force of the explosion was so powerful it took a neighboring ship with it.

The Varsarians, on the other hand, seemed to be having a whale of a time, concentrating their fire on the ships that didn't appear to be malfunctioning. In the distance, a lone vessel was being chased by over fifty flying saucers, all of which simultaneously opened fire. The vessel tried its best to take evasive action, but the force of the attack was too great, and it was soon destroyed.

"Open a channel to all remaining ships," Geoff ordered.

"What?" the officer said.

"Open a channel to the all remaining ships!" Geoff shouted.

"But, sir—don't you remember what Mai said? The aliens are almost certainly listening to our communications! They'll hear everything you say!"

"That's exactly what I'm hoping for," Geoff replied calmly.

The officer looked at him for a moment as if he was going to say something else before limping over to the communications terminal and wiping it clean with the sleeve of his uniform.

"I hope you know what you're doing," he said, pressing a small red button in front of him. "Channel open."

Geoff cleared his throat.

"Remaining Earth ships, your attention please! Prepare to activate the Death Bringer!"

Geoff looked up at the screen and waited. His heart was beating so hard he felt like his whole head was pulsating.

Just as he had hoped, the transmission seemed to have quite an effect on the Varsarian fleet. Ships that were previously circling around the last remaining battle cruisers appeared to break off their attack, and many of the capital ships began to swing around into a precautionary retreat, as if there was some nervousness about the meaning of Geoff's message. The only exception to this sudden display of panic was a lone flying saucer still gleefully taking pot shots at a crippled medical frigate.

"There," Geoff said, pointing at the craft. "Do you see it?"

"I do," the officer said.

"Lock on to that ship and open fire."

"What's a 'Death Bringer'?" the officer said.

"It doesn't matter!" Geoff shouted. "Lock on to that ship and open fire!"

"But, sir—weapons systems are offline! We've barely got enough power for propulsion."

"Then set a collision course!" Geoff barked. "We'll have to ram it!"

"Sir, I don't think…"

"Don't argue with me! We haven't got much time before they realize we don't have a Death Bringer! This is a priority four-seven-thingy-bravo-thingy order! Set a collision course for that vessel! Now!"

The officer nodded and hobbled over to the navigations terminal. He pushed a dead body off the seat so he could sit down and typed in a few commands as quickly as he could.

"Course set," he said. "Engines are powering up."

The bridge creaked as the *Concordia* began to accelerate toward its target. Another beam fell to the floor behind them, crashing through a row of monitors.

To the right of the screen, Geoff noticed one of the last remaining Earth ships drifting into their path.

"Get out of the way!" Geoff screamed! "I can't hit it if you're in the way!"

The ship appeared to respond, firing its secondary thrusters to maneuver out of the *Concordia*'s path.

All of a sudden, Tim walked from the stairwell, his gun pressed against Mr. Knight's throat. The rest of their contingent of armed guards marched in behind them, their rifles trained on the traitor's head.

"We got him," Tim said, kicking Mr. Knight to his knees.

"Where's Ruth?" Geoff said, running over to meet them. "And the Defense Minister?"

"They're still downstairs trying to fix the computer," Tim said, dabbing a cut on his forehead. "Doesn't look good."

Geoff looked down at Mr. Knight.

Mr. Knight looked back.

He had a serious wound to his leg and a nasty gash across his face, but he was smiling inanely, a gleam of triumph in his eyes.

"I don't know what you're smiling about," Geoff said, grabbing Mr. Knight's jaw and jerking his head to face the main window. "You see that ship dead ahead? The one we're about to ram into?"

Mr. Knight twisted his head free from Geoff's grip and spat out a mouthful of blood. He said nothing.

"That's the ship with your ancestors on it," Geoff said. "You were right: they were the only ones that didn't react when I told the fleet to activate the Death Bringer—they were the only ones who carried on attacking. Thanks to your little story, you made them easy for us to identify."

Mr. Knight's eyes widened, but his smile stayed fixed on his face as if he was too stunned to realize that he should probably change his expression.

"So here's a question for you: what do you think will happen if we destroy that ship?" Geoff asked.

Mr. Knight remained silent.

"Let me tell you what I think. If your ancestors are on that ship, killing them would kill you, right? If they die, you'll never have even existed. And if you never existed, you wouldn't have been able to sabotage Mai. Not only that—you wouldn't have been able to come up with this whole scheme to change history. The way I see it, if we destroy that ship, your entire race is finished."

Mr. Knight didn't look quite so pleased with himself anymore. He struggled to get to his feet, but it was a futile attempt. He fell back on his wounded leg and screamed out in agony.

"Don't even think about it," Tim said, grabbing Mr. Knight by the collar and pressing his gun into the back of his head. "One more move and I'll kill you on the spot."

The only problem with Geoff's little plan was that in its present state, the *Concordia* was about as maneuverable as an elephant drugged on sleeping pills stuck in heavy traffic, and wasn't having much luck in catching up with its target. It didn't take long for Mr. Knight to realize this, and he was soon smiling again as he watched his ancestor's ship accelerate safely away from its crippled pursuers.

"We're losing them!" Geoff screamed. "Can't we go any faster?"

"Engines are barely functional, sir," the officer replied. "If we go any faster, we'll fly apart!"

"Fly us apart, then!!" Geoff shouted.

The officer nodded and typed a few more commands into his console.

The *Concordia* began to pick up speed, but just as the officer had warned, computer terminals began to explode all around them, showering the bridge in electric sparks. Above their heads, rows of piping began to split, pouring out thick plumes of smoke. Geoff waved his arms to clear the air and hobbled back to his seat, determined not to lose sight of the one ship he was after.

Unfortunately, the extra burst of speed didn't seem to be enough—the alien craft was still managing to fly farther and farther away.

Mr. Knight began to laugh.

"Nice try," he said, his voice weak with exhaustion. "You had me worried for a moment."

The officer slumped back in his chair and shut his eyes.

Geoff stared at the screen and thought for a moment. What else could this ship do that might help?

"Um…you there," he said to the officer, not sure how to address him.

"Sir?"

"Does the tractor beam still work?"

The officer immediately opened his eyes and sat up straight again, spinning around on his chair to check a panel behind him. He ran his finger down a row of figures on a computer screen and smiled.

"Yes, sir!" he said. "Tractor beam is fully functional!"

"Then activate it, for heaven's sake!" Geoff shouted.

The officer twisted a small dial to the right and looked up at the main window. In the distance, a large ball of red light engulfed the escaping ship, stopping it dead in its tracks.

"Gotcha," Geoff said, watching as the alien craft dangled helplessly ahead of them like a fly caught in a spider's web.

"I don't know how long I can hold it!" the officer said. "We're on the verge of a ship-wide systems failure!"

"Then transfer all power to the engines!" Geoff said. "We've *got* to destroy that ship!"

"Even life support?"

"Everything!" Geoff shouted.

The officer spun around in his chair again and typed a few more commands.

"Here goes nothing," he said, pressing a final button on the console.

The *Concordia* began to pick up speed again, lurching toward the alien ship as fast as it could go. As Geoff had ordered, this final burst of acceleration came at the expense of everything else, plunging the bridge into darkness and powering down all nonessential systems. The only source of light now came from the main window, which was glowing bright red as the alien ship came closer into view, struggling to free itself from the tractor beam.

Geoff took a deep breath—the air was getting very thin.

"How long … before … we make impact?" he gasped.

"Thirty seconds," the officer replied.

"And how long … before the … tractor beam fails?"

The officer looked at the panel behind him and shook his head.

"It's gonna be close, sir," he said.

"Come on…" Geoff said, standing up from his seat, his body silhouetted against the glow of the oncoming ship. They couldn't have been more than a few miles away. "Almost… there…"

At their present course, the alien ship was going to smash straight through the main window.

"Sir!" the officer cried. "The tractor beam is failing!"

Everyone held their breath as the red glow began to flicker around the oncoming craft. There were two reasons for this—firstly, this was a pretty tense situation, and secondly, there wasn't actually much air left to breathe.

The tractor beam finally failed. The alien ship immediately fired up its engines, desperately attempting to pull away from the *Concordia*.

Geoff smiled.

"Too late," he said.

Geoff dived to the floor and shielded his eyes as the alien ship smashed through the main window, the weight of its hull buckling the walls to either side. The impact was catastrophic, instantly killing the last remaining officer and sending shards of glass and metal flying in all directions. Beneath Geoff, the floor began to split in two, sending him tumbling toward a bank of damaged computer terminals, and through the debris, he watched as the alien ship listed to one side, ripping the ceiling free from its few remaining supporting beams. Over on the other side of the bridge, Tim was pressed up against the rear wall, still holding on to Mr. Knight by the scruff of his neck.

Tim appeared to be shouting something at Geoff, but in the vacuum on the bridge, everything was silent. Geoff strained his eyes and tried to read his friend's lips. It looked like he was saying, "She's gonna blow," but Geoff was never any good at reading lips. For all he knew, he might have been saying "It's gonna snow" or "Let's tie a bow," but under the present circumstances he assumed his first guess was probably the most likely.

His feelings were soon confirmed as the alien ship ricocheted back out into space and folded in on itself, exploding in the characteristic flash of light they'd come to expect from every other ship they'd destroyed today. As the shockwave burned through the bridge, bathing everyone in its warm glow, Mr. Knight screamed out in silence, his body fading away into the thinnest of thin air. Geoff tried his luck at reading lips again—unless he was mistaken, it looked like he was saying, "Agggggghhhhhhh!"

This latest series of events was proving to be a real headache for the space-time continuum, which was struggling to work out what should happen next. Indeed, this was the question on everyone's mind as they lay suffocating on the bridge of the *Concordia*, basking in the pleasantly warm if somewhat radioactive glow of the explosion they had just witnessed.

TWENTY-EIGHT

Fortunately, the space-time continuum must have been in a pretty good mood that day because with Mr. Knight gone, it proceeded to undo everything he had done. As the shockwave faded, Geoff watched as the bridge began to rebuild itself—fallen beams rose back into the ceiling, the floor leveled off and joined back together again, and scorch marks erased themselves from the walls, leaving no trace of the damage that had just been done. All around him, crew members were coming back to life, their bodies rising up from the ground and floating back to their original positions, wounds healing themselves as they landed gently in their seats. The front of the bridge was also healing its wounds—the buckled walls straightening themselves out again, the scattered shards from the main window gliding back through the air, forming a solid pane of glass once more.

But it wasn't just the bridge of the *Concordia* that seemed to be benefiting from the fact that Mr. Knight never existed. Through the newly re-formed window, Geoff watched as all the other ships that had previously been destroyed began to restore themselves, the charred remains of hundreds of battle cruisers transforming back into pristine condition and the split hulls of so many collided ships joining up again, their engines flickering back to life.

Geoff got to his feet and walked over to Tim, who was no longer holding a gun. His leg didn't hurt anymore.

"Erm … what's happening?" he said.

"I don't know," Tim said, running his finger along the cut on his forehead as it healed itself up and disappeared. "I guess you were right about that ship—it must have had Mr. Knight's ancestors on board. And if Mr. Knight's never existed, the space-time continuum must be catching up with how events would have transpired without his interference."

"So why are we still in space?" Geoff said. "I mean, if Mr. Knight never existed, we wouldn't even be here, would we?"

"Beats me," Tim said. "Perhaps the space-time continuum has a mind of its own. Perhaps it needs us to destroy the rest of these bloody aliens before it can go back to normal."

That didn't seem to be too much a problem for the newly restored fleet, which, in its new lease of life, appeared to be doing just that—blowing up alien spaceships left, right and center. Through the window, hundreds of tiny explosions were joining the stars in lighting up the blackness of space, each one fading away to reveal the remains of a destroyed flying saucer.

Geoff walked over to the resurrected captain, who was sitting calmly in his seat, overlooking the battle.

"Well done!" the captain said, leaping out of his seat and shaking Geoff's hand. "Very well done indeed!"

"How's it going?" Geoff said.

"Much better than it was a few moments ago," the captain replied. "For a start, I'm no longer trapped in a corridor with those bloody Varsarians, and with your Mr. Knight out of the way, Mai is more than capable of handling the situation. Right, Mai?"

"Affirmative, Captain," Mai replied, her voice no longer stuttering. "We should be down to the last ship in a matter of minutes."

"Let me know when," the captain said. "I want to destroy that last one myself."

"Yes, Captain."

"Well, it looks like you saved the day," the captain said, reaching out to shake Geoff's hand. "Well done."

Geoff smiled and walked back over to Tim. Behind him, the lift doors opened. Ruth and the Defense Minister stepped out.

"What the hell just happened?" Ruth said, looking around the bridge. "One minute we were trying to put the computer back together, and the next minute, it just fixed itself!"

"You should have seen it," the Defense Minister said. "All the pieces just floated in the air and joined back together again as if they had a life of their own! It was … creepy."

"You two know something, don't you?" Ruth said, narrowing her eyes, sensing that Geoff and Tim weren't that surprised.

"Well, it's a little bit complicated," Tim said. "But we think we may have changed history."

"Oh," Ruth said, watching a flying saucer spiral past the main window in a ball of flames. "And how did you do that exactly?"

"I found the mother of all weak spots," Geoff said.

"What are you talking about?"

"Geoff worked out a way of identifying the exact ship with Mr. Knight's ancestors on board, and we destroyed it. So as far as history is concerned, Mr. Knight now never existed."

"He … never existed?" Ruth said.

"Nope."

"So how come we still remember him?"

"I don't know," Geoff said. "Maybe that will remain one of the great mysteries of the universe, like why you can eat an infinite number of cocktail sausages without feeling full."

"That's not quite the same thing really, is it?" Ruth said.

"Excuse me, Captain," Mai announced over the loudspeaker, "but you asked me to let you know when we were down to the last ship."

"Thanks, Mai," the captain said, turning to his navigations officer. "Where is it?"

"Two thousand clicks off the port bow, Captain," the officer replied. "Bearing 7-9-5 mark 2-6-6. Looks like she's trying to flee."

"Set a pursuit course," the captain ordered, getting to his feet. "We can't let them get away."

The officer typed all the commands necessary into his console to set a pursuit course before saying the somewhat predictable words: "Pursuit course set."

As he spoke, the *Concordia* banked to the left to face the final alien ship, which was darting about erratically in the distance as it tried to make its escape.

"Do we have a lock?" the captain said, walking over to his weapons officer and leaning on the back of her chair.

"Yes, Captain,"

"And all weapons are fully functional?"

"All weapons are armed and ready."

"Then let's hit this last ship with everything we've got," the captain said, walking back to his chair and sitting down.

"Torpedoes armed, plasma cannons primed, and particle beams ready, Captain."

"Fire!" the captain said, leaning on the arm of his chair and clenching his fist.

The bridge shuddered as the *Concordia* unleashed every nasty weapon in its arsenal, sending a barrage of destructive mass and energy swarming toward the fleeing ship. The torpedoes were first to strike, tearing through the center of the ship and ripping it in half like a fortune cookie, and if that wasn't enough, they were soon followed by a lethal burst of laser fire, burning through the two separated halves like molten lava through a paper plate. This really left the ship no choice but to explode, which it did in spectacular fashion, the two semicircular sides of the hull crashing into each other and detonating across the stars in a dazzling burst of blue light. It was by far the biggest explosion of the battle, and as the light faded, all that remained were a few splinters of hot metal drifting peacefully through the air to join the rest of the debris from the battle.

The crew of the *Concordia* leapt up from their seats and cheered, hugging each other ecstatically, and punching the air.

"Well, that was good, wasn't it?" Geoff said, slapping Tim on the back and smiling at Ruth.

"I don't know," said Tim. "I wasn't so keen on that middle part when we nearly died, but apart from that, you did a great job." He reached out and shook Geoff's hand. "Well done, mate."

"You were magnificent, Geoff," Ruth smiled. "Who would have thought it?"

"So what happens now?" Geoff asked.

"I'm not sure," Tim replied. "I suppose now that we've destroyed the final ship, there's no reason for us to be here."

"No?"

"Think about it. If the aliens never invaded the Earth, we would have no reason to come back in time to defend the planet. So, if the space-time continuum is correcting itself again, I guess we should be disappearing any…"

TWENTY-NINE

" . . . **S**econd."

Geoff looked around.

"Did . . . something just happen?" he said.

"I think so," Tim said. "I think we're somewhere else."

"Yes, but where?" Ruth said. "Where are we?"

That was a good question. They seemed to be back in the room where Geoff had first had his interview—the room that overlooked the London skyline. But something had changed. The room certainly looked the same—wine glasses and paper plates from last night's party were being swept away by an army of cleaners, and a group of workmen were dismantling the elaborate Roman decorations, but the view out of the window was very different. Whereas before, the London of the future had looked identical to the London of the past, it now looked like a new city: one that had evolved and grown over time like you would expect. There were still all the recognizable landmarks: St. Paul's Cathedral, Big Ben, and the London Eye, but they were joined by a whole host of new, futuristic architecture: beautiful glass skyscrapers towering into the air, their ergonomic construction reflecting the clear blue sky onto the streets below.

"Are we where I think we are?" Geoff said.

"I don't know," Ruth said. "It looks like we're back at headquarters, but everything looks so . . . different."

"Well it would, wouldn't it?" Tim said. "If the aliens were totally wiped out in the twenty-first century, they never would have been able to invade in the twenty-second century, and the original

London would never have been destroyed. What you're looking at is a different London—this city's no longer a memorial; it's a city that's been allowed to build up over the years and change as any normal city would."

"Looks pretty good," Geoff said.

"There's still one thing I don't understand," Tim said, turning to Geoff. "If Mr. Knight no longer exists, why are you still here?"

"Me?"

"Well, he was the one who thought up the Time Rep scheme, wasn't he? Without him, we wouldn't have thought to recruit people from different time periods to act as tour guides."

Geoff nodded to himself. Tim was right. Was he going to disappear again any second? He hoped not—today had been confusing enough as it was.

"What are you lot doing just standing there?" a voice said.

The group turned around. Eric was walking toward them, a computer disk in one hand and his walking stick in the other.

"Eric!" Tim said. "You're alive!"

"Of course I'm alive!" Eric said. "Why wouldn't I be?"

"Doesn't matter," Tim said.

"Let me just test something," Ruth whispered to the group. "Eric?" she said, stepping forward. "Where's Mr. Knight?"

"Mr. who?" Eric said.

"Mr. Knight. The chief exec."

"But…you're the chief exec, aren't you?" Eric said.

"I am?" Ruth said.

"Well, you're the one who thought up the Time Rep idea, aren't you?"

"I did?" Ruth said.

"Of course you are! That's why you're the one the Defense Minister appointed to the job!"

Ruth looked at the others and raised her eyebrows.

"What is this, some sort of joke?" Eric said. "Look, I've got no time for this—I've got to get down to the paradox-scanning facility right away."

He turned to leave.

"Why do you need to go there?" Ruth said.

"To upload the new algorithm," Eric said, holding up the disk in his hand. "I was telling you about this yesterday, remember? My new code removes a fundamental loophole in the system. Once this is uploaded, no one will be able to cheat the computer."

"Good," Ruth said, looking at the others. "We wouldn't want that."

"I don't know," Eric muttered under his breath, hobbling toward the lift at the back of the room. "I spend all this time telling them about the work I'm doing to improve my code, and they *still* don't listen."

"Will you excuse me a moment?" Ruth said. She ran over to Eric and gave him a hug, then whispered something in his ear. Eric smiled, gave her a wink, and left.

Tim frowned.

"What was that about?" he said as Ruth rejoined the rest of the group at the window. "I didn't think you two were that close?"

"Oh, nothing," Ruth said, smiling to herself as she looked across London's new skyline. "Just checking something."

"Well, I guess that explains why I'm still here," Geoff said. "Ruth *did* think up the idea for Time Reps after all. Must have come up with it independently."

"And now you're the boss of the company as a result," Tim said, turning to her. "Congratulations."

"Thanks," Ruth replied, touching Tim's hand.

Geoff inflated his cheeks with air, held it there for a moment, then blew it out again.

"Erm…would anyone object if I went home now?" he said. "After all this excitement, I think I need a holiday."

"Well, we have a number of great locations for you to choose from," Tim said. "Have you ever thought about visiting the Great Fire of London?"

"No," Geoff said. "But my fist is thinking of visiting your face."

THIRTY

Geoff walked up the garden path to 23 Woodview Gardens with his house keys at the ready, his legs barely able to carry the weight of his body. It was late—the night sky looking remarkably peaceful considering the epic battle that had just taken place above his head. Indeed, reminding himself of the date, he realized it must have been around this time that the Varsarians were being defeated, and as he looked up, he just caught a glimpse of a small explosion lighting up a corner of the sky briefly with a glint of blue.

As he fumbled with his keys in the door, he thought about everything he'd been through today. Not only had he witnessed the extinction of the dinosaurs, he'd travelled over one thousand years into the future, seen the Great Fire of London, uncovered a conspiracy to change the course of history, and saved the entire planet from an alien invasion.

Not bad for a first day's work, he thought, twisting his key in the lock and pushing open the front door.

He stepped into the hallway and slammed the door behind him, hanging his coat on the end of the banisters. As much as he wanted to climb into bed and go to sleep, this process involved going up the stairs, which was a big no-no at the moment. So he staggered into the lounge and collapsed on the sofa, burying his face into the nearest cushion that didn't smell of newspaper.

It had certainly been a long day, and to make matters worse, he had an early start tomorrow. Apparently, he had to meet thirty-three tourists outside a modern art gallery at nine in the morning and explain to them why twenty-first century people considered a piece of litter stapled to a canvas to be a work of art. He wasn't really sure what to say: by that logic, had any passerby caught a glimpse of the front room, they wouldn't have thought they were walking past an animal enclosure—they might have thought they were walking past an art installation.

Today had certainly been a long day, and yet inside he felt refreshed, confident—a changed man. Would this get him into trouble? After everything that had happened today, would Ruth really fire him for feeling a little better about himself? For knowing his purpose in life? He yawned and shut his eyes. Perhaps, if he saw Zoë tomorrow, he would ask her if she wanted to go down to the lake with him just like they used to do in the old days.

THIRTY-ONE

"So, how you keeping?" Zoë said, sitting next to Geoff on a bench, overlooking the lake. "Found another job yet?"

"Actually, yes," Geoff said, brushing his hand against some long grass growing next to his feet. "Remember that one I applied for the other day?"

"The holiday rep?"

"Yep. I got the job."

"You did?" Zoë said, running her fingers through her hair. "That's fantastic!"

"Thanks," Geoff said.

Zoë stopped stroking her hair and narrowed her eyes.

"They were very quick, weren't they?" she said.

"Quick?" Geoff said.

"Well, you only applied for the job yesterday, didn't you?"

"Did I?" Geoff said. All this traveling through time had made him lose track of what day it was.

"Definitely."

"You sure it wasn't last week?"

"No, it was definitely yesterday," Zoë said. "I was delivering you that letter, remember?"

"Ah yes. I remember."

"Who was that from, by the way?"

"Oh … nobody," Geoff said. "Just some … thing."

"So, they didn't even ask you in for an interview?"

"No, they did."

"When was that?"

"Yesterday."

"What do you mean yesterday?" Zoë said. "You only applied for the job yesterday! You mean to tell me they asked you in for an interview on the same day?"

Geoff was sweating.

"Yep," he said, tugging at the collar of his t-shirt. "I er… delivered the letter by hand. It was the last day they were accepting applications. Since I was there, you know, they said I might as well sit for the interview."

"And they offered you the job on the spot?"

"They did."

"Wow," Zoë said. "That's amazing. It's not normal for places like that to make a decision so fast. You must have really impressed them."

"Well, you know," Geoff said. "I was just being myself."

"That's even *more* amazing," Zoë said.

Geoff laughed.

"So what do you have to do?" Zoë said. "Does it involve any traveling?"

"Kind of…" Geoff replied. "Mainly, I'm just showing tourists around London, but now and again I have to go… elsewhere."

"Shame it wasn't for somewhere exotic," Zoë said, "like the Maldives."

"I know, I know. But you've got to start somewhere, haven't you?"

"Well, I'm really happy for you," Zoë said, picking a stone up off the floor and tossing it into the lake. "I always knew you'd do well."

"Thanks," Geoff said, shuffling a little closer. "Listen—can I ask you something?"

"Sure, what is it?" Zoë said.

"Well…"

"Hey, look at that," Zoë said, interrupting Geoff to point up at the sky. "You don't see many seagulls around here, do you?"

"No, you don't," Geoff said, watching as the bird circled in the air. "Most unusual."

"Sorry," Zoë said, turning to face him once more. "What were you saying?"

Epilogue

Eric leaned back on his chair and watched as the video simulation disappeared in a puff of vapor. He looked at his watch—how long had they been down here, sweating away in the paradox-scanning facility?

"Well, now we know why Mr. Knight didn't want you double-checking his choice of candidates before you sent those letters out," he said, turning to Ruth. "If he finds out you came down here…"

"He won't," Ruth said, folding up a piece of paper and sticking it in an envelope. "If he didn't find out when he ran this simulation himself, he won't find out in real life, will he?"

"I suppose not," Eric said. "What's that in your hand?"

"The letter I'm about to send to Geoff," she said. "I wrote down exactly what he read aloud at the beginning—don't want to start changing anything now. I just hope he can read my handwriting—I had nothing to lean on."

"What do you mean?" Eric stammered. "You're not actually going to get him in for an interview, are you? We should be calling the police! Mr. Knight needs to be stopped! You've seen the simulations he's been running down here—he's dangerous!"

"Why should we try to stop him?" Ruth said. "It's clear what will happen—if we call Geoff in, every alien on this planet will be wiped out once and for all. On the other hand, if we move in on Mr. Knight now, there'll still be hundreds of them out there. We've got no choice."

"But… he's going to kill me."

Ruth put her arm around Eric.

"I know," she said, "but things turn out all right in the end, don't they? You come back to life, don't you? You've seen it for yourself. And you've seen how pleased I was to see you…"

"You just want to be chief exec of the company."

"That's not what this is about," Ruth said, "although I'll admit that is a fairly nice bonus. There's just one thing…"

"What is it?"

"We'll have to behave *exactly* as we did in that simulation," Ruth said, pointing at where the screen had just been. "And there were a few moments when both of us nearly gave the game away. I'm pretty sure everyone saw you wink at me at the end, for goodness sake. If we let anyone know that we're onto something, or do anything remotely different, things may not go the way we think."

Eric sighed.

"I hate to admit it," he said, "but you're right. It's the only way we can stop them."

"There's just one thing I don't understand," Ruth said.

"What's that?"

"Well, since we know Mr. Knight must have watched that simulation as well, why does he still want to go ahead with this? I mean, if Geoff is ultimately responsible for foiling his plan and wiping out the entire alien race, why does he still want to interview him?"

"I don't know," Eric said. "Perhaps he only had time to watch the simulation up to a certain point and assumed the rest would turn out okay."

"That's ridiculous," Ruth said. "You mean to tell me that after all that planning, he didn't take the time to sit down and watch it through to the very…"

ABOUT THE AUTHOR

Peter Ward was born in 1980 and studied English Literature at the University of Southampton. He lives in London with his wife Lucy. He is the author of *Note to Self* and the Time Rep trilogy.

Website: Peterwardauthor.com

Blog: https://peterwardauthor.com/blog/

Email: peterwardauthor@hotmail.co.uk

About the Publisher

This book is published on behalf of the author by the Ethan Ellenberg Literary Agency.
https://ethanellenberg.com
Email: agent@ethanellenberg.com